Lost Beneath the Tide

A Tide Harbor Suspense

Where love and murder lie just below the surface.

Book 2

By Zara West

Tidal Waters Press

New York

Dedication

To those that work in the sea.

PROLOGUE
Minas Basin, Nova Scotia

They found the body floating facedown, washed up against the side of the fish pen closest to the shore. An accident, Alex Harris thought. Had to be. A swimmer caught in the tide as it rose. Or an inexperienced boater fallen overboard in the dark. It was July, and there were plenty of out-of-towners in the area who didn't understand the danger of the high tides in the Minas Basin.

Behind him, the flashing red, blue, and white lights of the emergency vehicles brought back too many bad memories. He shaded his eyes with his hands and focused on the Royal Canadian Mounted Police officers who stood on the dock, waiting for the Cowling Fisheries boat to approach the pier with the body.

The battered, red-and-white aluminum boat that serviced the salmon pens docked, and the paramedics lifted the body over the side and placed it on a gurney. It couldn't be someone he knew. It couldn't be . . .

He shoved his boss's frantic phone call and gut-twisting request to the back of his mind and moved forward. He'd find out in moments.

Chapter 1
ALEX

1ˢᵗ Sunday in August

As Alex Harris steered his pickup onto the bumpy road leading to the abandoned dock, he looked over at his daughter. "This will just take a minute, Ellie."

Wearing a pout worthy of the starring role in a kid's TV drama, the five-year-old crossed her arms in front of her and shook her head. "But you promised we'd go. There's gonna be popcorn and ice cream and everything."

"Soon as I check out what's going on at the fish pens, we'll head right over to the town hall. We still have time." He squinted at the clock on the dashboard and grimaced. Between working overtime and doing extra leg work for the boss, he would have to step on it to make it to the annual Tide Harbor ice cream social. Not that he had any desire to sit around, chatting with the local moms while the kids got wound up and sticky, and the divorcees who eyed him like he was tastier than the ice cream they were doling out. But he hated to disappoint his daughter.

She was why he got up in the morning. Why he worked at a job he despised. Why he was driving down this dead-end, sand-buggy track to check out what was probably a great big nothing for a paranoid boss who saw eco-terrorists around every corner.

He jerked the wheel to avoid a pothole. The ancient pickup he'd inherited from his father needed to be coddled, not gunned down a washed-out dirt road. But the spit at the head of the harbor had the best view of the fish pens from land. If some eco-freak was messing with the pens, he'd see them. His boss had made it clear. Cowling Fish Farms didn't need another dead body tainting its reputation.

Thomas Cowling had also made it clear that if he was going to promote him to the lucrative head of security position at the Halifax offices of Cowling Fish Farms, despite their boyhood friendship, nothing else had better happen on his watch. So, if Thomas wanted him to check on the pens after hours, then check the pens he would.

He clutched the steering wheel tighter. Two more weeks of peace and quiet. That was all he needed to snag that job and be on his way to Halifax, leaving Tide Harbor and its haunting memories behind.

He glanced over at Ellie. His daughter would have so many more advantages in the city. She'd go to a big fancy school. Make new friends who weren't going to grow up to be fishermen. Best of all, with an office job, he'd be home every night. No more dragging his little girl with him on wild goose chases. He could be the father she deserved.

The truck thudded over a rock in the road and came down hard.

Ellie latched on to his arm. "Daddy, why we driving down this bumpy road? Dorchester doesn't like it."

"Huh? Who's Dorchester?"

"My puppy."

Alex made a quick scan of the cab then raised an eyebrow. "Where're you hiding a puppy?"

Ellie laughed. "Dorchester's not real, Daddy. He's a pretend puppy." She moved her hand as if she were petting a dog. "I'm practicing so I'll be ready for a real puppy someday. And don't you worry. Dorchester is very good. He won't cause any trouble."

Alex slowed the truck to a crawl and put a hand on Ellie's shoulder. He didn't have many bright spots in his life, but his daughter was one of them—the most important one. "I promise we'll get a puppy as soon as I get that promotion. Say, why don't you be my lookout and tell me if you see any more rocks in the road."

Ellie sat up straighter on her booster seat and gave him a salute. "Aye, aye, Daddy. I'll pretend I'm Uncle Matt in the crow's nest, looking for swordfishes." She made a tiny barking sound. "Dorchester can help look, too."

With Ellie and her imaginary pet guiding them, and by inching forward at the speed of a sea slug, Alex managed to avoid several more rocks and a pothole the size of a dory. Finally, they arrived at the site of the old dock.

Alex stomped on the brakes, and the old pickup rattled to a stop, all four tires thankfully still intact and a few feet away from where the rickety boards began. He peered out the windshield. A postcard-perfect sunset loomed on the horizon, the kind his mother used to call a soda pop sky, because the oranges, purples, and golds illuminating the clouds mirrored the artificially colored sodas she refused to buy for him and his brothers.

He glanced over at Ellie, who was talking in a tiny voice to her imaginary pet. He sure missed having his mama around. He had no idea how to handle pretend pets or a little girl who longed for her dead mother. But the one thing he did know, he needed to do better at being a father.

Letting out a huff, Alex pulled out his binoculars from his pack and rolled down the window. From here, the five, ninety-foot-diameter circular net pens that held the Cowling salmon fry were only several hundred feet away, as close as one could get without using a boat. Which was fine by him. He hadn't been in a boat in a long time—being out on the water brought back the day he'd watched his beloved wife sink beneath the sea . . . every single time.

Alex scanned the water around the nearest pen. Nothing.

Then the next. Nothing.

He focused on the third ring.

There. A black object bobbed up and down near it, making occasional splashes.

His boss had been right. Something was out by the pens.

His stomach unclenched slightly. Something alive, thank goodness.

Now, was it a seal or a shark?

He adjusted the binoculars' focus.

Behind him, the passenger side door squealed open then slammed shut.

He spun around, only to see his daughter dash toward the old wooden pier.

"*No!* Ellie, come back. The dock's not safe." Heart in his throat, Alex jumped from the truck and charged after her.

"Ellie, sweetheart, stop." He grabbed her arm just as she stepped onto the rickety planks of the old dock and pulled her back.

"Let go, Daddy." She shook off his hand. "I'm just going to get that shell. It can be Dorchester's water dish." She pointed to a small clamshell wedged between the planks, just a few feet from the shore.

"You've got plenty of shells like that one at home. Now stay right next to me."

Ellie looked up at him, her hazel eyes so like her dead mother's. "Can you get it for me?"

He looked at the gleaming white shell and the water slapping against the seaworn concrete piers. A cold shiver ran down his back. It might as well be on the outer islands.

He put the binoculars up to his eyes. "No. It's just an old shell. I'm here to make sure the salmon are safe."

She scuffed her sneaker in the gravel. "Stupid fish. All you ever do is worry about the salmon."

"The salmon pay our bills, Ellie." He watched the bobbing object disappear under the water. "Might be a big bad seal out there, trying to eat them. We can't let that happen, can we?"

For a few moments, she stood quietly next to him, then she pulled on his sleeve. "We aren't going to make it to the ice cream social, are we?"

He shook his head.

Her little mouth puckered. "I never get to have any fun. Aunt Olivia was gonna take Rory, Peter, and Teddy. You should have let me go with them."

"I'm sorry, Ellie. Tell you what. We can stop at the supermarket and buy popcorn and ice cream and have our own party at home. I'll read you your favorite book."

"The one about the mermaid that Mommy bought me?"

Heavens, he hated that book, and the memories it rekindled, but what choice did he have?

Alex nodded. "Whatever book you want."

"Okay." She tugged on his sleeve. "Can I look, too?"

How could he refuse after letting her down?

Alex lowered the binoculars and placed the strap around her neck. Then he stood behind her and held the lenses to her eyes as he adjusted the focus. Narrowing his gaze against the glow of the setting sun, he guided her to the spot he'd last seen the object. "There. That black blob. Can you see it?"

She gave a little jump and pointed. "Yeah, there it is. Oh, it's coming toward us." She bounced up and down. "Here, Mr. Seal." She wiggled her fingers. "Here. Don't eat my daddy's fishies."

Alex peered out over his daughter's head. The seal—or whatever it was—dipped and splashed toward the shore. Now, that was rare. Sea mammals usually moved sleekly through the water.

A bad feeling washed over him.

"Can I use the binoculars for a minute, sweetheart? Not sure that's a seal."

Ellie passed them up, and he went back to studying the creature as it neared the far end of the crumbling pier. For a moment, it sank below the surface then popped up again. With a twist, a black-suited scuba diver hitched up onto the dock and sat with his feet hanging over the side.

Silhouetted by the setting sun, the diver removed his facemask, tore off his hood, and shook out his hair. Long, wavy strands of hair glowed pink in the sunset.

Alex focused in. The swimmer was all feminine curves. Not a he. A *she.*

For a second, he was stunned. Then he gave himself a shake. What was a strange scuba diver doing nosing around the fish pens, especially after that out-of-town student had been found dead out there? It didn't matter that it was a woman, a gorgeous one, at that.

Whoever the diver was, she'd better have a good explanation, or she would be in deep trouble. Nobody was going to mess with Thomas Cowling's fish pens and steal his promotion away.

Ellie slipped her fingers into his and tugged.

He glanced down. His daughter's face was round in wonderment. Her eyes fixed on the diver.

"Look, Daddy. It's a mermaid. Maybe she's seen Mommy?"

He gazed again at the woman. She'd removed her oxygen tanks and was now busy checking the gauges. In a minute, she'd turn and see them.

His heart raced. Ellie didn't need her memories of her mother crushed by some tourist.

Alex scooped up his daughter and hurried back to the truck. He'd talk to Miss Scuba tomorrow, when Ellie wasn't around.

He took one long look back.

Scuba Diver Lady would be trouble, all right. Trouble he didn't want to have.

Chapter 2
CAT
Sunday Evening

Cat Silva shook out her hair and took several deep breaths. Despite the August heat, the water in the harbor was much colder than she'd expected, and murkier, especially around the fish pens. That would make completing her research much harder. She might have to stay a few days more than the week she'd budgeted. Not that she minded staying longer.

This had to be one of the most beautiful places in the world. Across the harbor, the sun, in a fiery display of red-orange, golds, and violets, slowly set behind the gray, weathered, cedar-shake houses that lined the shore. Tide Harbor, with its peacefulness and friendly people, was the kind of place she'd dreamed of living in as a child. Even now, she'd love to leave the city behind and settle here. But, what would she do about Momma?

Momma. Yikes. She'd promised to call every day at six, and it had to be well past that.

She yanked off her flippers, tossed them onto the dock, and then unzipped her wet suit.

Zoom. An engine roared to life behind her.

Cat spun around just in time to see a banged-up pickup with a noisy muffler backing up and pulling away from the dock.

The hairs on the back of her neck rose. Had someone been spying on her?

She climbed to her feet and tried to make out the driver, but the last light of the sun glared blindingly off the windshield.

The truck straightened out, and a small child, her oval face surrounded by a mass of unruly black curls, leaned out the passenger side window, waving furiously.

Cat gave herself a shake and waved back. Just a girl and her parent taking in the glorious evening. Foolish her. This was friendly Tide Harbor, Nova Scotia, not New York City.

Humming her favorite pop song, she picked up her tank and fins and headed up the dock, gingerly avoiding the rotted planks. Then, following the well-worn footpath, she reached the paved road where she'd parked her rental car and stowed her scuba gear in the trunk. She slammed the lid down and stared down the road.

Why had the pickup driver driven right down to the dock, anyway? Only a fool would risk damaging their vehicle, no matter how battered it was. And his truck had sure been battered.

She ran a hand along the shiny red finish of her rental. She'd taken one look at the boulder-strewn lane with potholes that rivaled the best New York City had to offer and resigned herself to hauling fifty pounds of gear down to the water. Still, it had been worth taking a dip late in the day at the turn of the tide. The ocean had been so still and quiet, the gentle flow and ebb relaxing after her flight from the city and the almost two-hour drive to Tide Harbor.

She unlocked the door just as her cellphone rang, the hard-rock ringtone piercing the silence of the evening and bringing her back to the reality of her life.

Digging in her backpack, she found her cell and flicked it on.

"Catalina. You there?"

She jerked the phone away from her ear. "Yes, Momma. You don't have to yell." She didn't have to call her Catalina, either. She hated that name, and the memories it brought.

Catalina had been the silent girl who wore thick glasses and hid from the stares. Cat was hip and bold, and she gave people in-your-face reasons to stare.

Her mother's voice lowered to semi-truck loud. "But you are so far away."

Cat peered out toward the mouth of the harbor, seven hundred miles from Larkin Avenue in Brooklyn, and lied a little. "Not that far, Momma. And I'll be home in a few days, as soon as I get my samples. Why d'you call?"

"I can't find the TV clicker."

She rolled her eyes, glad her mother couldn't see her full-of-sass reaction. This was the kind of thing she'd worried about before setting out. Sure, her brothers said they'd check in on their mom, but there were all the daily little things she did to keep Momma happy, like put the TV remote in the cute pink fish-shaped holder she'd given her for her birthday.

She pictured the small three-bedroom house she'd grown up in. The remote couldn't be that hard to find. "Go look on the coffee table."

She could hear her mother huffing her way down the hall.

"Nope."

"How about on the sofa?"

Another nope.

Cat leaned against the car and ran through the litany of places the remote might be. "The sink top."

"No."

"The cupboard."

"No."

"The refrigerator."

"No."

Just as she was about to give up, she heard a shout of success.

"Found it."

Finally. Dare she ask?

"Where was it, Momma?"

"In that ugly plastic fish thing you gave me for my birthday."

Cat stifled a groan. "Great. Next time—"

"Got to go. *Law & Order* is on."

"*Law & Order*? Since when—"

The phone clicked off.

Cat gawked at it. Now that was weird. Two days ago, her mother wouldn't have been caught dead watching *Law & Order*, claiming those police dramas made her scared to walk down the street.

Cat slipped her cell into her pocket. Well, one disaster avoided. Later, she'd call her big brother, Rob, and make sure he came down from his fancy penthouse apartment in Manhattan to check on their mother. Maybe he could put a string on the remote and tie it to the leg of the coffee table so she couldn't wander off with it. And maybe he could find out why she was suddenly watching *Law & Order*, too.

She drove over the rise and drew the rental car to a halt. Indigo and purple clouds scudded across a fading lavender sky. Gentle waves lapped at a stellar crescent beach, the sand white against the dark of the sea. Seagulls swooped overhead. A cotillion of terns floated on the rollers. Beauty. Peace. Water. If she could, she'd quit clawing after the full-time teaching position at New York University and move here in a New York minute.

But with her dad gone, how could she leave Momma by herself?

Cat turned down the newly graveled drive. Up ahead, surrounded by a stand of scrubby pines, their tips bent in the direction of the prevailing winds, stood a traditional Nova Scotia house with a single-peaked dormer rising above the front door.

Wearing weathered-silvered cedar shakes and slightly tilted to one side, Captain Fletcher's looked like it had been there forever, battling winds. But, actually, it had been built in the sixties, on boggy ground by an overly optimistic pair of entrepreneurs.

Behind the house, and as incongruous as a row of log cabins on Park Avenue, a string of newly renovated bungalows sported a whimsical mix of red, orange, green, and yellow siding, bright enough to be seen from across the harbor, and probably by the passengers on the jets streaking by overhead on the transcontinental flyway. Which was the point, according to Rosie Masden, the overly welcoming transplant from Ottawa.

How else could she lure tourists to an out-of-the-way, small seacoast town on the Minas Basin? And, Rosie insisted, it was working. Captain Fletcher's Seaside Bungalows were booked nearly solid for the entire summer. Although Cat had a hunch the bookings were more likely due to Rosie's enthusiastic listing on every vacation rental site on the web—that's how she'd found it. With the spectacular sunset view of Fletcher's Cove and a weekly rate lower than the B&B in town, who could resist?

Not her.

The dreamy photos and the discovery that the largest salmon farm in the Minas Basin sat out in the harbor had drawn her to provincial Canada when she could have been sampling fish pens off the coast of Maine, several hundred miles closer to her momma.

Cat parked in the lot and headed toward her bright orange bungalow. Rounding the corner of the house, she surprised her landlady, who was drinking iced tea on the back porch.

Rosie held up her glass and yelled, "Come and join me."

Cat hadn't escaped her momma to replace her with another watchdog, so she gave a wave and said, "Off to take a shower."

"You do that, girl. After, come on over and have some cool mint tea and a chat. Give you the low-down on the hot spots in town. I know Tide Harbor's pretty quiet, but we do have some nightlife and good-lookers, you know."

Good-lookers. Just what she didn't want.

She ran her finger over the scar marring her upper lip. Good-lookers took a good look at her and turned away.

She wanted to head down to the beach and watch the last of the sunset. Alone. Listen to the rhythmic roll of the sea. Alone. Lie beneath the stars. Alone. And that was exactly what she would be doing this evening.

Cat trudged up the gravel path to her cottage. She didn't need a good-looker to feel complete. She'd checked off almost every box on Cat Silva's Six-Step-Plan-for-Happiness.

One, she'd gotten her degree in marine biology when everyone in her family had said she'd never succeed.

Two, she'd earned her Master Scuba Diver rating.

Three, she'd beat out the guys and was first in line for the highly competitive tenure track position at New York University.

Four, she was going to get that position. She had a well-funded research project underway that would produce a surefire report on salmon farm pollution and her much-needed publication.

The fifth thing on the list was to get a place of her own. Somewhere with a view of the ocean.

Cat unlocked the door of her rental cottage, stepped inside, and smiled. Somewhere like this compact bungalow with its windows facing the cove and the delightful sea-themed décor.

She threw her knapsack on the bed and winked at the orange fish painting hanging over the headboard. The cartoon fish had fins in impossible places and a grin better suited to a Cheshire cat than an inhabitant of the ocean's depths. Whoever had painted it had surely never seen a real fish. But she loved how it made her laugh. She'd even named it with the highly unoriginal but totally appropriate Goldie.

She wanted a poster just like it to hang in her own place when she got one.

But that step was on hold. Right now, taking care of her momma was more important. At least, until she recovered from her father's sudden death. And step six? Find a man who loved her for who she was and not how she looked. That lay in the distant future. The so far distant future that it might never happen.

But, at this moment, none of her dreams mattered.

Momma came first.

Chapter 3
ALEX
Monday Morning

Holding his breath against the fishmeal stink of Cowling Fish Farm's landing bay, Alex headed down the hall to his boss's office. He stopped in the doorway and peered inside. Thomas Cowling was wielding a fly swatter and yelling at the top of his voice.

Alex hung back. Bad timing. Boss Man was on another one of his rampages. But then, it was always a bad time to see Thomas.

"Take that." The swatter smacked down. Thomas swept up the crushed fly and dropped it in the wastebasket. Flyswatter in hand, he spun around and caught view of him. "Alex. Get in here. Now. They've identified the body."

Alex hesitated. He didn't want to know who had died out there, nor how.

Thomas slapped another fly flat then wagged the swatter at him. "Come in already."

He forced himself across the threshold and stood before the monster mahogany desk that took up most of the office. It looked totally out of place, surrounded by fish crates and safety posters. But nothing was too good for Thomas Cowling, the boyhood friend who'd never been told no by anyone.

Alex gnawed the inside of his cheek. "So, who was he?"

Thomas swatted another fly. "Some college kid from Toronto. Here with his buddies to go kayaking. RCMP found a knife on him. *A knife.* One of those daft eco-terrorist types, for sure. Probably planned on slicing the pens open and letting the salmon escape."

Alex nodded in agreement. But the idea that a college student would cut the netting didn't sit well with him. Anyone set on destroying fish farming would know that releasing genetically modified fish into the natural environment would cause even more environmental damage. He'd have to do some further digging into that story.

"And this." Thomas shoved a newspaper at him. "Halifax paper has another stupid article about toxin levels in farmed salmon. Crazy eco-alarmists. I raise a good product here. Healthy. High in protein and omegas. In tightly controlled pens. No escapees from one of my fish farms. But these outsiders get everyone riled up with scare-mongering. It hurts business."

"And gets boys killed."

Thomas scowled. "Kid's own fault. All this outcry has to stop, Alex. I've done a good thing here." He turned to peer out the window at the harbor. "Look out there. Fish just waiting for us to gather them in. Don't have to go out to sea for days at a time. Don't have to freeze our fingers and butts off in winter."

Thomas spun around and faced him. "Remember when we had nothing, you and I? Thought we'd have to break our backs fishing like our poppas did? Now I employ over forty people. Never have to put my toe in a boat. And I add some oomph to Tide Harbor's non-existent economy at the same time."

Alex nodded his head. As a boy, he'd dreamed of being a fisherman, captaining his own longliner. But that dream had died along with his wife.

Now he had a new dream, one hitched to Thomas's. He was going to make it big in fish farming like his childhood friend had done. He just needed to get his shaky finances in order and gather enough capital. If that meant he had to uproot from Tide Harbor, then that's what he'd do.

He sucked in a breath. The timing couldn't be worse, but he had to ask now or it would be too late. "About that head of security job you have open at the Halifax terminal? I want it."

Thomas came around the desk and put an arm over Alex's shoulders, the way he used to when they were kids and he wanted to wheedle him into doing some troublesome prank, like stealing the laundry off his mother's wash line or sneaking out in his cousin's moss boat.

"Now that's what I have been hoping to hear. So, you're ready to move on, buddy. That's great."

Alex's gut clenched. He'd never be ready to leave his siblings and the town he'd grown up in, but he had to . . . for Ellie's sake.

Thomas's arm slid off his shoulders. "One thing, though. This is a big step up in terms of responsibility. The Halifax position will put you in charge of a crew of twenty security personnel at the shipping docks. I have to know you'll show up, that you'll follow my orders. No going off on your own or coming up with some 'creative' solution."

Alex focused on the smashed fly. "I know I let you down in the past, but I've made up for it. I've done everything you've asked. Went for counseling. Even hounded that ecologist out of town for you last year. Though he was harmless—doing research on black-headed gulls."

Thomas snorted. "Anyone with the word eco in their job title is not harmless, witness that dead body." He frowned. "You didn't get rid of that for me, did you? Like I asked. Brought in the police."

Alex clasped his hands behind his back to keep from smashing his boss's face in. "They'd already been called by the sanitation crew."

"But you could have at least moved the body away from the pen like I asked, before anyone else called it in."

Alex's chest constricted. And there was the crux of the matter. His aquaphobia made him totally unqualified for the position he held, and everybody in Tide Harbor knew it. He owed Thomas everything—allowing him to stay head of security after Helen died, ignoring his bouts of depression, and not demanding payment on the mortgage. But to ask him to move a body floating in the water, when he knew Alex didn't go near the sea, had either been a test of his loyalty or another chance to make him feel guilty.

His old buddy gave him a half-smile that looked more like a sneer. "Take it easy, Alex. It all worked out. It's just you're too soft-hearted sometimes." He sat down. "It's what Helen loved about you, you know. Said so when she turned down my proposal."

Alex rubbed his finger where the wedding ring used to sit. "I'd rather starve with a man with a tender heart," Helen had told him when he'd asked her why she'd married him and not Thomas, "than grow fat with a man with one made of stone."

Thomas thumped the desktop. "So, I let her go—for you. Because we are best buddies, right?"

Alex fought the pang of guilt that rose unbidden. She should have married Thomas. Then she'd still be alive.

Once, not so long ago, he'd have stormed out and done one of his famous disappearing acts—gone inland to his family's hunting cabin and hole up for days at a time, fighting depression. But Helen was gone two years now, and he had hardened his heart, at last.

He peered at the man who'd been his rival on the ball field, in the classroom, and in love. He would not lose this opportunity because of stagnant jealousy or debts owed. Having Thomas on his side was key.

Alex took a deep breath and forced out the long overdue apology. "Helen said a lot of things. I'm sorry she hurt you."

Thomas fiddled with the flyswatter. "Time we all moved on. I'll pencil your name in for that job. At least, it doesn't involve water. Gus retires at the end of the month. Think you'll be able to move to Halifax by then?"

Four weeks. To pack. Find an apartment. Enroll Ellie in a new school. Sounded daunting. But he could do it—he had to—before there was another dead body he refused to get rid of.

"Sure. Just let me know the date, and I'll be there."

"That's set then." Thomas smacked another fly. "By the way, did you discover what was out by the pens this time, or do I have to wait for the police to show up again?"

Alex pictured the woman he'd seen at the dock. She seemed harmless enough. "Thought it was a seal, but looked to be a female tourist out scuba diving. Someone staying at Rosie's, I bet. Probably gone by now."

He sure hoped she was gone. When he'd spied that sleek figure with her hair flowing down her back, his heart had done a little flip, something he hadn't felt in a really long time. Something that felt a lot like attraction. Not that he was interested. Not at all.

Ellie was the only female in his life, and he owed it to her—and to Helen—to keep it that way

Whack. Thomas took out another fly.

"You said she was scuba diving? Seems odd. Tide Harbor is not a Caribbean underwater paradise. Got all kinds of nasties down there"—he flicked the dead fly off the desk—"as you know."

Yes, he did know. Still, her equipment had been none too fancy.

"I'm no expert on scuba, but the woman looked like an amateur to me."

"That doesn't make me feel any better." Thomas huffed. "A newbie diving alone? Idiot gets hurt out there, she'll probably figure out some way to sue me. Whether she's a rank amateur or a master, either way, any stranger out by my pens is a problem. I want you to keep a watch on her, Alex. I don't want to read another eco-attack in the paper or discover another tourist's body floating by my pens."

"No problem. I'll go find out where she is staying right now."

"In fact, Alex, make that your main assignment." Thomas's lips twisted into a semi-smile. "I want to know everything this 'scuba diving tourist' does, everyone she talks to, and every time she dives into the water until the minute she drives out of town. Got that, Mr. Softy?"

Alex squeezed his hands into fists. Thomas knew all the buttons to press, but giving him a punch in the nose like when they were kids was no longer an option. He forced his hands to relax.

"I think you're overreacting, but I'll do my best."

"You do that, old buddy. Prove to me you can follow orders and deserve that promotion, and I might even give you a going-away perk, like buy that house of yours. I can't pay you top dollar for all that custom work you did, but with the real estate market the way it is, you'd be lucky to sell it at all."

Tail some tourist? Sell Helen's house to Thomas, whom she hated? Alex strode down the steps and out into the parking lot. He had no taste for any of it. If he could, he'd quit this job in a minute.

But he couldn't. He was tied to Thomas and his eco-phobias and often-illegal whims if he wanted that promotion.

Alex glanced at his watch. Running late again. Ellie would miss the read-aloud at the library if he didn't put a move on.

He shoved thoughts of Thomas and an annoyingly attractive scuba diver, who was making his job a headache, to the side and focused on picking Ellie up from his sister's. Ellie was what was important in his life.

Everything else was a big joke life had played on him.

Chapter 4

CAT

Late Afternoon, Monday

Cat trailed her feet in the ankle-deep water and soaked in the warmth of the sun. In front of her, a long stretch of mudflats, stinking of hydrogen sulfide and teaming with life, beckoned.

For a marine biologist, this was a research bonanza. For a dreamy girl from the city, it was paradise. It was only her second day in Tide Harbor, but she knew for sure she'd never be able to finish her research in a week. There were just too many wonderful distractions. Instead of analyzing her water samples like a good researcher, muddy sand squished between her toes and sucked on the soles of her feet.

She studied the grayish-tan goop of the tidal flats.

There. With a skill born of years of practice, she scooped up a *Tritia obsoleta*. The tiny mud snail, its rough, wet shell glistening in the sun like some precious jewel, crept across her palm.

She smiled. "That tickles, little one." The shell guidebooks might be full of prettier snails, but Cat had always been drawn to the less showy creatures—ones that blended in with their surroundings. Maybe because that was something she'd never mastered.

"Hey there." A little girl stood on the shore, jumping up and down and waving.

Cat squinted against the sun. She couldn't be sure at this distance, but it looked like the black-haired child she seen in the truck yesterday. Must live around here.

She waved back then stooped down to return her find to its home. "There you go, *Tritia*. Let's hope that there's nothing in this harbor to make you sick."

She peered out over the water at the circular fish pens floating like giant life preservers on the swells of the outgoing tide and hoped the direction her tests were pointing was wrong. The last thing she wanted to do was hurt the livelihoods of the people who lived here.

Behind her, feet splashed through the water. Cat swirled around. Uh-oh. The clayey mudflats, bared by the tide, were slippery with algae and no place for running.

Sure enough, before she could even yell *stop*, the child's legs flew out from under her, and she toppled face-first into the mud.

The child came up screaming, mud dripping from head to toe.

Cat hurried forward as fast as she could without slipping herself. She waved again. "Don't move. I'm coming."

The child screamed louder.

Please don't let the girl be injured. Although the surface looked smooth, anything could be buried beneath the watery muck—broken shells, jagged rocks, even old pieces of metal. She'd learned long ago to look where she walked and test every step before putting her full weight down.

Cat reached the crying child. She brushed the muddy hair from the girl's face. "Are you hurt, little one?"

The girl shook her head.

"Let's make sure." Cat picked up each small foot, wiped it with a wet hand, and examined the soles. Then she checked the exposed skin of her legs and arms. "Good, you're not bleeding anywhere I can see."

The child cried harder. "But I'm all stinky."

Cat offered her hand and helped her stand. "No biggie. Mud washes off."

A sob broke out. "But Daddy will know I came to the flats." She swiped a muddy hand down the front of her T-shirt, managing to spread the mud more. "I'm not allowed here."

Cat's heart went out to her. She knew exactly what it felt like to be caught breaking parental rules. In twenty-eight years, she'd broken nearly every one her parents had laid down.

"I have an idea. It's a warm day. Let's head over to the sandy beach on the other side of the spit and rinse off. That will make you feel better. Then we'll go explain to your dad it was an accident."

The child rubbed her hands down her legs as if she could make the mud disappear. "No. Can't go there, either."

"Ellie," a voice called from somewhere farther up the dunes.

The child seized on to her like a leech and pressed her face against her. Cat fought to keep her balance against the muddy onslaught. Wet mud squished between them and soaked through her shorts. The nose-wrinkling rotten egg smell intensified. So much for keeping the vacation clothes she'd splurged on clean.

But that was nothing new. She was famous in the Silva family for being the one who came home smelling like she'd rolled in a garbage bin. But then, that was probably because, as a kid, she had discovered hiding in one was a great way to escape her annoying brothers.

The little girl's arms tightened around her. Cat looked down. Tears streamed through the mud on the girl's face. Her experience with injured children might be nil, but something told her this one needed a hug. As her dad always said, *hugs made everything better.*

Ignoring the mud caking her pink shorts and tee, Cat squatted down and wrapped her arms around the small body. "Are you Ellie?"

The head nestled against her moved up and down.

"Is that your dad calling?"

The small head moved again.

"So, I think we'd better go find him." She stood and took her by the hand.

The child planted her feet.

Cat looked into the child's eyes. "Ellie, your dad is not going to hurt you, is he?"

The girl frowned. "Nuh-uh. He's gonna be sad."

Sad? In her family, coming home covered in mud and tar was a laughing matter. They'd been laughing at Dirt Ball Cat for ages. Still, the child had to face her father.

"Well, sad or not, muddy or not, you have to tell him what happened." She offered her hand again.

The child didn't move. "No. It's too yucky. I'll slip again."

Cat glanced down at her newest funny T-shirt find. This one read, "*Sorry I Can't. My Fish Need Me.*" So perfect for a marine biologist. She'd been looking forward to wearing it to class. Oh well, it was already spotted with mud.

She squatted down. "Okay, Ellie, let's deal with getting to solid ground first. I'll carry you." With a huff, she lifted the child out of the mud, surprised to find the girl weighed less than her scuba gear.

The child's muddy black curls draped over her shoulder. Her arms came around her neck. Her legs wrapped around her waist.

Back home, Cat would spend her lunch hour in Washington Square, watching toddlers crawling on the grass and their older siblings playing in the fountain. But she'd never held a young child this close before. Despite the mud seeping through her T-shirt, having this small, warm body huddled against her made her feel needed in a way she'd never felt before. Not that she knew exactly what to do with a child. Mothering was not one of the skill sets her current career required. Item seven on her Happiness Plan—having a family—had been crossed off long ago.

Watching her footing, Cat trudged across the flats toward the high ground. The man's shouts came closer.

A little voice sounded near her ear. "Your hair is so pretty."

Cat smiled. Not too many people complimented her hair with its wacky hipster dye job. *Flamingo Pink*, the hairdresser had called it. Pink was her favorite color. In the city, people stared then looked away, and that was just the way she liked it.

In honor of her completely pink wardrobe and because of her research focus, her students had dubbed her Dr. Salmon. She liked that, too. But for her trip to Tide Harbor, she probably should have forgone the hair dye. Here, people stared and walked into things when they saw her. Well, at least, the guy bringing in the carts had done that when she'd stopped at the local supermarket to pick up some shampoo and ended up buying some wild shade of pink nail polish.

The little girl's fingers crept into her hair. "It smells good, too."

Cat laughed. "Well, it definitely smells better than this mud."

"My puppy's gonna like it."

"You have a puppy?"

"Uh-huh. His name is Dorchester."

"Lucky girl. I always wanted a puppy."

"Don't be silly. You're supposed to have a pet seahorse."

"Oh, I do have pet seahorses. They're one of my favorite sea creatures."

Ellie nuzzled closer. "Of course, they are."

Just as they reached the dry sand, a man came over the rise and halted in his tracks.

Cat stopped and caught her breath. Oh my. This was the girl's father? He must be one of Rosie Maden's good-lookers. Silhouetted against the blue of the sky, his shoulders broad, his hands clenched, black hair flying wild, he looked like one of those sexy models on the covers of the romance novels she loved to read.

Despite the shiver skipping down her spine, Cat gave a wave, and he waved back. Then he was running down the shoreline, feet pounding, his hair blown back from his face. It was the face of someone near panic.

She clutched Ellie tighter. Oh dear, the girl's poor father must be thinking the worst.

"She's okay," Cat called. She clutched the child more securely and hurried toward him as fast as she dared in her bare feet.

By the time she reached him, she was out of breath and splashed from head to foot with mud. Not the best way to make a professional impression. Not that it mattered. All his attention was focused on his daughter.

The little girl held her hands out to him, and despite the mud, he took her in his arms and drew her close. "Ellie, are you all right?"

Cat stood back. She was an outsider, after all.

Up close, the man looked less like a superhero and more like someone who had forgotten how to smile. The worry and fear etched on his face broke her heart. It was the look her father had worn the last time she'd seen him, standing on the pier as the research vessel, *Atlantis*, sailed out of Woods Hole. A look that said he loved her more than life itself and would miss her.

He held his daughter the way her father had held her, his strength gentled, as if he were holding a rare seashell. Seeing them together made her miss her father even more.

Cat shook off the grief that had been hanging over her like a cloud ever since her father had died last year. Her dad wouldn't want her to mourn, as he'd always been her cheering gallery. Dad would want her to be doing exactly this—pursuing her research, exploring the sea.

She wiggled her toes. "Your daughter's fine. Just slipped in the mud."

"The mud?" He turned and glared at her. "You took my daughter on the flats?"

He might be a concerned father, but he had no right to accuse her in that tone of voice.

"*I* didn't take her anywhere. She lost her footing. I rescued her." Cat hooked a stray hair behind her ear.

His eyes fixated on her hair. Okay, she was used to that. Her hair *was* weird.

"Cat Silva." She stretched out her hand. He made no move to take it. She glanced down. "Oops. Little muddy." Maybe it wasn't her hair he was staring at. She'd forgotten she was covered in rather odiferous mud. She wiped her palm on her shorts and offered it again. "I'm staying in one of Rose Madsen's summer bungalows. Just over the rise there."

This time, he took her hand and gave it a shake. "Alex Harris. I live up the road. You were the scuba diver out by the pens yesterday?"

"Yeah, doing a practice run."

"Practice?"

"First time out in a while." She gazed at the harbor. "Cold out there. Never dived this far north before. Do you dive?"

The creases in the corners of his eyes deepened. "Uh, no. Not interested in anything to do with the sea." He hesitated. "Your hair really is pink. Thought it was just the sunset."

Okay, so he *was* mesmerized by the hair and bold enough to admit it. She liked plain talk in a man.

She gave him her sideways smile, the one that said don't-take-me-seriously. "Yeah. Matched my outfit until the mud happened." She brushed the drying mud off her arms. "So, you were the guy in a hurry in that bilious green truck?"

Ellie raised her head. "Daddy thought you were a seal. But I know better. You're a—"

"Hush, Ellie."

For a moment, it looked like he would say something more. Then her phone emitted the ear-jarring hard-rock ringtone she'd assigned her mother, and Alex Harris winced. She really had to change the music. It worked fine when she had to hear her mom's calls over the roar of the subway. Out here, drums and a guy screaming got way too much attention.

The ring repeated, and Cat yanked it from her back pocket, hoping it wasn't bad news. She held up her hand like a stop sign. "Sorry. My momma. Might be a problem. Got to take it."

The guy frowned at her. "And I've got to go. Get Ellie cleaned up. Uh, and thank you for your help." He looked her up and down. "You could do with a wash, too." With that, he turned his back to her and strode away.

Cat flicked on the phone, wondering what the girl had been about to say that her father didn't want her to hear. She hoped it hadn't been something rude. An imperfect bookworm who tripped over her own two feet, in a family of star athletes, she'd been called plenty of names in her life. She hoped Ellie's dad had raised his daughter better than that.

With the phone to her ear and her momma yammering something about the garbage, Cat trudged up the slope. But she couldn't help glancing in the direction Ellie and her dad had headed. Foolish as the idea was, she sure would like to get to know Alex Harris better.

She liked that he said what he thought. She liked that he loved his daughter. And she really wished to know why he wanted nothing to do with the sea when he lived in the beautiful seaside town of Tide Harbor.

Chapter 5
ALEX

Monday Night

Alex tucked his daughter into bed then turned out the light. He took a last peek at her sleeping profile before shutting the door.

Seeing her yesterday, clinging to a stranger in the middle of the tidal flat where she'd been specifically told never to go, had cinched his decision to move to Halifax. His pulse still sped up at the thought of what might have happened. What if that woman hadn't been there? What if the tide had been coming in instead of going out?

He could have lost his daughter, too.

Then there'd been that mermaid business. Why had his sister comforted Ellie on the loss of her mother by telling her that Helen had become a mermaid, swimming in the sea? Despite curves in all the right places, Cat Silva was no mermaid, and she'd soon be gone. Ellie didn't need her heart broken again.

Alex ran his hand down the smooth oak molding of the doorframe then moved into the high-ceiling living room with the fish mobile Helen had insisted he hang from the exposed rafters. He'd worked so hard to build this seaside home for Helen. He'd gone head-over-heels into debt, just like he'd gone-head-over heels for her. He'd believed they'd have a forever here. But he'd been greedy, and the sea had been greedy in return.

Now he would have to sell his dream house, probably to Thomas who, ever since boyhood, had always wanted everything of his. Well, good old Tommy Boy could have it. There was no forever for him, just bad luck.

He headed to his bedroom. Time to clean out the closets and start packing.

Alex stopped. *Idiot*. He'd need boxes and tape to do that. At this hour, he'd be better off checking online for apartment rentals in Halifax.

He returned to the kitchen to retrieve his laptop.

Thump. A knock sounded on the front door.

Alex started. Who came calling all the way out here this late?

Another knock.

He hurried to find out before the noise woke Ellie.

He pulled the door partially open. Rose Madsen, the new proprietor of Fletcher's B&B, stood on the deck.

"Rosie?" He opened the door and put his finger to his lips. "Shh. Ellie's sleeping."

Rosie slipped inside and gazed about. "I knew this was a cool place from the outside, but the interior is really incredible." She spun around then headed to the floor-to-ceiling windows at the front and slid the drape aside. "Must have an amazing view of the cove in daylight. Even in the dark, you can see the lights of the town."

"Interested in buying?"

She turned to face him. "What? You're not selling, are you?"

"Thinking that way. Have a job offer in Halifax."

"You've been a great neighbor, helping me settle into the community. I will miss you and Ellie. She always brightens up my day when she comes over to visit." Rose studied the huge open-plan living area. "You went all out on this place, didn't you? Wish I hadn't tied up all my money in that moldy old wreck I bought. I'd move in here faster than a gull after a tourist's French fry, if I could. But I'm sure you'll find a buyer. Though, perhaps not from here—the locals knowing the story and all." She walked over to the mantel of the stone fireplace and picked up the only photo he displayed of Helen.

Taken just days before she died, Helen stood in front of the house, holding a much younger Ellie. It broke his heart to look at it, but his daughter needed some links to her mother.

Rosie gave him a hard stare. "Your wife was beautiful." She set it down. "But she's not the only woman out there. Don't you think you should get out some?"

Alex turned away. No one could ever replace his dead wife. "I have Ellie."

"Well, that's what I came over to tell you. With the cottages all rented, I can't just pick up and leave, so if you need a sitter, I'm available. And I just adore Ellie. She is always bringing me drawings of your dog." She looked around. "Where is that rascal, Dorchester? Such a clever name."

"We don't have a dog. She's just pretending we do."

"Oh. That's disappointing. Ellie sounded so excited." She lifted her chin. "I guess the story about the mermaid is made up, too?"

Alex clenched his teeth. "Definitely."

Rosie laughed. "Kids do have active imaginations, don't they? Gets them in trouble all the time. Speaking of trouble, I wanted to talk to you about my renter in the Orange Cottage—Cat Silva."

"Yeah, I've met her. Seemed pleasant. Some hair on her."

"Shame to dye blonde hair pink like that. But I guess it's the latest fashion in New York City."

"She's from New York?"

"That's what her passport says. And that's why I'm worried about her. She went off this morning with her scuba gear. A city girl like that, diving alone. Dangerous, I should think."

"You have the right of that."

"I don't want to get her in trouble. Aren't you the security supervisor at Cowling? Couldn't you keep a watch out?"

"My focus is the fish pens and compound, not wayward tourists." No way was he going to admit he'd been watching her . . . from a distance.

Rosie pressed her palms together. "It's just . . . I'm not sure she *is* a tourist. When she's not diving, she spends all her time in her cabin. Never goes sightseeing or even to town much. Tried to get her to test the nightlife, but she shrugged me off."

Rosie gave him a once-over. "You wouldn't be interested in stepping out with her now, would you? Despite the pink hair and the wacky clothes, she's quite attractive. Maybe find out what she's doing in my rental. I tried to peek in, but she has the curtains drawn." She glanced over at the front windows. "Something she has in common with you."

She dug in her pocket. "The tourist board was handing out these complimentary tickets to the Tide Harbor Theater production of *The Tempest*. You could take her. Enjoy the play. Heard somewhere you were an English major in college. Wrote poetry." She laid the tickets on the coffee table.

Heaven save him from small towns where everyone, even recent arrivals like Rosie, knew everything about him. Moving to Halifax was looking better and better.

Alex strode across the room and yanked the drapes together. "It's kind of you to think of me, but I'm not interested in entertaining tourists or listening to Shakespeare at the moment. I plan to be out of here in a month. Got packing to do."

"Well, do think about it. Might be fun." Rosie rested her hand on the doorknob. "You sure you want to sell this house? It could be a wonderful legacy for Ellie. The love you had for her mother is in the very bones of it. Have you considered renting it in case it doesn't work out in Halifax? So you can come back?"

He gazed at Helen's photo on the mantel. Remembered Thomas's willingness to have him move dead bodies. No, he was never coming back.

He shook his head. "I'm selling. So spread the word. Let your contacts in Ottawa know. Could be a fine vacation home." And perhaps, he wouldn't have to sell it for next to nothing to Thomas.

Rosie nodded. "That it could. It could also be a fine place to raise a daughter." She stepped outside and waved. "Call me if you need a babysitter."

He gave a nod back. "Will do."

Alex leaned against the door and glared at the tickets on the coffee table. Seemed like everyone wanted to know about Cat Silva. Some batty New Yorker with pink hair and apparently the habits of a hermit. Someone who'd be gone in the wink of an eye.

He really didn't want to give her a hard time, but the woman was a bit odd. Scuba diving in the harbor. Walking on the flats. And she'd said her name was Cat. What kind of name was that?

It fit her, though. She had a smooth, sleek way of moving. It had been the first thing he'd noticed about her on the dock. Well, right after he'd ogled her curves. Then there was the way she had bantered with him, all while covered head-to-foot in stinky mud. Few women would have been so relaxed about it. She'd almost made him smile, and he wasn't much on smiling.

Forget the woman.

He strode into the kitchen, flicked on his laptop, typed, "*Halifax apartments*," into the search bar, then deleted it. Shaking his head, he typed in "*Cat Silva*" then waited. The images came up slowly.

Turned out there were a lot of cats named Silva, and even a handful of people with the appellation Cat Silva. But none of the faces glaring at him off the computer screen resembled her. No woman had the same pink hair and cute upturned nose.

Was Cat Silva even her real name?

He shut down the computer and slid back his chair. He might be making a mistake not finding out more about her like Thomas wanted. If Miss Silva was up to something having to do with the fish pens and he missed it, goodbye Halifax. Thomas would make sure he spent the rest of his life doing security patrols around Tide Harbor, and worse.

Maybe Rosie had the right idea. Maybe he should spend more time with Ellie's pink-haired mermaid.

Chapter 6
CAT

Tuesday, Midday

Cat climbed out of her car and carefully set her sample bag on the deck of Orange Cottage. Five more days to go, and her sampling of the water around the fish pens would be complete.

"Whatcha doing?" The little girl from the mud flats bounded up to her. With her hair in pigtails and dressed in denim shorts and a blue cotton pinafore top, covered with white rabbits, the child looked adorable and a lot cleaner than yesterday.

"Hi, Ellie." Cat tipped back her baseball cap. "How are you today?"

"Auntie Rosie is babysitting me while Daddy is fixing the truck so he can take me to summer camp." She wrinkled her nose. "He doesn't trust me after I broke the rules and got all muddy."

"You're all cleaned up now."

"Yep." Ellie climbed up on the deck and pointed to the sample case. "What's in there?"

How in the world could she explain her research on bio-pollution, caused by intensive salmon aquaculture, to a child? She might be able to teach graduate students, but children? She had never dealt with children. If anything, she avoided them. Children had no place in her future.

Cat glanced at the earnest little face. Well, she'd just have to do her best.

She opened the case and took out the plastic tubes filled with murky samplings from the perimeter of the pens. "I'm collecting sea water. I want to find out if there are any chemicals or pollution in the water that might hurt the plants and animals that live in and around the harbor."

The girl pressed her fingers against her lower lip. "Like poison?"

"Yes. But I won't know for sure what's in the water until all my testing is done."

The child studied the tubes. "That water's so dirty. Is that the bad stuff in there?"

"Not necessarily." Cat held one of the samples up to the sun. "See all those flecks floating around? Some of that is algae. Some is silt stirred up from the bottom. And some of what you see are bits of waste from the animals that live under the water. None of those are dangerous. Thing is, you can't always see bad things in the water with your eyes. Sometimes, water can look perfectly clear and yet contain chemicals or bacteria that can make you sick."

"So, how do you find out?"

"That's my job. I use my microscope and other tools to study the water and the creatures that live in it."

"Helen," Rosie called across from the main house. "Don't you bother Miss Silva."

Cat called back, "It's okay. We're just talking." She turned her attention to the child. "I thought your name was Ellie?"

"Well, it's really Helen, like my mommy. But Daddy says Ellie is shorter."

"So, it's a nickname."

The girl nodded.

"Well, Cat is a short way to say my name, too. My full name is Catalina Maria Silva."

"That's pretty."

"Helen's a lovely name, too."

Ellie peered down at her feet. "I like to be called Helen—that's what my teacher calls me—but it makes Daddy sad."

What a strange thing for a child to say? But she knew how important names were. Cat was an extremely different person from Catalina.

"So, what do you want me to call you?"

"Ellie is okay. I'm used to it." The girl tipped her head back and looked at her. "Usually, Aunt Olivia babysits me, but she had to go to the lawyer people. She doesn't want to be married to Uncle Sid anymore."

Cat drew back. *Whoa.* This conversation was getting way too personal.

She eyed the girl. Tide Harbor sure taught their offspring how to gossip at a young age. The last thing she wanted was her starry-eyed view of the locals spoiled. Time for a distraction.

"Would you like to see what lives on the bottom of the harbor?" Cat scurried to the trunk of the car, took out the bucket of bottom-dwelling marine life she'd collected from around the pens, and set it on the deck next to her sample case. She lifted off the lid.

Ellie stood on tiptoes, peering into the bucket. "*Ooo . . .* what's that?"

Cat leaned over behind her. "That's a *frondosa*—a sea cucumber." She reached in and picked it up.

Ellie stepped back. "Yucky."

"No, look at his cute little feet. They're called podia."

"Those little bumps are feet?"

"They are for a sea cucumber. Sea cucumbers help keep the sea clean." Cat turned the creature in her hand. "There's his little mouth. He sucks in algae and tiny, microscopic creatures and sand with those reddish tentacles. The food and sand pass through his body. The waste comes out this end. It looks like poop, but it's really mostly sand."

Ellie giggled.

"What's so funny?"

"You said *poop*."

"So I did. All animals poop, you know. The scientific word is *excrete*."

Ellie gave a little wiggle. "Are you a scientist?"

"Uh-huh. You want to hold him? He can't hurt you."

Ellie wrinkled her nose. "He's ugly. Like a fat wormy thing."

"He can't help that he's not as pretty as his cousins—the sea stars. He looks like this because it helps him survive. His muddy brown color makes him hard to find on the ocean floor. Scientists are curious about all kinds of creatures, no matter how they look. You're not scared of him, are you?"

The little girl shook her head. "My cousins made me hold worms, and it was okay."

"Well, if you are brave enough to hold wiggly worms, I bet you're brave enough to hold Mr. Frondosa."

Biting her lip, Ellie held out her hands. Cat gently placed the sea cucumber on the small palms.

Ellie looked up at her. "*Wooo.* He's really light and slimy."

"Yep. That's the way sea cucumbers are made. All hollow inside so they weigh very little. And the slime helps them stick in one place when the tide turns. But we'd better put the little guy back. He can't breathe out of water."

Together, they slid the creature back into the pail.

A familiar pickup truck with a noisy muffler zoomed into the parking lot.

Cat glanced over. "I bet that's your daddy."

Ellie nodded. "Can I show him Frondodi?"

"Frondodi? Oh, Frondosa, the sea cucumber. Sure."

"Yippee." Ellie took off at a run, her pinafore flying out around her, her pigtails bouncing.

Cat slammed the trunk down. Such excitement over a lowly sea cucumber. She'd had the same curiosity about the world as a child.

Cat shaded her eyes as the man from the mudflat encounter picked up his daughter and spun her around until she laughed.

The way he held Ellie reminded her of her own father, whose arms had always been ready to swing her high when he returned from work, or to hug her tight when the cruelty of the other children got to be too much. She drew in a breath as the old hollowness washed over her. She missed her dad terribly. Ellie was a lucky little girl to have such a loving father, even if he was overly protective around water.

Why was he dressed in an all-gray outfit? Boring. Probably a uniform of some sort. Fitting, she supposed. Alex Harris came across as the type of guy who liked rules and wasn't appreciative of mud-covered strangers with pink hair.

Ellie grabbed her father's hand and pulled him toward her. The closed expression on his face shouted that he really didn't want to talk to her. Well, too bad. She had no intention of disappointing his daughter.

Cat pasted on a big smile and walked over to meet them. She put out her hand. "Good to see you again, Mr. Harris."

He gave her hand a brief shake. "Ellie says she has something for me to see."

Up close, he wasn't a bad-looking man, just a sad one. He'd definitely seem a lot more pleasant if he just smiled. Something terrible must have carved those hard frown lines on his face.

It wasn't his daughter. It was obvious from the way he held her and paid attention to her chatter that he loved her. Did he have some job he hated? His gray garb was too clean for him to be a mechanic. Though she didn't need his fashion choices to tell her that. Based on the state of his truck, he wasn't into auto repair.

She glanced at him again. Not a fisherman, either. Uniforms were definitely not their style. Perhaps, a policeman? Nope. Not right. The Canadian Mounties that she'd seen in the tourist brochures wore those funny cowboy-type hats and red coats. Oh well, it was a small town. She'd find out what he did sooner or later.

Ellie tugged on his sleeve. "It's over here, Daddy. See? It's a frondodi."

"She means frontosa. You probably call it a sea cucumber."

He bent over the bucket, his frown darkening. "Yah sure, that's what it is. A pickler. Good eating, I hear."

Ellie's chin dropped. "Oh no. Is that true?"

Cat nodded. Unfortunately, it was. But it was a harsh fact to share with a young child who'd just met a living one, nose-to-nose.

Ellie's father straightened up. "Just heard tell they've started a big commercial sea cucumber operation down on the southeastern shore. It's considered quite a delicacy in Japan and China."

Ellie gripped the rim of the pail and stared down at the *frondosa*. "Don't worry. We aren't going to eat you. Dorchester and I won't let them get you."

Cat laughed. "Definitely not. Besides, *frondosa* are very important in the ecosystem. They're known as nature's vacuum cleaners. They help keep the ocean floor from being littered with decaying waste."

Alex looked her way. "What do *you* plan to do with it? You leave it out in the sun in that bucket, and you'll have one stinky fish stew, for sure."

Ellie wrinkled her nose. "Daddy, that's gross."

Cat grimaced. She had intended to dissect the creatures she'd collected and take samples to be tested for pollutants, but seeing how upset Ellie was about eating the sea cucumber, she dare not say that.

She had no idea how to explain that sacrificing a few animals for scientific research could help save millions. Didn't matter. She could get another tomorrow. Better to model respect for living things.

"I was planning to go out on the dock and dump him back in. Want to come?"

Alex rested a hand on his daughter's shoulder. "Ellie's not allowed near the water."

Cat nodded. "Yes, I remember. But surely, she can come if we both go with her. You can swim, right?"

He gave a half-nod.

Ellie scuffed her foot in the gravel. "But if you dump Mr. Frondodi off the dock, how will he find his home?"

"As long as he has food and water, he'll be happy. Back in the sea, he'll move around the harbor, happily doing his vacuuming job."

Ellie's father gave her a rock-hard look. "How do you know so much about picklers?"

Cat pulled out her phone and thumbed up a *National Geographic* article about overfishing of sea cucumbers in Maine. She passed the phone to him. "Give me your email, and I'll send this to you."

He grunted and handed the phone back. "Don't bother. How did you catch that one in the first place?"

"I found it at the bottom of the harbor."

Ellie looked up at her. "You swim under the sea?"

"Yep, I use this scuba equipment." She patted her wet suit drying on the deck. "I wear that to keep me warm, and I have air tanks to help me breathe and a face mask so I can see."

Fingers in her mouth, Ellie curled up against her dad. "What's it like down there with the fishies?"

"It's beautiful. Calm. Quiet. Full of amazing creatures. That's why I scuba. I've dived all over the world. I've seen coral reefs, and sharks and stingrays, and once, out in the Pacific, I even saw a giant squid, bigger than a car."

The girl's eyes widened. "Wow. Have you ever seen a mermaid?"

Cat winked at the dad. "Not yet."

Alex Harris gave her another stiff-faced look and took his daughter's hand. "Time to go, Ellie. Say thank you to Miss Silva for showing you her creature."

His daughter tugged her hand loose. "But we have to put Mr. Dodi back in the harbor."

"I'm sure Miss Silva can handle that on her own. Now, come. You've bothered the lady enough." With that, he again took the little hand and set off toward his truck, walking so fast that Ellie had to jog to keep up.

Cat shaded her eyes and stared after them. Well, that was rude. How could he act so kind and loving to his daughter and be so off-putting to her? His mouth hadn't shown a wisp of a smile when she'd winked at him.

She glanced down at her T-shirt. The uptight man hadn't even made a comment about her bright pink tee, which showed a picture of a narwhale holding a sign that read, "*Not a Unicorn.*" Most people found her funny, yet Harris seemed immune. Probably thought her unattractive. He wouldn't be the first man to do so.

She ran her tongue along her upper lip. Her brothers insisted the scar was no longer visible, but in her mind, it would always be there. It was why she loved the sea. It didn't matter what you looked like underwater.

Cat turned back to her specimen bucket and stared down at the ugly creature. "Guess I get to dissect you, after all." Though she would have much preferred throwing the sea cucumber back in if it meant she got to spend a little more time getting to know Ellie and her father. Not that she was interested in dating grumpy Alex Harris or anything—she sure didn't have time for that. But Ellie didn't deserve to be kept away from the water so rigidly.

For one thing, making something forbidden also made it more tempting, and thereby, more dangerous. More importantly, he was denying his daughter the opportunity to explore the wonders of the world she lived in, and that just wasn't fair.

Maybe if she shared her own experiences as a child growing up by an ocean much rougher than Tide Harbor, he'd relax a bit and let Ellie walk on the beach, or at least get her swimming lessons.

The sound of Harris's muffler-challenged truck rattling its way out of the driveway made her turn. She gave a wave, but he didn't wave back.

Cat shrugged. She needed to forget the man. Alex Harris wouldn't listen to a stranger soon-to-be gone, anyway.

Chapter 7
ALEX

Tuesday Afternoon

Alex stared out the window. Outside, tractor trailers hauled away the latest crop of Cowling's prime Atlantic salmon. The shipment was going off without a hitch. Thomas would be happy, and a happy Thomas was a lot easier to abide than an angry one.

But all he could think about was his daughter's current obsession—Cat Silva and sea cucumbers. It was the last part that worried him.

What kind of tourist collected picklers?

He gave himself a shake. Didn't matter. The annoying woman would be gone by Sunday.

Alex refocused on the paperwork littering his desk. He hated shuffling papers and filling out payroll. As long as he didn't have to go on or near the water, he much preferred doing the rounds, checking in with his men, and driving along the service road with the window open and a fresh breeze washing over him as he checked out the security around the pens.

And for the next few days, eyeballing a cute but puzzling scuba diver.

He shut the payroll book. With a larger staff, the Halifax job would mean even more hours at a desk. But he'd do it for Ellie's sake.

He added another paper to Thomas's stack. He couldn't keep working for a man he didn't trust.

It was well past two when he finally got to the day's mail. Alex slit open each envelope with the scrimshaw letter opener that his wife had given him as a birthday present the year after they had married. He ran the pad of his finger over the bare-breasted mermaid carved into the bone handle. Helen had winked at him when he'd unwrapped it. "Looks like me, don't you think, with those long curls?"

He'd nodded.

She'd angled her chest and threw back her hair. "I want you to picture me every time you grasp it in your hand."

And he did. Every single time. And every single time, tears filled his eyes and his gut pinched as if clasped in the claw of a lobster.

He wiped his eyes with his sleeve, lined up the envelopes, and began the tedious process of extracting each missive and deciding where to file it.

He was near the bottom when he saw it—a letter from the RCMP. This would be the report of the inquest into the young kayaker's death. He hesitated before opening it. He really didn't want to revisit that tragedy. Should he just dump it on Thomas's desk and let him deal with it?

Alex held it over Thomas's stack then stopped. What if he was accused of negligence? The pen tender crew had called in the sighting, not him. He'd wasted time debating whether to move the body away from the pen, as Thomas had demanded.

He lifted the folded papers, opened them, spread them out on the desk, and set to reading.

By the time he was done, the packing plant lay quiet and the parking lot was empty. He took a gander at the clock. Six. His sister was going to be furious—he'd be late picking up Ellie again. But this wasn't something he could rush.

He reread the report again. The student had cut his femoral artery on something sharp and bled out in the water, not drowned like everyone had thought. The police were calling it an accident.

He wiped his hands down his face. That should quell the rumors circulating around town about a murderer on the loose. In the past, no one would have thought such a thing in Tide Harbor. But after last year's bombing of the tidal turbine and the murder of the old man, Owen Young, everyone had become more wary.

The victim had been an Ontario college boy, camping with his friends. They'd found no ties to anything criminal or even any interest in ecological issues. What in the world had the kid been doing at the pens that he'd get cut so severely? Nothing like that had ever happened in the harbor.

He reread the last page. What was troubling was they hadn't found the boy's kayak, hadn't uncovered the reason he'd gone out alone without his buddies, nor did they have any leads on what he might have been cut by. Their search of the water around the fish pens had turned up nothing deadly.

Well, he'd leave it to the police to find the answer.

Alex pushed up from his chair, strode down the hall, and peeked into Thomas's office. He let out a long breath. Boss Man was gone for the evening. No need to discuss the police report. Alex threw the papers on the overloaded desk then went out to his truck.

He climbed in and started up the engine. The harbor sky glowed golden in the sunset, a sight that once would have filled him with chilling awe. Tonight, the chills creeping up his back felt a lot more like fear.

He swallowed hard. And what about this Cat Silva who was hanging around? He'd have to keep a closer watch on her, for sure. Or better yet, get her to stop diving in the same place that boy had died.

He accelerated out of the parking lot. Thank goodness he was leaving this town. Something strange was going on, and he had a daughter to protect.

By the time Alex drove into the gravel drive leading to Olivia's, he felt more in control. There were plenty of keen-edged objects, like broken-up boats and jagged rocks, that might snag and cut an unwary swimmer on the sea floor. It was a freak accident. That was all.

He stopped next to the big old ship captain's house that had been his parents and his grandparents before them and leaned on the horn. Then he jumped out, strode to the passenger side, and opened the door.

Olivia came out onto the porch and gave him a wave. "Ellie's on her way. She's fetching that *puppy*."

"Hey, Daddy." Ellie raced down the path, scrambled up into the truck, and settled on her booster seat. She patted her thighs. "Come on, Dorchester."

Alex chewed his lower lip and reminded himself to be patient. "I thought Dorchester was a puppy. That's a pretty high jump for a pup."

Ellie wrinkled her nose at him. "He's growing bigger."

He grasped the door handle. "Okay. So, is he in?"

"Uh-huh. He's right here on my lap." Ellie giggled. "See? He's licking my face."

Alex fastened her seat belt then closed the door before rounding the truck to get in on the driver's side. It was time to prepare her for the move.

"So, I have some exciting news for you." He started up the truck. "Daddy's got a new job. We're going to be moving to Halifax in a few weeks."

"Moving?" Ellie's voice went really small. "From our house?"

He looked over at her. If Helen had lived, she'd be devastated to see her child dressed in washed-out hand-me-downs and sitting in a fifteen-year-old truck. He'd promised her better. The Halifax job was his chance to make good on it.

"We're going to get a new house. Well . . . an apartment at first. You'll love it there. It's a big city. You'll go to a brand-new school. Make lots of friends. Have pretty clothes. Get to visit museums."

"But what will happen to my things? And Mommy's things?"

"We will take everything with us."

She wrapped her arms around herself. "Even Dorchester?"

This imaginary dog business was getting worrisome. He had to wait while she walked him in the morning. Be careful not to forget him when he drove her to summer day camp. And at night, she insisted he couldn't sit on her bed while he was reading to her because he might squash the puppy. Any day now, she'd be begging him to buy dog food. Even his usually easy-going sister had complained.

"Bad enough to have four children underfoot," Olivia had said. "An invisible dog is impossible. One of the boys is always stepping on it, setting Ellie on a crying jag. Please do something and save my sanity."

Alex rotated his shoulders to release the tension. "Ellie, you'll be starting first grade in September. You're too old to have an imaginary friend. I'll tell you what. After we're settled in our new place, we can get a real puppy. Would you like that?"

She hunched over and shook her head. "I'm not going if Dorchester can't come."

"Well, let's talk about that later."

"You always say later." Ellie scrunched down more. "I don't want to move. I don't want a real puppy. I want my Dorchester." She squeezed her arms tightly around her imaginary pet. "He's the best. He's not alive, so he can't die and leave me like Mommy did. Or you will."

His heart twisted so tight he could barely breathe.

Alex patted her knee. "I wouldn't leave you, Ellie. Never."

She gazed up at him, her blue eyes wet with tears. "Promise?"

All he could do was nod and pray there was nothing dire in his future.

Chapter **8**
CAT

Wednesday Morning

The jarring ringtone Cat had assigned her mother reverberated through the small bathroom. Why did she keep forgetting to change that horrid music? She made a quick mental note to find something more subdued as soon as she hung up. Then she jumped out of the shower, ignoring the water dripping onto the floor, and grabbed the phone off the sink top.

"Hi, Momma." She flipped her wet hair off her nape. Leave it to her mother to call at the most inconvenient time.

"Where are you, Caterina? Why aren't you home yet?" her mother sputtered. "You didn't leave the country again, did you?"

Cat's stomach did one of those oh-no clenches like she got after eating too many Coney Island hot dogs. She hated to lie. She grasped on to the bathroom vanity. But no way could she tell her mother the truth.

"No, I'm in—" She stopped. Maine would be too far. "Massachusetts. Doing my research, remember?"

"Don't we have enough fish here for you to study? You've been away forever, and the food those Wheels people deliver is tasteless. I need you here to cook for me."

"I told you it would take a week, at least. It's only been three days—well, four and a half. I'll be home before you know it."

Her mother's voice rose. "Now you listen here."

Cat held her cell away from her ear.

"You come home today. I'm coming down with something. I can tell. Probably caught the flu from those strangers delivering the glop they call food."

Cat's stomach clenched tighter. "I'm sorry you are not feeling well. Have you called Rob? He promised to look in on you."

"Rob has his business to take care of. I need you, my darling girl. No one else cooks lasagna like you."

She sighed. This was what it always came down to. Until she married and had children, her mother would consider her a live-in do-body, not the accomplished marine biologist she was. Still, she loved her mother.

In the past, she would have abandoned her work, packed her things, and rushed home. Not this time. This time, her career was on the line. Without her professorship, she'd have nothing to call her own.

With one hand, she grabbed a towel and wrapped it around her. She stepped into the bedroom and sat down at the small desk littered with samples and testing materials. She peered at her computer and the stack of notes. She only had three more days to finish.

Cat controlled her voice. "I can't come home yet, Momma. I explained how important this research is. If I don't publish an article by the end of this year, they won't renew my contract at NYU."

Her mother coughed. "You care more about those stupid fish of yours than you do me." She coughed again. "I'll just sit here all by myself, feeling sick." The phone clicked off.

Cat gazed at the blank screen. Her mother could be manipulative. But was she wrong this time? Was her mother truly sick? Fingers trembling, she hit the icon for Rob. There was a rustling, and then her big brother came on the line.

"I'm trying to catch a cab. What's up, sis?"

"Rob, Mom called. Says she sick."

"You know Momma—she always says she's sick when you do something she doesn't like. She complained she was on death's door the entire time you were off doing research last summer. She didn't die, did she?"

Cat sunk down on the bed. "No, Dad did." The hole in her chest reopened. He'd passed away when she had been out in the middle of the Pacific Ocean, carrying out her postdoc research. She hadn't even made it back in time for the funeral. "Momma's all alone now."

"That's what she tells you. She's not senile—she's manipulative. Time you stood up to her. All the rest of us did. Or are you as boneless as those fish you study?"

"I think you mean jellyfish. Fish have bones."

"Well, *you'd* know, what with that fancy degree. Think of what you went through to graduate. You had no trouble standing up to your chauvinist professors and cutthroat colleagues. Apply that same courage to dealing with Mom."

"But what if Momma really is sick? She's getting old. Can you check on her?"

"I'll call her later. Look, I'm meeting a client in . . . twenty minutes. Cab's here. Got to go." The phone went silent.

Cat glanced at her suitcase. She could leave now and fly home. She could be there in six hours.

The phone rang. Momma *again*. She flicked it on.

"So, you coming home?" In the background, she could hear voices. Now, that was odd. Momma had just said she felt sick.

Cat stared at the phone. "Momma, what's going on there?"

"Nothing."

She listened closer. Yeah, definitely someone was talking in the background, and it wasn't the TV.

"You have someone there."

Her mother sniffed. "You left me all alone, so I invited some neighbors over."

"I thought you were sick?"

"I am. See?" Her mother coughed into the phone.

Despite the *Dr.* in front of her name, Cat was no physician, but even she could tell that cough had been fake.

She had to stop letting her mother get her way. Time to add another step to her plan: make Momma less dependent on her.

"Look, I will be home just as soon as I get all my samples. I promise to cook your favorite recipes for you." And freeze them so she could go out once in a while and have a life of her own. Her brother was right—time to stop being Momma's jellyfish.

There was a snuffle, and then her mother came back on the line. "Okay. I want a huge pan of your lasagna first. And don't forget to call at six."

"Will do, Momma."

Cat clicked the phone off and gave the orange fish painting a thumbs-up. "One for the boneless invertebrate, Goldie. Now I think I will get some boots so I can explore the mud flat some more."

Tide Harbor Marine Supply had a rather limited assortment of wading boots. Cat stuck her foot in a knee-high rubber wader and wiggled her toes. Too big. She'd have the skin rubbed off her heels in no time. She shook it off and moved down the line. The next pair fit better. She took a step. Then another. Yes. Now, if only this pair were pink or some color other than sour olive green.

She looked longingly back at the other pair. At least those had red toes. She imagined the blisters and huffed. Sometimes, you just had to be practical.

"New footwear?"

Cat glanced up. Ellie's father stood beside her. Today, under the fluorescent store lights, Alex Harris looked less like a Coney Island lifeguard and more like a respectable community member. With his too-long black hair combed smooth, his jaw clean-shaven, and garbed in a nondescript gray shirt tucked neatly into a pair of identical gray trousers, this was a man whom she could easily resist. Good. She could deal with Mr. Ordinary as long as she forgot what he looked like with his hair windblown and his biceps showing.

Cat gave him a full-face smile. "Good morning. No Ellie today?"

"She's at her school's summer program."

"And you're free to go shopping?"

"Came in for some strapping tape." He looked down at her footwear. "You're not planning to go out on the flats again, are you? I would have thought you'd not want to get covered in that mud a second time. It stains terribly. I had to throw out Ellie's T-shirt."

"I have a well-supplied suitcase." Cat did a little curtsey to draw his gaze down to her outfit of the day. Her silver leggings with the pink flamingos, the filmy pink miniskirt, and the pink camisole with its sequined flamingo design that read *"Majestically Awkward"* never failed to set her students tittering when she walked into a classroom.

He gave her a once-over, his face expressionless, or was that a twitch at the corner of his eye?

"So, I see. Very, uh . . . pink."

"Pink's my favorite color."

His lips moved up—slightly. Definitely a twitch. "Maybe a little fancy for wandering across mudflats." His mouth settled into a firm line. "Not that the seagulls mind what you wear, I'm sure."

"Seagulls? I don't dress to please birds."

One eyebrow rose. "No?"

She shook back her hair. "I dress to match my crowning glory."

No laugh. Oh well, Alex Harris was made of sterner stuff than first-year biology students. But of course, he was a man.

With a daughter.

Though, according to Rosie, no wife.

Still, what was she doing flirting with him?

She kicked off the boots and shoved her feet back into her pink, clunky-heeled sandals. She then picked up the waders. "That's why I'm buying these."

He studied her footwear. "City girl?"

Cat wagged her head. "New York City, born and bred. Have a problem with that?"

"Not at all. We love tourists here in Tide Harbor. Here, let me." He took the rubber boots from her, the muscles in his forearms flexing, and she caught a whiff of his aftershave, something clean and citrusy, and way too enticing.

She followed him up to the counter, noticing other things she shouldn't—broad-shoulders, narrow hips, a purposeful stride. Alex Harris was a pulled-together man. Fine to look at, but not the man for her. No way would she allow herself to be attracted to a grumpy Mr. Ordinary who wouldn't let his daughter explore the ocean.

Her phone made a soft chiming sound—the new Momma ringtone. She stopped and tugged it out of her purse.

Alex set the waders on the counter, next to a pile of rope and tape. "Put these on my tab, Adam."

"What?" Cat ignored the ringer and put her hand out, moving the boots back. "No, you mustn't. I can afford them."

"I'm sure the shorts and shirt my daughter ruined were far more expensive. Please, let me do this to repay you." He moved the boots back and grinned at her.

"All I did was pick her up after she fell." To the right of the counter was a display of children-sized boots. "Say, how about I buy her a pair of waders?" She headed to the rack and picked up a cute yellow pair with ducks on them. "What's her size?"

His smile faded. "No. She doesn't need them. The mudflats are off-limits. Ellie knows not to go there again." He gathered up his stack of tape. "Enjoy your stay in Tide Harbor."

Cat frowned. Well, really. She bet Ellie would be right back out there the minute her dad turned his back. That was what she'd done as a child.

She pictured Ellie's foot in her hand then examined the boots. These would do fine. And if they didn't fit, Mr. Grumpy could return them.

Cat clunked the boots down on the counter. A pile of T-shirts, marked down fifty percent, sat on a rack beside the cash register. She ought to get some more practical clothing if she planned on clomping over the mud flats again.

She sorted through them. The colors were blah—white, gray, black—but she liked the slogans. Obviously, someone in Tide Harbor had a sense of humor, even if Alex Harris didn't. She picked out three and added them to her bill.

With a smile at the cashier, she hefted her bag and turned to leave.

The door popped back open. Alex Harris stuck his head in.

"Uh, I was wondering . . ."

Cat stilled. Had he seen her buy the kid's boots? Was he going to chide her?

She scrunched her nose. "Wondering what?"

"I have some tickets to the local theater production. They're doing *The Tempest* tonight. Would you like to come with me?"

"You barely know me. Don't you have someone else you could ask?"

"I haven't dated anyone since my wife died."

"Oh, I'm so sorry." How sad. No wonder he was so protective of his daughter. No wonder he looked so lost and sullen, and dressed like he wished to disappear into the fog. No wonder Ellie didn't want to get him upset.

She wanted to throw her arms around him and hug him. Good thing her arms were loaded down with her purchases. She'd probably scare those awful gray pants right off him.

"Thank you. So, how about it? We could get to know each other better." His mouth twitched. "Maybe find out if you have anything in your suitcase that isn't pink or has flamingos on it."

"You might be disappointed."

"Surprise me. Shall I pick you up at seven?"

She caught her tongue between her teeth. Why not? She'd be gone in three days.

"Fine. Just be sure to bring a foghorn."

"What?"

She eyed his gray clothing. "Don't want to miss you in the fog."

Chapter 9
ALEX

Thursday Afternoon

Alex turned down the road to his sister's house. He hoped Olivia hadn't heard her reclusive brother was taking someone to the play tonight. She'd have the whole town bubbling over with that hot tidbit.

He pulled to a stop in her driveway and shook his head. *Idiot.* When he showed up at the tiny theater with a pink-haired tourist on his arm, the gossip mill would go wild anyway. Luckily, he was moving in a few weeks.

Ellie waited outside on the porch.

Olivia stuck her head out. "Late again."

He climbed out of his truck and made a sad face. "Sorry."

"*Right.*" His sister wagged a finger at him. "Good luck finding someone to watch Ellie for you in Halifax. It's only because of my sisterly love that you get away with arriving late."

"I know. And do I appreciate it." Alex pinched his lips together. That was another thing he'd have to do—find a sitter for Ellie. The idea of leaving her with a stranger sent chills down his back.

Olivia disappeared inside, and Alex relaxed the shoulders he hadn't realized had tensed. There'd be no confrontation with his sister today about his date, and if he were smart, he'd cancel it before she heard about it.

Ellie shuffled down the steps and slowly walked to him.

He kissed her on the tip of her nose. "No Dorchester today?"

She shook her head. "He's hiding."

"Hiding?"

She sniffed. "He doesn't want to go to Halifax. I don't want to, either. Aunt Olivia said dogs don't like living in apartments with nowhere to run and play."

Alex closed his eyes and counted to ten. Olivia was going to hear a word or two from him shortly. But first, he had to fix things with Ellie.

"Lots of dogs live in apartments. There are parks where they can have fun. I know the idea of moving to a new place is upsetting, but Dorchester will be fine there, and so will a real puppy when we get one. But we are going to move. We don't have a choice. That's where my new job is."

She shook her head so hard her curls bounced. "But . . . you have a job here."

"I will have a better one in Halifax. And I won't be picking you up late either."

"You won't?"

He tousled her curls. "No, I won't." And he would keep that promise no matter what other sacrifices he had to make. "Now, you go fetch Dorchester, and let's go home. I have a surprise for you."

Ellie looked up at him, her mouth a wavy line that made her look young and unsure.

His heart did a little half-hitch. He'd put that insecurity there. Of course, Ellie would be afraid to leave all she'd ever known behind. He had to chase away those worries for now, and he knew one way to do it. So much for canceling his date.

He squatted down to her level. "Mrs. Madsen is going to babysit you tonight."

The quivery line straightened then turned up. "Do you mean Aunt Rosie?"

"Right. She'll make you dinner and watch a movie with you."

"Goody! Can Dorchester come?"

"Sure. Just make sure he behaves. No more hiding him, okay?"

"Super. I'll go get him. He's always a good boy at Aunt Rosie's. She bakes dog biscuits for him and lets me eat them, too." Ellie raced around to the back of the house.

Alex watched her disappear. *Dog biscuits?* They were probably cookies, but he wished Rose Marden didn't encourage his daughter's fixation on the invisible dog. Not that he'd ever say anything to Rosie now that he knew why Ellie had invented the dog.

Ellie beamed at him as she skipped back to the truck, her hand holding an invisible leash. Alex helped her get settled then got in the other side of the cab.

He backed out of the driveway and turned the truck toward home. He patted Ellie's leg. From now on, he was going to work hard to keep that smile on his daughter's face, even if it meant letting Rosie spoil her and going on a date with Cat Silva.

Ten minutes later, Alex steered the truck into their driveway and parked. He reached across and undid Ellie's seat belt.

She looked at him. "Are you coming to Aunt Rosie's, too?"

"No, I'm going to the play the Shakespeare Club's putting on. Taking Miss Silva, the lady who pulled you out of the mud and showed you that pickler."

Ellie made no response.

He glanced at her. "That okay with you?"

She chewed on her lip. "You gonna be nice to her?"

"I'm always nice to people. I'm nice to you, aren't I?"

She giggled. "You have to be nice to me. You're my daddy. But you don't like her."

"Who? Miss Silva? Well, her hair *is* very pink."

"See? You don't like her." Ellie jumped out and took off for the house.

"Wait." He hustled after her. "I shouldn't have said that. We shouldn't judge people by how they style their hair or by what they wear. It's just that Miss Silva and I have barely met. We need to get better acquainted. That's why I'm taking her to the play. I promise, I'll try to like her."

Ellie spun around. "Good." She bent down and petted a space about a foot above the floor. "Now, Dorchester, be the best puppy ever at Aunt Rosie's so Daddy doesn't worry about us, and he can have fun with Cat."

Fun? Right. Alex marched off to the bedroom to change for his pseudo-date with the Pink-Haired Wonder. It was cute how Ellie worried he didn't like the perplexing tourist. Not liking her wasn't the problem. For some strange reason, he liked her just fine. Despite the hair and her odd taste in clothes, she was funny and entertaining, and she stirred up all kinds of interesting feelings he hadn't felt in a long time.

By the time Alex arrived at Rosie's to drop off Ellie and pick up Cat, the fog blanketed the harbor. Not that it bothered his driving. Navigating in the fog was second nature. After all, Tide Harbor was one of the foggiest places in Nova Scotia, and he'd lived here all his life. Still, he'd hoped for a clear night for Cat's sake.

Tourists always complained about the damp and poor visibility, and he wasn't looking forward to escorting a whiney New Yorker.

He left Ellie with Rosie and hurried over to Cat's bungalow.

She finished locking her door then looked up. "Hi there. Heard your truck pull in." She gave a little twirl. "So, what do you think?"

Alex glanced back at the main house. He knew what he'd told Ellie—you really shouldn't judge someone by what they wore—but there was no way he could show up in town with the yellow apparition in front of him. On the positive side, she'd covered her pink hair with a yellow scarf, and her shapely legs sported yellow leggings decorated with orange goldfish. A little loud, but nothing beyond the realm of tourist fashion.

On the negative side, she was sporting a neon-yellow T-shirt, emblazoned across the front with a large fish and the words, "*Size Matters.*" He'd never live down the teasing.

"So?" she asked again. "I'm not wearing pink. Even covered up my hair."

"Uh . . . nice. For sure, I won't be losing you in the fog." Or anywhere.

Alex swallowed. It would be okay. He'd survive the jokes. He was moving in thirty days and never coming back, and he was doing this for his job, right? Besides, Miss New York City intrigued him. What made this lady tick?

Cat looked him over. "Might lose you, though. Is everything you own colorless?"

He looked down. The local theater production was nothing fancy, but he'd tried to spruce up. He was wearing his gray chinos and a gray plaid shirt.

"Nothing wrong with gray. It's a perfectly fine color."

She sniffed. "If you can call it one. Lead the way, Fog Man."

As they walked up the gravel path to where the cars were parked, Alex glanced at her red rental. It looked a heck more comfortable than his truck. "Wouldn't you prefer to take your car?"

"Oh, no," Cat said. "I love old trucks."

"That's good. Because this one is definitely old." Alex opened the creaky passenger side door, and Cat slid in.

She ran her hand over the childish stickers decorating the glove box. "But much loved."

"Yah, sure, Ellie had some trouble for a while going to kindergarten, so I came up with letting her put up a sticker every time she stayed the entire day."

"How clever." She looked at him with those wide-open eyes of hers. "You're a good dad, Alex."

No, he wasn't. Just ask anyone in town. But, luckily, she didn't know anyone to ask.

He tapped his hand against his thigh. Exactly. Miss Outrageous New York didn't know him. He could relax with her. Be a whole new self. After all, in a few days, she'd just be a memory.

He climbed into the cab and started up the pickup.

Cat leaned forward and swiped the moisture off the windshield with the side of her hand. "It's awfully foggy out."

"Gets that way here. But don't you worry. I'm an old hand at this. I'll drive you there and back safe as can be. I guess you don't get much fog in the city where you live?"

"Not much."

"Tide Harbor is famous for its fog. Sometimes, it hangs around for days."

"They didn't put that in the tourist brochure. I sure hope it lifts, though. I'm only here three more days."

Three days. The worry Thomas had laid on him uncurled slightly.

"Hopefully, you'll get some more sunny days before you go. Too bad you can't stay longer. Have a job to get back to?"

"I teach, and it's summer break. It's my mom I have to hurry home to. She's alone."

"Yeah, I noticed she calls you a lot." More tension dissipated from his shoulders. A teacher. No threat to Cowling that he could see. Time to enjoy his evening. "Couldn't help but notice your T-shirts. You seem to like bright colors and"—how to say this diplomatically—"clever sayings?"

Cat clapped her hands. "Oh, you finally noticed." She turned slightly. "I collect funny T-shirts. This is one of my favorites."

Did she know how sexy she looked in that shirt and how off-color the slogan was?

He concentrated on keeping his face still and his eyes on the barely visible centerline of the foggy road. "It's, uh .. . nice?"

"*Nice?*" She fell back in the seat with a huff. "You don't like it."

He gripped the steering wheel. "Didn't say that."

"But you're supposed to laugh. It's a joke. Fishermen always lie about the size of the fish they catch, right?"

No one could be that naïve.

He braked and pulled the truck over to the side of the road before he hit something. "I get the joke, Miss Silva. It's just kind of over-the-top for around here."

She clasped her hands under her chin. "Oh. Sorry. Didn't mean to embarrass you. Maybe you should take me back to Rosie's."

Ellie would be so disappointed if he didn't at least make an effort at being nice.

Alex touched her upper arm. Mistake. Despite the dampness of the evening, her skin was warm to the touch and soft beneath his palm. He pulled his hand away. "I'm made of tougher stuff. As far as I'm concerned, you can wear anything you want."

"Really? You're not just humoring me?" She fingered the hem of the shirt and peeked up at him through her lashes. "I could put it on inside out."

"No." He gripped the steering wheel and squeezed his eyes shut against the vision of her pulling off the shirt. "I'd still know it was there."

She grinned. "That you would."

He tamped down the laugh that threatened to burst free and started up the truck. "Look, let's just go have a good time."

Chapter 10
CAT

Thursday Night

Tide Harbor's theater group performed in a sawdust-scented, former shipbuilding warehouse. Cat had seen *The Tempest* before, acted out by big-name actors in the city. In comparison, the town's production had numerous glitches and fumbles, yet the cast made up for it by their passionate performance of the Bard's work.

For two hours, despite the uncomfortable folding chair and the minimal set, she'd been transported to a wondrous island in the midst of the ocean. Her whole being felt as light as seafoam. She joined the standing ovation then followed Alex out of the theater and into the night.

She turned to him. "That was wonderful. Thank you so much for bringing me. I love it when the performers emphasize the romantic elements over Shakespeare's social commentary. Ferdinand and Miranda truly related as lovers. That kiss looked real."

Alex lowered his voice. "That's because it was. Those actors are lovers. It's the local scandal. Both were engaged to other people when they started rehearsal."

"Oh my. A real theater romance makes it even more delightful." She caught a glimpse of Alex's frown. "You don't agree?"

"No need to be polite. You must have seen far better performances in New York."

She glanced down at her tee. "I'm wearing this shirt, and you think I'm polite? Believe me when I say I enjoyed it. You can't hear Shakespeare's verse without feeling it intensely. 'We are such stuff as dreams are made on—'"

"'And our little life is rounded with a sleep,'" he finished, putting a hand on the small of her back. "Say, shall we get some coffee over at Kate's?" Alex indicated a cozy-looking café across the street. Several other couples were already heading that way.

Why not? It had been forever since she'd been out with a man. And she was liking this one. Probably too much. He was a loving father, he lived in this beautiful place by the sea, and he knew his Shakespeare. He'd put up with her eye-blinding wardrobe, too. Even introduced her to people he knew, despite the looks they gave her shirt. A real gentleman. A good-looking one. Why not let herself dream a bit? Neither of them expected anything more than a casual evening out, and she deserved a cozy ending to her date as much as any girl.

She looped her arm into his and gifted him her brightest smile. "Sure."

They dashed across the street and hurried inside. The little coffee shop was nothing fancy—some tiny tables, a modern Formica-topped, glass-fronted counter, and hand-lettered signs detailing an amazing array of tantalizing coffees and spiced teas.

Cat inhaled the delicious scents. How wonderful. Cinnamon, vanilla, and fresh brew all mingled together in utter deliciousness.

The only attempt at décor was a series of stained and outdated navigational charts tacked to the walls. She couldn't wait to study them and compare them to the new ones she was using.

Alex guided her to a table near a map showing the head of the harbor. "See anything you like?"

"I see a lot I like."

His mouth quirked up on one side. "Do you?"

Her cheeks heated. Had he thought she was referring to him? How embarrassing. She'd meant the maps and the food.

"Sorry, that came out wrong." She avoided his eyes and studied the plastic menu on the table. "I'll have a cappuccino."

"Have to order at the counter. Be right back."

Cat turned her attention to the nautical chart on the wall beside her. There had definitely been changes on the sea bottom. From what she remembered from the current map, the harbor end nearest the fish pens had once been much deeper. She would have to check the dates against when the Cowling fish farming operation had started.

"Got us some treats." Alex placed two cappuccinos and a plate of assorted cupcakes on the tabletop. "Kate makes delicious baked goods. Always something different. I didn't know which you might like, so I got one of each."

Cat selected the cupcake with chocolate icing and took a bite. Inside, it was filled with rich chocolate fudge that melted in her mouth. She licked her lips. "Oh my, what is this?"

Alex swiveled in his seat to check the sign. "I think that's the one Kate calls Done to Death by Chocolate."

"It's deathly good."

Alex laughed. "Shall I get another?"

Cat surveyed the assortment on the table. "But I haven't tried the rest yet. Which one do you want?"

"None for me."

"But I can't eat all these by myself. Pick one." She slid the plate toward him.

He pushed back a little on his chair. "They are all for you. I just want to watch the expression on your face when you taste them."

"Do you now?" She lowered her gaze and focused on the cupcakes. Oh my, Mr. Grumpy was not only smiling and laughing, he was flirting with her. Well, what would it hurt to flirt back a little? It wasn't as if there could be anything serious between them. They were merely strangers passing the time.

Cat studied the small, exquisite cakes in their red-and-white striped paper wraps. "Let me see. How about this?" She chose the one topped with plain vanilla icing and bit into it. Luscious salted caramel oozed into her mouth. "Oh." She held it up so he could see the filling. "This reminds me of you."

"Huh?"

"All plain and ordinary on the outside, but surprising on the inside. For example, you seem to know everyone in town." She took a lick of the caramel then leaned forward. "So, tell me about yourself."

Alex rested his elbows on the table. "Not much to tell. Grew up here. My dad was a lobsterman and part-time boat builder. I have one older sister, Olivia. She watches Ellie while I work. And a trio of annoying brothers."

"Amazing. I have three brothers, too. Drove me bonkers as a kid. So, are you all lobstermen like your dad?"

"No. My little brother is studying at Dalhousie. Nick"—he glanced over his shoulder—"is out west, despite having Kate here waiting for him to pop the question." He turned back around. "My oldest brother, Matt, is the fisherman in the family. Inherited Dad's seventy-five-foot longliner, the *Emma Mae*. Catches mostly lobsters. Haddock, swordfish, tuna, and such in the summer." He took a sip of his coffee. "I worry about him. It's dangerous. Sudden storms, heavy fog—like tonight—boat accidents." He hesitated. "My mother worried about my dad. Now I worry about my brother."

Cat set down the pink-iced cupcake she'd been just about to bite into. "But everything we do has risks. I could get hit by a taxi on the way to class. My father . . . fell off a ladder last summer, fixing our gutters, and died."

He reached across the table and laid his hand over hers. "I am sorry about your father."

Warmth seeped into her. She'd received many condolences from acquaintances and colleagues, but this off-the-beaten-track stranger had offered the one thing few others had—a gentle touch, simple words. He'd lost his wife. He knew what grief felt like.

She brushed the side of her other hand over her eyes. "Thank you." She slipped her hand out from under his. "But you're right. Going out to sea is far riskier."

Alex nodded. "Fishing is among the most dangerous jobs in the world. Go down and look at the seamen's monument at the end of Water Street. Study all those names. There are eleven Harrises on it, including my grandfather and my father."

Cat leaned across the table and placed her hand on his. "I understand how you feel. The sea is dark, and deep, and dangerous. But it also gives life. Eighty-six percent of the water we drink comes from the sea. Billions of people rely on the world's oceans to provide them with food to eat. The average consumption of fish in the States alone is over twenty pounds per person per year."

Alex slid his hand out from under hers. "You have no idea how I feel about the sea." He rapped his fingers on the tabletop. "If people want to eat fish, fine. But instead of sending men out in small boats and risking their lives, we can farm-raise what we need using aquaculture. Fish pens, like the ones in the harbor, are the future of the industry."

She stuffed the rest of the cupcake in her mouth and swallowed. "So, if you are not a fisherman, what do you do?"

"I'm head of security at Cowling's Salmon Fishery."

The cupcake turned into a pinched, hard knot in her stomach. "Security? What does that entail?"

"I make sure no one bothers the pens or our processing plant." He touched the corner of her mouth. "You have some filling right there."

"Oh." She wiped the icing off then threw her napkin on the table.

Alex Harris was not who she'd thought. He worked for Cowling. He supported open-pen fish farming that was polluting this harbor, and so many others. The aura of happiness she'd been enjoying faded, replaced by an unwelcome suspicion.

"So, is that why you were spying on me the first night I went out scuba diving?"

"No, not spying. Just checking on things. It's what I do. Someone scuba diving alone can get into all kinds of trouble out there. We had a young man turn up dead just a few weeks ago, right in the same area you're swimming. My boss asked me to keep an eye on you. Maybe suggest you stay away from the pens. Nothing more."

Cat gritted her teeth. Of course, Cowling's CEO would sic his security guy on her. Her newest test results showed the company's fish pens were a polluting nightmare.

She placed her palms flat on the table. "Was that what this 'date' was about—getting me to stop scuba diving?"

Alex stood, his face set in hard lines. "No. Rosie had extra tickets, and I thought you'd enjoy the play. See some of Tide Harbor's community life. It had nothing to do with my job."

His simple answer caught her off guard. Was Alex Harris telling the truth? Was it merely bad luck that someone who showed an interest in her happened to work for Cowling? Other than his dour thoughts about the sea, she had enjoyed his company, and he had relaxed in her presence. Even laughed.

Cat rose from her chair. If she told him her real reason for being in Tide Harbor, maybe shared some of her test results, would he be all right with it, or would he run, tattling to his boss?

She gazed across at him. No, she couldn't risk telling him. Three more samples, and she would have all she required to complete her research study. No way could she leave Momma alone for another week while she started over somewhere else. Better to soothe Mr. Security Officer into believing her the tourist he assumed she was.

She gave him a small smile. "I enjoyed the play, and the cupcakes."

"As did I." Alex glanced at his watch. "Best we be moving along. I promised Rosie we'd be back before ten." He held the door open for her. "But, you know, even Rosie worries about you diving alone. If you want to scuba 'round here, sign up at one of those tourist outfits where you have a guide."

She stepped out into the fog and shivered. It seemed thicker and colder than when they'd entered. "No one need worry. I'm an experienced diver. I know what I am doing."

"That's what fools say."

She was no fool.

Cat stopped dead in her tracks and turned on him. "Appearances can be deceiving. I'll have you know I'm an NAUI-certified master diver. I have hundreds of dives under my belt. I teach scuba. I have led underwater surveys. I probably have way more experience underwater than any of those scuba tour guides."

He held up a hand. "Easy now. Be that as it may, you can't continue to dive around here alone. Cowling doesn't want a lawsuit if you get hurt."

The knot in her stomach twisted into a ball of heated anger. So much for trusting Alex Harris. He would side with Cowling no matter what.

"There's no law against scuba diving in the harbor—I checked."

"No. But as head of security, I have to warn you to stay away from the fish pens."

"So, now you have."

Nerves jingling, Cat hurried toward where his truck was parked, her lips clamped firmly together to keep from speaking her mind. Thank heavens she hadn't told him her purpose for being here. He might like her, but he wasn't going to stand up against his boss for a New Yorker who had pink hair and wore wacky T-shirts, even if they had some kind of unexpected attraction to each other.

She wished she'd never learned he worked for Cowling. She had been so happy for a few hours, bathing in his attention. Dreaming stupid dreams.

Fool. She had even turned off her phone so Momma couldn't interrupt and spoil her evening.

Cat pulled the cell out of her pocket and checked her voice messages. Nothing. Uh-oh. What was going on? Her mother never let three hours go by without a phone call.

She held up the phone. "Got to check on my mom."

"Let's get out of the fog first."

Alex laid his hand on her waist and opened the truck door for her. Minutes ago, his touch had felt so right. Now she wanted his hand gone. She wanted him gone.

She climbed in and called her mother then sank into her mother's convoluted story about a neighbor's cat needing a home. For once in her life, she was glad her mother never stopped talking, because there was no way she was going to talk to the man sitting next to her.

When the truck came to a stop, she didn't wait for him to come for her. She opened the door and slid out. But then she leaned back in. "Thank you for the lovely evening. The play was great, and so were the cupcakes." She pulled the kerchief off her head. "And look at the bright side: no one said a word about my shirt." She slammed the truck door shut then ran up the path to her bungalow. Fog thick and tasteless wrapped around her heart.

Luckily, she'd be on her way home in just a few more days. Time to put her energies into her research. No more leaving the cabin except to acquire her samplings. She'd do her dives at dawn when visibility was low, and if she were lucky, she wouldn't run into Cowling's security officer ever again.

Chapter 11
ALEX

Thursday Night

Alex carried a sleeping Ellie into her mermaid-land bedroom and tucked her in. Pale light from the three-quarter moon highlighted her cherubic face. Black ringlets sprawled across the pillow. She looked so much like her mother that his heart broke.

He should have been the one who had drowned that day. Not Helen.

Helen should be here, raising their daughter. A little girl needed a mother to wipe her tears and teach her how to be a successful woman in the world.

Alex wandered into the living room and took up Helen's photo on the mantel. With an advanced nursing degree and a rising career in emergency health services, she had saved people's lives.

Then she'd made the biggest mistake of her life. She'd married *him*. The man who'd let her die.

He set the photo down. What she'd ever seen in him he'd never know.

Seven years ago, she'd barged into his life like a rogue wave. He'd been nursing his beer after losing to Thomas in the local sea kayak races, when a curly-haired firecracker of a woman bounced up to him and gave him a quizzical look.

She'd flicked her hand toward Thomas, who was regaling anyone who would listen about his big win. "That man cheated, you know. Purposely pushed the lane line into your path. You should report him."

He did know. He'd been friends with Thomas forever. The Cowling scion always had to win. Always cheated. But Thomas's parents had been there for him and his siblings when his father, and soon after, their mother had died. The Cowlings had handled the funeral arrangements and taken in the four shaken teens all on the strength of his friendship with Thomas.

In return, he'd vowed to always be there for their son.

He gave the girl staring at him a crooked grin. "We're buddies, and he enjoys winning more than I do."

Helen wrinkled her nose. "Well, I like winning, too, and I need a partner for the mixed doubles."

"I finished second."

She'd held out her hand. "Sometimes, second is the better choice. Join me."

How could he resist? Those bold blue eyes looked like a glimpse of heaven, and her wide smile warmed every corner of his soul.

He'd set his hand in hers and never let go, until . . .

"Daddy." Ellie's voice echoed down the hall.

He hurried to her room and gave her a hug. "It's okay, sweetheart. You're home in your very own bed. Time to sleep."

"Did you make Miss Cat happy on your date?"

Happy? He doubted it. The cupcakes had been a hit, but she hadn't taken his scuba advice well. She'd clammed up tighter than a wet knot and said nothing on the way back to Rosie's, just plastered her phone to her ear and gabbled on and on with her mother.

But he couldn't tell Ellie that.

He kissed her on her nose. "Yah, sure. She really liked the play." Even if she didn't like him much. "Now close those eyes and dream sweet dreams."

She scrunched beneath the covers. "Okay, Daddy."

He kissed her again then backed out of the room.

Time to forget the past and resume the search for an apartment in Halifax. He set up his laptop on the kitchen table and settled in for another fruitless hunt.

Crunch.

The sound sent his heart racing. Someone was coming up his driveway.

Alex rubbed his forehead and rose from the desk where he'd fallen asleep. He cupped his stiff neck and scowled at the time on his computer screen. Past midnight. No one ever visited him this late. Everyone knew he was an early-to-bed guy.

Pounding on the door echoed through the house. Had something happened?

He hurried to the door and threw it open. His stomach turned over. "Thomas."

"You dare leave this sitting on my desk like it was junk mail?" Thomas shook the RCMP report in his face. "You should have called me at once. We got to talk."

"I agree. But I thought we'd go over it in the morning. Ellie's asleep, and I was on my way to bed." He raked his hand over his mouth and pretended to yawn.

Thomas strode past and ensconced himself on the sofa. "Better here. More private."

Private? Alex's roiling stomach snapped into a tight rubber ball. He didn't want to hear what Thomas had to say. Knowing the man, it would be something distasteful.

He crossed the room, removed Ellie's discarded sweatshirt, and sank into the side chair. Why couldn't the body have been found after he had transferred to Halifax?

Or not found at all.

He tipped his head toward the paper. "So, you read it?"

"Read enough." Thomas tossed the report at him. "They're accusing me of murder."

Alex worked at keeping his voice calm. "It doesn't say that. Something terrible happened to that young man, for sure. But they didn't say it had anything to do with the fish farm. What's likely is that the tide carried the body there from somewhere else, and it got wedged against the netting. Besides, these are preliminary findings."

Thomas shook his head slowly from side to side. "You are so naïve, Alex. That boy's parents are all over me, ready to sue. The body was found on *my* property, tangled in *my* netting. And it is all *your* fault." He jerked to his feet and circled the room. "I told you to move the body."

"I couldn't."

"Of course, you couldn't." Thomas's voice raised a decibel. "You're afraid of the water. You're broken, Alex—broken." He seized Helen's picture off the mantel. "I should fire you. But, for Helen's sake, I'll give you one more chance. I want you to find that kid's kayak before the police do. Then get rid of it." He slammed the photo facedown on the mantel. "I don't care how."

"But . . ."

"No buts. Do it."

"Why?"

Thomas faced him. "Because you want that job in Halifax. And even more, because you are my closest friend."

A pitiful cry came from the bedroom.

Alex glanced toward the hallway. "That's Ellie, having a nightmare. I have to go to her."

Thomas pursed his lips together. "Only after you promise to do as I said. Find the kayak. Destroy it."

Ellie cried again.

Alex clenched his fists and vowed to let the police know the minute he found that kayak. He'd do just about anything for his friend, but not something illegal. and, right now, he just wanted him gone. "Fine. I'll do my best."

"Great, old buddy." Thomas ambled to the doorway. He stopped. "Heard you took the crazy scuba diver lady to the theater. That true?"

Alex backed toward the hall. "Yeah. Found out she's a science teacher. So, no worries there."

Thomas raised an eyebrow. "Good to know. Might stop over at Rosie's and meet the woman myself. Invite her out on my boat."

Alex inhaled deeply. He shouldn't care what Cat Silva chose to do, but for some reason, he did. And he hated the idea of her spending time with Thomas.

"She's pretty shy."

Thomas laughed. "Not what I heard. *Size matters?* Maybe I'll be a better fit." He put his hand on the doorknob. "Find that kayak, pronto. See you at the office."

Then he was gone, and Ellie's whimpers filled the emptiness.

Alex hurried to Ellie's room. She was standing in the doorway, clutching the stuffed mermaid Helen had given her and crying. He swooped her up and gathered her warm little body against his.

"It's okay, sweetheart. Everything's okay."

"I was scared, Daddy. There was a big monster in the water. He was going to eat me."

"Just a dream. You're right here in your own bed, with me to protect you."

"Always?"

"Always." He settled her back under the covers, crooned her favorite lullaby, "Fishing for Love," until she was back asleep, and then tiptoed out of the room.

Alex stood in the hallway and fought the overpowering need to yell and scream, to hit something. He was a lying scumbag.

He'd told Ellie everything was okay, but it wasn't. Thomas hoped to bully him into doing something illegal—destroying evidence. Why? Was he purposely trying to get him in trouble? That made no sense.

He went to the mantel, picked up Helen's photo, and then set it back up. He'd told Ellie that he'd be with her always. But if Thomas had his way, he could end up in jail. Then who would be there for Ellie?

Chapter 12
CAT
Friday Dawn

Cat wiggled into her wet suit. Only two more days of this, and she'd be done and on her way home.

She stood on the far end of the dock and slipped her air tanks over her shoulders. Fog shrouded the water. A shiver crab-walked up her spine. She usually enjoyed her dives, but having to go out before sunrise when the sea was dark and black felt more like a chore. Still, working in the pre-dawn was better than riling up the local fish cop.

She glanced back, but the fog hung just as heavy over the land. Perfect. No one could see her, and she'd be in and out in no time.

She tucked in her hair, tightened the chinstrap, and dived in.

Bubbles rose up around her then dissipated. The cold, still world of the sea embraced her. Cat floated for a moment, savoring the gentle rocking motion of the tide.

She loved the feeling of weightlessness and the way her body ebbed and flowed with the currents. The tension that had plagued her since Alex had warned her off scuba diving whisked away. She turned on her headlamp and kicked toward the fish pen.

The fog lifted just as Cat arrived at her sample site. Rays of light filtered through the water, creating a wavering fan. The silty sea bottom swirled in the sweep of the incoming tide. She savored the momentary beauty and dived into the cloudy water surrounding the pen.

She kicked down until she reached the muddy bottom beside the net and stilled for several minutes to let the sediment settle. Then she unscrewed the top of collecting jar number five and let water seep in to the measure mark. She affixed the top and thrust off the bottom.

As she rose, something caught her eye a little farther out in the water—a person-sized tangle of fishing gear scrapped along the bottom. Something about it looked wrong. Usually, the sea quickly claimed anything left in its grip, encrusting it with seaweed and barnacles. But the mass of yellow polypropylene rope and blue netting looked pristine like it had just been tossed overboard.

She swam nearer, squinting through the silt for a better view of the tangle. Definitely fishing gear. She could make out an array of hooks, swarths of netting, ragged strips of plastic, and even a sharp-tipped grapnel anchor.

And what was that?

She grabbed a protruding loop of rope and drew herself closer. Some poor animal had been trapped in the mix, too. Perhaps a seal or was it a baby whale? Whatever it was, it shouldn't have died in such a horrible way.

The twisting mass of debris was a hazard to wildlife and to any scuba diver or swimmer in the area. She couldn't leave it here.

Cat grasped the rope tighter and tugged. The knot of derelict gear shifted, raising more silt and blinding her, but it didn't move.

She swam closer and gave another tug. The ball of debris jerked then hurtled right into her.

She flailed in an attempt to swim clear, but one of the loops of rope wrapped around an air tank and affixed the ball to her back like some monstrous sea creature. Anchored under its weight, Cat shuddered, panic rising in her gut.

She fought the stomach-knotting fear with all her willpower. It wasn't a creature. It wasn't alive. She could deal with this. Like she'd told Alex, she was no novice. She knew what to do in an emergency.

Sucking in careful, controlled breaths of her precious oxygen, Cat held herself still and assessed her situation. The tanks were almost full. The tide was coming in. It was daylight, and she was barely a few hundred feet from shore. All she had to do was cut the entangled rope away from her tanks.

She drew out the serrated diving knife that every trained diver carried and sawed at the rope passing over her shoulder. It was a laborious process with the incoming tide pushing her toward shore and the horrid tangle of gear twisting and dragging her down, sharp hooks and pieces of metal just inches away from her body. Still, she sawed away.

In seconds, that felt more like hours, the rope split. Freed, she rose to the surface. She cleared her mask and kicked off for shore. Someone else would have to deal with that deadly monster.

Back on the dock, Cat took a moment to regain her composure, shucked her wet suit, hefted the air tanks, and raced to her car. For all her boasting, diving alone, even under the mild conditions of Tide Harbor Bay, was foolish.

If she hadn't been able to stay calm and slice herself free, or if one of the hooks or that anchor had gouged her, she could have bled to death.

Cat pinched her lips together and gazed back at the fish pens. Two more days. She could risk it for two more days. She just had to be smart about it and not try to do any more good deeds. But she'd have to tell someone about the gear tangle out there. Who that someone would be, she had no idea.

Five hours later, Cat wondered if she was doing the right thing. She stared up at the house. According to Rosie, this was where Alex Harris lived. For some reason, she'd expected a weather-beaten, traditional-style Nova Scotia house with cedar shakes and gabled dormers, not this magnificent contemporary home, tucked up in the pine forest above Fletcher's Cove.

She clutched the yellow boots to her chest and rethought her spur-of-the-moment idea to visit Mr. Fish Cop and drop a hint about the ball of debris. A man, whom Rosie said, designed and built a house like this wasn't going to be easily outwitted.

She glanced out at the fish pens sitting so innocently in the harbor. She had no choice. Someone could die out there.

Cat climbed up onto the deck, stamped the sand off her feet, and knocked on the door. Mr. Grumpy answered.

Today, he was decked out in a faded, green plaid flannel shirt and worn blue jeans and looked less like he'd disappear in the fog than he had last night. Still, the way he stood, glaring down at her like she was some interloper, made her want to stomp right off his deck.

But Cat no longer let people intimidate her, and besides, she was on a mission.

She raised the plastic bag she was carrying. "I bought these boots for Ellie." She held them out to him. "I know about your rules, but maybe you'd like to take her down on the flats sometime."

He frowned at her.

Okay, he was a rules-were-not-to-be-broken guy—she got that.

She softened her tone. "Or she could wear them to school on a rainy day."

Slowly, his hand came up, and he lifted them from her hold. "Thank you. That was kind of you to think about her."

"I also wanted to thank you for inviting me to the play. I truly enjoyed it."

His mouth quivered slightly. Maybe he wasn't as cold as she thought.

She couldn't help herself. She peered over his shoulder in a blatant attempt to see inside. "Rosie says you built this house yourself."

"I did."

"Is it as beautiful inside as it is on the outside?"

For a moment, she thought he'd slam the door in her face. But some element of courtesy surfaced.

"Would you like to see it?" He stepped aside. "Come in. Just be quiet. Ellie's taking a nap on my bed."

One glance told her the house was like something out of one of her dreams. Through a wide archway off to her left, she glimpsed a huge, modern kitchen. A glass-surrounded eating nook revealed the pine forest surrounding the back of the home.

In front of her, the living room, with its soaring cathedral ceiling, took her breath away with its elegance. Pale maple boards, matching the kitchen cabinets, paneled the walls. Light filtered in through a row of clerestory windows running across the top. It was like being inside an amphitheater. A well-stuffed sofa and chair invited sitting. Lamps made of driftwood brought the sea inside.

Cat walked across the room to the wall of drape-covered windows and ran her hand along the smoothly sanded window ledge. Just imagining living in this house, cooking in the elegant kitchen, and relaxing on the sofa in front of the fireplace sent tingles running down her spine. Everything was flawless except for the drapes, hiding what had to be a spectacular view of the cove. Rosie had told her about the way Mr. Grumpy kept the curtains closed all the time. Well, it was time to shine some light on Alex Harris and find out what made him tick.

Cat flung open the drapes and gasped. It *was* a view to die for.

From the house, the land sloped down gradually to the dunes that surrounded the cove. White sand glistened in the sun. The water in the harbor shone blue. The sky bluer.

"The house faces west. The sunsets must be incredible." Cat leaned closer to the glass. "Are those islands out there?"

"Uh-huh."

She peeked back at her host. Alex's hands were tightly fisted. The skin beneath his eye twitched. Coldness radiated off him. She could tell he wanted her gone.

She stepped back and faced him. "And you built this? By yourself?"

"I learned a lot about carpentry from my father—building boats."

"You could make a career designing houses. I've never seen anything like it. The mix of woods. The unique way you've crisscrossed the paneling to create a herring-bone effect."

He stared down at his feet. "Never thought about it."

"But surely—"

His head jerked up. "Don't. Let's just say I lost my interest in carpentry."

"Oh. Well, can I have a peek at the rest?"

He hesitated then nodded. "Of course."

Cat followed Alex down the hall, peeking into the white-tiled bathroom and bypassing the door to what must be his bedroom. Ellie's room was the epitome of a little girl's room—colorful posters of mermaids hung on the walls and a pink, frilly bedspread matched the curtains.

Cat clapped her hands. "Look at that. Your daughter loves pink as much as I do."

Alex grunted. "I think it's the influence of the mermaid movie. She's got a fixation on mermaids."

Cat laughed. "Then I guess it's good that she's settled on an imaginary dog. What if she'd decided to have an imaginary mermaid as a pet?"

Alex rubbed his forehead. "About the mermaid thing. It has to do with her mother. I'd appreciate it if you didn't encourage her interest in them. I worry she'll try to go into the water on a mermaid search."

"Oh. Is that why you have the no-water rule?"

He nodded. "I have to keep her safe."

Cat picked up a pink stuffed mermaid. "Of course, you do. Though, I strongly advise you to get her swimming lessons. That's what my parents did when they caught me sneaking down to the shore."

He grimaced. "Sometimes knowing how to swim makes you overconfident."

"Not if you're taught properly." Cat gave him her stern-professor stare. "I bet you never had swimming lessons. Learned by jumping off a dock."

Alex snorted. "So? I am an excellent swimmer. I used to hold the record for swimming across the harbor and back."

Cat shrugged. "Key words are 'used to.' I, on the other hand, hold no records, but I do have a Red Cross lifesaving certificate. I don't just swim. I know how to be safe in the water."

"And you think scuba diving alone is safe?"

After her morning scare, he had a point.

She rubbed her thigh. This was when she should tell him about the debris ball. Own up to disobeying him. But she couldn't. He was acting like every other man and questioning her strength and skill. She refused to provide him with ammunition.

She set her hand on her hip. "Yes. I am perfectly safe paddling around a few hundred feet from shore. My equipment is top-notch. I check it before and after each dive, and I'm not going so far nor so deep that I can't pop up to the surface if I run into a problem. The sea is our friend. Even our bodies are attuned to its ebb and flow."

"You have no idea what kind of problems are out there in the water."

"And you do?"

"*Yes.* Too many of my friends—people I loved—have sunk below those waves never to rise again. My wife drowned out there in your *friendly* sea."

Cat's pulse soared. She held a hand to her heart and took a step back. How could she have been so callous?

"Oh, I'm so sorry. I didn't mean to sound like a know-it-all. Of course, the sea can be dangerous."

Alex flicked his fingers as if to chase the memory away. "It's okay. You didn't know."

But she should have figured it out. He'd given enough hints, and it explained his distaste for the water.

Barely looking him in the eyes, Cat edged her way to the door. "Thank you again for inviting me to the play and for the cupcakes. It was the high point of my stay here. And condolences on the death of your wife. I apologize for my lack of sensitivity. I lost my father last year, and it still hurts."

The hard planes of his face softened slightly. "It's okay. It was a pleasure taking you to the show."

"That's very kind of you."

"I'm happy I asked you. The local actors deserve our support."

But he didn't look happy at all. She tucked away the information about the hazard by the pens and hurried down the deck steps.

She rushed toward the beach. *Stupid, stupid, Cat.* She'd done what she always did—berated a man for a perceived slight. Challenged his swimming ability. His wife had drowned, for heaven's sake.

Her chest tightened. Had he been unable to save her? If so, no wonder he was so concerned about safety and afraid of letting his precious daughter near the sea.

Cat took refuge in the cove. She sank down on the sand, wrapped her arms around her knees, and watched the waves dance in and out. Despite his charming daughter, she should never have gone to the theater with Alex Harris.

She ran her fingers through the sand. She was mouthy, and he was closed-lipped. She loved the sea, and he hated it. And for good reason, she had to admit.

She'd drop off a note at the Cowling offices tomorrow. The dangerous debris taken care of, she'd leave on Sunday and never see or think about Alex Harris again. And if that thought made her stomach twist, she refused to analyze why.

Chapter 13
ALEX

Friday Morning

Perched on the roof of his truck, Alex fine-tuned the focus on his binoculars. Just what was Cat doing now? For one thing, she was back to sporting pink, which made her easy to spot against the vast expanse of the mud flats. But finding her was one thing. Figuring out what she was doing was driving him nuts.

She slogged along the edge of the water, outfitted in the boots he'd bought her. Every few steps, she bent down and came up with a handful of mud. Then she'd toss it down, take another step, and repeat. She wasn't acting like a tourist.

Tourists liked sandy beaches and getting tans. They went out to restaurants, and they purchased ceramic lighthouses that read, *"Tide Harbor,"* on the base. They didn't wander up and down the stinking mudflats.

Could she be clamming? But, where were her shovel and bucket?

A fishy-smelling pickup pulled up next to him. "Hey, brother. Checking out the wildlife?"

Alex lowered his binoculars and peered into his brother, Matt's, grinning face. "The boat's in?"

"That it is, landlubber. Brought in a haul of haddock and halibut and two fine swordfish."

Alex jumped off the truck and gave his brother a hug. "Crew hale and healthy?"

"It's summer—a great time to be out on the water. Not that I can convince you of that. So, who's the girl who's caught your eye? Did you pass the size test?"

Alex adjusted his baseball cap. Darn T-shirt. Did the town gossips ever take a break?

"Wasn't like that. I was doing my job."

"Yah, sure, checking out whether the Shakespeare Club made off with some of Thomas's salmon. Then looking for them inside Kate's pastries."

Alex slapped his brother on the back. "You been talking to Olivia."

"Could be."

"I'm not looking for a girlfriend. Ellie and I are relocating to Halifax end of the month."

Matt rocked back and forth on his feet. "Aye, heard that, too, little brother. You'll hate it there, you know." He poked him in the ribs. "You won't have us around to keep you from going looney."

"And good riddance to that."

His brother gave him a serious look. "No, really, what will you do in a city full of strangers? Who will care for Ellie when you're working? What if you get sick? Family is everything, Alex."

Matt rested a hand on his shoulder. "You've had a rough time of it. We get that. Maybe we can't stop the hurting.

Maybe the pain of losing Helen will never go away. But we're here for you. All of us—me, Logan, Olivia, Nick. Well, Nick has his own demons buried in the sand out there in Alberta, but he'd come at a moment's notice if you asked him. Don't give up on Tide Harbor. Don't abandon your family."

Alex pictured Ellie racing across the mudflats. It was too risky living so close to the sea. He had to get her away from here.

"I am doing what's best for my daughter."

"Are you? Ellie loves Olivia and the boys. They're her second family. She'll miss them. Think about it, bro."

Matt wagged his head in the direction of the flats. "Say, looks like you've been sighted."

Alex spun around. Cat was storming toward them, shouting and waving her arms.

He glanced at his brother. He didn't need a witness. Living down her date T-shirt would take months, if not years. He hated to see what zany slogan she was wearing today.

"You'd better go."

"Ah, no. This should prove interesting." Matt squinted. "She sure likes pink."

"It's her favorite color."

"Sounds like you know the lady well."

"Hey, I took her to the play to find out what she's doing here because Thomas asked me to. He's whack-a-doodle crazy afraid of anyone messing around his fish pens. That's all."

His brother raised his eyes skyward. "And we all know how you do everything Thomas tells you because you are best buddies and all."

Alex clenched his fists. "I do my job."

"Right. Playing at being a pretend cop because you're afraid to do what you really want to do."

"I'm doing what I want to do. I am taking care of my daughter. I'm all she has."

Cat reached the road and clomped toward them. Every step she took made him feel smaller and smaller.

"Besides, Miss Silva is leaving in two days."

Matt leaned against the truck. "Introduce me to your lady friend, bro."

Alex shut his eyes. The last thing he wanted to do was introduce the Pink Lady to his brother. But it was too late.

Cat pulled up in front of them, panting hard, her face flushed, the pink strands of her wind-tossed hair flying out all around her face. She looked absolutely gorgeous and energetic, and bright and glowing, and full of life. Then he read the slogan on her shirt and nearly choked. Beneath a picture of a tuna about to bite the hook it read, *"Men and fish are alike. They both get in trouble when they open their mouths."*

She jabbed her finger at him. "I saw you, Mr. Cowling Security Man. Up there, watching me with your binoculars. Spying. And I wasn't even near your precious fish pens."

"Just making sure you were okay."

"Stop it. I'm fine. Believe it or not, I can do most things without your supervision. Tie my sneakers. Put my lipstick on straight. Tell the difference between a clam and a salmon. And walk on mud flats. Especially with these lovely boots."

She turned toward his brother and held up her foot. "I don't know who you are, but don't you agree these are lovely boots?"

"I'm Matt." He pointed at Alex. "This idiot's my brother. And to be honest—because he won't be—the boots clash horribly with your outfit. Which, by the way, is quite lovely and informative and very, very, *very* pink."

"Hmm. That's what I thought, too, when I saw these boots. Not even a spot of pink to draw the eye. But alas, these were the only pair they had over at Lebranche Marine that fit. However, your brother was kind enough to buy them for me."

Matt laughed. "Amazing. Pretty sure you're the first lady my tight-fisted brother ever bought waders for. Not the most romantic thing to do, but it's something." He tilted his head to the side. "You must have made a real impression on him."

Alex found his voice. "Ellie ruined her clothes. It was the least I could do."

"I'm sure it was." Matt tipped his hat. "Well, I've got a boat to clean. Pleased to meet you, Miss Silva. If you are still here Sunday, we'd love to have you at our family get-together. We're having a barbeque to celebrate the record haul we caught."

Cat grinned. "Ah. You must be the fisherman brother." She glanced at Alex. "My plans are to leave early Monday morning, so that works. But I will only come if Mr. Fish Cop wants me to." She turned and gave him a wide-eyed glare.

Alex fingered the strap on his binoculars. Leave it to his brother to push the two of them together. Sure, he found the Pink-Haired Wonder interesting and a bit enticing. But that was all. Mostly, he just wanted her and her wacky T-shirts gone.

"You want me to come?" Cat repeated.

Alex squeezed his eyes closed so he wouldn't have to look at her tee. "Yah, sure. But could you wear a different shirt?"

Matt laughed and headed for his truck. "You go right ahead and wear that one. Olivia will want to know where she can get one just like it. Oh, and don't forget to make sure Alex invites you to the festival." He jumped in his cab and took off, leaving them staring at each other.

Cat glared at him. "So, Mr. Fish Cop, explain the spying."

"Nothing to explain. I'm doing my job—watching the coastline around the pens."

"Rubbish. You sat up there, training your binoculars on me for a half-an-hour. And in case you didn't notice, the fish pens are on the other side of the sand spit. You can't even see them from here."

"People try all sorts of ways to get out there and see what we're doing."

"Cowling has something to hide?"

"No. Not at all. Company's got a great record."

Her eyebrows rose. If anything, that made her look cuter. "Record for what?"

"Producing clean, healthy salmon."

Cat shook her head. "You're a real flag waver for Cowling, aren't you? You think open-pen fish farming is the future?"

"Yes, I do. In fact, in a few years, as soon as I have the capital, I plan on investing in a fish farming operation of my own."

"You do know the aquaculture industry has problems?"

"It doesn't have to be that way. Cowling's operation proves that. Passes all the criteria set out by the government."

Cat huffed. "Any time you put a mass of specially bred, genetically modified animals in close confinement, there are going to be issues. It's not natural for them to live fin-to-tail in pens. Despite the high tides, the water exchange in a harbor like this isn't enough to clear out the pollution caused by their fecal matter and the uneaten feed that builds up under the pens. Then again, if you locate them farther out, where there's more flow, the pens get damaged in storms, allowing the fish to escape and destroy native salmon fisheries. It's a no-win situation."

Alex gritted his teeth. Who was this woman? Surely, not a simple teacher. A school teacher might be an expert diver, but Cat knew way too much about the sea and marine life. She was on top of the latest research on salmon farming, and she hated fish farms.

Warning signs flashed inside his head. Miss Silva might be exactly whom Thomas feared—an eco-activist out to get dirt on his operation.

But the woman was also delightful and amusing in her own way. He'd enjoyed watching her on the flats, moving with the smoothness of a cat and making a face every time she examined a handful of mud. Even now, standing here with her berating him, he couldn't see any bad in her.

Besides, she was leaving in two days. He wanted to ignore the hair-raising clues he was picking up. Yet, despite the warning on her T-shirt, and with that search for a missing kayak hanging over him, he couldn't risk a mistake, so he had to ask, "You're not merely a tourist, are you?"

"Sure, I'm a tourist. I'm visiting a new place to sightsee and meet interesting people, get away from my demanding mother for a week." Her phone buzzed. "Sort of."

Alex started to relax, but she wasn't finished with him.

"And I teach at New York University in the biology department. My specialty is marine biology. My research focus is salmon farming." She scuffed the toe of her boot in the sandy gravel. "I should have told you the other night when you said you worked at Cowling." She licked those luscious lips. "I planned to tell you last night, and you told me about your wife, and I chickened out. But I hate being dishonest. I couldn't sleep—I felt so guilty. Sorry, Alex."

"So, out there on the flats, you were collecting samples?"

"Yes, I am examining the relationship between the nitrogen levels in the fish pen sediments and the overall nitrogen levels in the harbor. High nitrogen levels cause marine die-off and create dead zones where nothing can live."

Alex bit his lip. The harbor was polluted? Was that why Thomas was so worried about ecologists sniffing around the pens?

"So, what have you found?"

"The testing is all preliminary at this point. I have to send my samples to the lab. But it seems like the process is well underway here. I've studied several other fish farm sites in the last two years, and Tide Harbor has the highest nitrogen levels so far. The islands at the mouth of the harbor slow the exchange of water that might keep the levels in the safe range."

Alex rubbed the crease between his eyes. Please let her be wrong. He didn't want anything bad to happen to Tide Harbor. He might be leaving, but he loved the place.

"Can it be stopped?"

"That's what I'm trying to find out. Though the easier solution is to get rid of the open water fish farms and go to raising salmon, or even better, Arctic char, sustainably in contained tanks on land."

"Thomas Cowling won't like what you're doing."

She shook her head. "Of course not. Do you want me to go explain the problem to him? Perhaps make some suggestions to alleviate the nitrogen buildup? I have my research proposal and the results of my initial tests, and an invitation to go out on his boat with him tomorrow."

Alex gazed off at the sunlight glinting on the water. If she told Thomas what she'd just shared with him, Thomas would go ballistic. He would blame him for not uncovering Cat's purpose here sooner. Kayak handled or not, he'd lose the Halifax position.

He readjusted his ball cap and watched a tern dive for a fish. Did he really need to tell his boss about her? Cat would be here two more days. All he had to do was get through the weekend without Thomas finding out what she was doing. Sunday, he could keep her busy, visiting with his family. Tomorrow, he could take her to the festival.

He shifted his gaze back to Cat. "No. Don't talk to Thomas at all. My boss hates scientists nosing around. Might demand you turn over your findings to him or something. I'd advise you to wrap up your research then just enjoy the rest of your stay. Would you like to go to the Whirligig Festival with me and Ellie tomorrow?"

The smile that lit up her face was as blinding as the sunlit sand in Fletcher's Cove.

Cat pressed her hands together. "That festival your brother mentioned? I thought you'd never ask."

Alex's gut tightened. He couldn't let himself be taken in by that smile. Cat was a problem. One he didn't know how to solve. And it didn't help that he liked her more and more each time they butted heads.

Chapter 14
CAT
Saturday Morning

Cat studied the T-shirts spread out on the bed. She had no idea what to wear to a whirligig festival. Actually, she didn't even know what a whirligig was. Didn't matter. She was going to spend the day with Alex and Ellie and enjoy herself. By Monday, she'd be gone, back to the city, back to her mother, back to her cutthroat battle for a full-time position.

Before, that would have been enough. But now her future was looking a lot grayer and duller. Her Happiness List more pitiful.

Somehow, a man named Alex, and a little girl named Ellie, had filled her up with liquid sunshine, and she wanted to store up every happy memory she could.

A familiar truck with a rattling muffler pulled into the parking lot. Cat glanced out the window. They were here.

She grabbed the tee she thought least offensive and yanked it on. Then she spun around, swiped up her knapsack and sunglasses, and stepped out onto the porch.

"Hi, Cat," Ellie shouted. "Let's go." The child popped out of the truck and sprinted toward her. Two small arms wrapped around her waist in a hug. Then Ellie seized her hand and dragged her back to the pickup.

Alex came to help her in. He gave her a half-wink. "Nice shirt."

She peered down at the black tee with a goldfish sporting a policeman's hat and holding a baton in its fin. "I picked it out with you in mind. What do you think, Ellie? Does the policeman fish look like your dad?"

Ellie giggled. "Yep. That's what Daddy does. He guards the fishies."

Cat helped Ellie snap in her seat belt. "Got it at Lebranche Marine. It didn't come in pink, unfortunately."

"Oh, we bought you something," Alex said. He reached behind the seat and drew out a plastic bag. "We saw this at Guy Frenchy's and thought of you."

Ellie bounced up and down on her seat. "Dorchester and I helped pick it out."

Cat opened the bag and peeked in. "Oh my. It's perfect." She drew out the pink sunhat and plopped it on her head. "Now that brightens up this so-not-pink T-shirt."

Alex picked up the strings hanging down. "You'll have to keep it tied on. With this wind a-blowing the way it is, it's a great day for whirligigs, but not for keeping one's hat out of the harbor." He lifted the ties, crossed them, and tied them into a bow under her chin.

The brush of his fingers against her skin sent warm currents flooding through her. Their eyes met and, for a moment, Cat felt a connection that she'd never experienced before. Alex Harris might look like an ordinary man, but beneath that plain surface was someone who cared. Someone who was interested in her.

She touched the scar cutting through her upper lip with the tip of her tongue. He hadn't even said anything about her off-kilter mouth. It was usually the first thing people commented on.

Ellie bounced up and down. "Come on. We don't want to miss a single thing. There's gonna be breakfast at the lighthouse, and a parade, and a boat race, and lots of whirligigs. I have one entered in the contest."

Cat fastened her seat belt. "Just what is a whirligig? Some kind of children's toy?"

Alex laughed. "Oh no. A whirligig is, uh . . . more like a weather vane. But much more exciting." He started up the engine. "You'll see."

An hour later, Cat, her stomach full of pancakes doused in local maple syrup, joined the crowd milling up and down Seaview Street, which ran along the shore. She'd never felt so happy. The day was faultless. The sky azure blue. The water a scintillating turquoise. But the most amazing thing was the hundreds of whirligigs mounted on stakes all along the street.

Gusts from the south raised a smattering of white caps and spun the blades of clever wind-powered inventions of all designs. Wings fluttered on tiny hummingbirds. Lobster claws snapped and rotated. Inside a huge whale, Jonah desperately swam, his arms flipping around faster than the eye could see.

Cat spun around, her mouth open. "Oh, look at them all." She bounded across the grass, stopping to examine each one and to talk with the people who'd made them. The best was a complex wood carving, depicting a man sitting in front of an empty dish. His arms flew up and down, banging the table, while behind him, his wife turned a meat grinder handle and a dog waiting below opened and closed its mouth, snapping at the sausage hanging down.

Alex came up beside her. "Poor guy. Looks like he'll be missing dinner. Speaking of food, it's near noon, want me to get you something to eat?"

Cat lifted her chin up. "Noon already? I'm still full of pancakes."

"By the time we get to the food vendors, you'll be hungry enough. If we wait too long, they'll run out of the good stuff. Happens every year."

She poked him in the arm. "Well, we can't have you ending up with an empty plate like that guy up there."

Ellie ran over from where she'd been peering through a telescope trained on the harbor. She tugged on Cat's sleeve. "Come see my whirligig now."

"You made one of these?"

Her head bobbed up and down. "In summer camp. They're over there." She pointed to a group of small, colorful spinners displayed in front of the local historical museum.

Alex put a hand on his daughter's shoulder. "How about I get us something to eat while you show Cat your creation?"

Ellie grabbed Cat's hand. "Okay."

"So, what should I get you?"

"Hot dog," Ellie shouted.

Cat searched in her purse for a twenty. "A coffee is fine for me." She held out one of the slippery Canadian plastic bills. "My treat."

Alex waved away her money. "Buy yourself a souvenir." He headed off toward the food trucks.

Twining her little fingers into Cat's, Ellie dragged her in the direction of the children's whirligig display.

Cat glanced over her shoulder. "Will your dad be able to find us again?"

"Silly, he knows where we are going. Oh, I see my teacher, Miss Paquette." She took off running.

"Wait up," Cat yelled, hurrying after.

Ellie stopped under a pole and pointed up. "There's mine."

Cat smiled. All the children had used the same basic cardboard fish shape, but Ellie's had been transformed into a pink mermaid, her tail flippers flopping up and down, long pink yarn hair flapping in the wind.

Ellie raised her hand. "That's you. Swimming in the ocean with all your sea friends."

"Oh." For a moment, Cat was speechless. She couldn't believe she had made that much of an impression on the child in three days. She took Ellie by the hands and spun her around. "I love it. You've captured me perfectly."

Ellie's face turned suddenly serious. "Do you think it will win?"

"Win?" Oh dear. Only one child could win, and she didn't want Ellie to be hurt. She knew just how that felt. As hard as she tried to win her sports events growing up, she rarely crossed the finish line first, much to the amusement of her star-athlete brothers.

Cat squatted down. "You know winning isn't the important thing. Knowing that you imagined that wondrous creature, that it made you happy to create it and share with me, that's better than winning any time. And the thing is, for one person to win means that everybody else loses."

"Oh." Ellie gazed around. Other children were showing their whirligigs to their families. "My friends made these. I don't want anybody to feel bad."

Cat stood. "Tell you what. How about you go and say something nice to each of your friends about their whirligigs while I talk to your teacher."

Ellie ran off to her friends, and Cat watched her go, so full of life and hope. It must have been devastating to lose her mother at such a young age. Now, where was that teacher?

Several minutes later, Alex came up alongside her and held out a cup and a paper dish of fries covered with what looked like white bits. "Your coffee."

Cat took the cup from his hands, her fingers brushing his. She gave him a quick glance. The inexplicable attraction between them would only make leaving Tide Harbor harder.

She inclined her head toward Ellie, who was in animated conversation with another girl about her age. "You've done a wonderful job raising your daughter. She's so caring about others."

"She's my everything."

"She must miss her mother."

"She was only three. But yes, there's a big hole in our lives. My sister, Olivia, has filled in as much as she can, but it's not the same." He held out the dish. "Here, have one."

Cat frowned at the strange-looking concoction. "What in the world is on these fries?"

"Cheese curds and gravy." He grinned at her. "This is real honest poutine."

"Never heard of it."

"Well, now you have." He picked up a fry and handed it to her. "You haven't been to Nova Scotia if you haven't eaten poutine."

She stuck the fry in her mouth and savored the taste of the melted cheese. "Yum. My dad always said cheese on top of anything was a sure winner." She took another. "But calling a local dish after the head of Russia? How did that happen?"

Alex choked on his fry. "Not *Putin*. Pou-tén. It's French-Canadian."

The *rat-a-tat* of drums echoed off the walls of the buildings lining the street. Cat spun around and did a double-take.

"What in the world?"

Down the street, the crowd had moved to each side of the road to let a parade of men in Revolutionary British uniforms march by.

She turned to Alex. "Why are there British Red Coats here?"

Alex laughed. "It's your turn for a lecture. Much of Nova Scotia was settled by Loyalists and freed slaves after the American Revolution. That's our local reenactment militia." He pointed out toward the harbor. "Over there is our privateer, *The Tide Harbor*, out to sink a Yankee long boat. On the anniversary of the town's founding, we stage a battle and burn the American ship."

"You set fire to a boat?"

"It's just a slapdash thing we make out of old wood and anchor out there. That guy at the helm of the *Tide Harbor*? That's my brother, Matt. He's the captain."

Cat lifted the brim of her hat to get a better view. "What an incredible boat. It's a gaff-rigged schooner, right?"

"You know boats as well as fish, it seems."

"When you study marine biology, you get to go out on lots of boats. I once took a trip down the coast of North Carolina in a schooner much like that one. It's a marvelous way to travel."

"Yeah, that was always the plan."

"Plan?"

"To travel. My dad and I built that boat. Modeled it on the sailing ship on the Canadian dime, *The Bluenose*, but built it shorter at sixty-five feet. The dream was we would sail to different ports in the Maritimes and New England, maybe even visit New York City. When I was a boy, I would picture us sailing into New York Harbor, going right by the Statue of Liberty. Kind of like in that movie *Romancing the Stone*."

Cat elbowed him in the ribs. "You watch chick flicks?"

"No, but my mom did. She'd make us sit through her movies as punishment for all the sports events she had to put up with. The Stone movie wasn't bad, though. I was a kid. I liked the alligators."

"They were crocodiles."

"Same thing. Big sharp teeth and all."

"Not really. Alligators live in freshwater and are native to the United States. You find them in the Florida Everglades. The crocodiles in the movie are *crocodylus acutus* and live in Central America. Sorry, there I go again, spouting off."

Alex laughed. "Think I need some teaching, do you?"

His laugh transformed his normally dour face into one that begged to be kissed.

Her cheeks heated at the thought.

She turned and peered out into the harbor. Time to change the subject. "So, anyway, what happened with the schooner? Obviously, you finished it. Did you get to go on any trips?"

Alex shaded his eyes as he followed the course of the boat sailing across the harbor. "No. My father passed before we could finish it, and I guess we just don't have the will to do more than bring it out for the local events and give people rides. It's never been out of the harbor."

Cat watched the schooner's sails fill with wind. "So, why aren't you out there with your brother? A boat like that needs more than one man."

"Matt's got help. All the teens around here can't wait to get a chance to crew the boat. He doesn't need me."

One of the men from the militia, dressed in an elaborate officer's uniform and a white wig, broke away from where the soldiers had gathered to drink and talk to the tourists. He came over and stopped in front of Cat. He sized her up.

"Well, Alex. This the teacher you're dating?"

"We're not—"

Alex put a hand on Cat's arm. "Yes. This is Cat Silva. She's visiting from New York City. Staying at Rosie's. Thought I'd show her some of our local color."

He turned to her. "Cat, this is my boss, Thomas Cowling."

She scrutinized the man. So, this was the owner of the fish farm operation. He appeared pleasant enough. Large and well-built, with clean-cut features and pale blue eyes, most women would find him super handsome.

She glanced at Alex from the corner of her eye. Call her crazy, but she much preferred her brown-eyed, black-haired Mr. Ordinary, especially when he had a smile on his face.

Thomas Cowling gave her a good look over then turned his gaze out to the water. "Saw you admiring Alex's sloop. Some boat. Spent half his teen years working on that schooner. I'd go over to his house and try to get him to come play ball with me, and he'd be too busy sanding or varnishing, or some other boring thing. I remember one time he got annoyed with me because I threw the ball at him, and it accidentally landed in a can of paint. Remember that mess, Alex?"

"How could I forget? Had to spend the rest of winter break sanding the railing and deck again."

Cat slanted her head. "But why if it landed in the can?"

Thomas slapped Alex on the back. "Well, I had to get the ball out, didn't I? So, a little paint spilled on the deck in the process, and maybe I got some handprints on the railing."

Alex's lower lip turned in. "The whole can spilled. My dad was none too happy what with the sloop being near finished."

"Yah, sure, it was sad your dad never got to see her in the water. But it all worked out in the end. Look at her go out there." He leaned in closer to Cat. "I have to tell you what a good man Alex here is. He never told his father it was me who made that mess. Took all the blame himself. Couldn't ask for a better friend. I rely on him totally to protect my interests."

He elbowed Alex in the ribs. "Say, buddy, you'll have to bring Miss Silva over to dinner tonight. I serve a mean grilled salmon with lemon sauce. Then I can tell her more Alex and Thomas stories."

Cat gave a nod. Thomas Cowling seemed down-to-earth, like all the Tide Harborites, not at all how she expected a CEO of a multi-million-dollar fish farm operation to be. Maybe Cowling would be understanding if she shared her discovery of the debris ball with him?

She opened her mouth to accept his invitation. "I—"

"Thanks, Thomas," Alex interrupted. "Hate to miss that salmon, but we already have dinner plans." He gave her arm a squeeze. "Right, Cat?"

Now, what was Alex up to? Was he trying to keep her away from the man? They appeared to be old friends. Still, she much preferred the idea of dinner with her Fish Cop.

"Uh, sure. But thank you for the invite, Mr. Cowling."

"Call me Thomas, please. We're not so formal here in Tide Harbor."

Ellie ran up. "Everybody did such a good job on our whirligigs that my teacher says we all get a prize." She clutched a piece of paper. "Look. Free ice cream." She grabbed Cat's hand. "Come on. Let's go."

Cat barely had time to wave goodbye to the owner of Cowling Fish Farm before she was being dragged across the town park to the farmers' market.

By the time they reached the ice cream vendor, Cat had bought a knitted shawl for her mother, a pewter seashell necklace for Ellie, and a small model of the Bluenose for herself, to remember this day and Alex and his boat.

She fingered the delicate model. What had happened when his wife drowned that scared him so much he wouldn't even take a ride on that glorious boat he'd built?

How could someone be that afraid of the water?

Chapter 15
ALEX

Saturday Afternoon

Alex let out a sigh of relief as Thomas headed off to the kayak races.

That had been close. The last thing he wanted was for Cat to spend any amount of time in his once-upon-a-time friend's company.

Surely, she'd be uncomfortable visiting with the owner of the fish farm she was investigating. But, more importantly, with her level of honesty, she might even inadvertently alert Thomas to her true purpose for being in Tide Harbor and destroy not only her research but also his opportunity to work in Halifax.

Ugh. Not a pleasant thought. He'd better keep an eye on her.

Alex shaded his eyes then set off in the direction of the ice cream cart parked at the back of the farmers' market. Halfway there, someone called his name.

"There you are." Olivia hurried over. Three little boys in swimsuits ran in circles and poked each other behind her. She shouted over her shoulder, "Cut it out, boys. Let

Mommy talk." She turned back. "Alex, the family is planning to go out on the sloop tomorrow at sunset. It's ten years since Dad passed. We're going to circle Pine Tree Island in his memory. We'd love you to come."

Every muscle in his body tightened. Sweat broke out on the back of his neck. Just the idea of being on a boat risked a panic attack. He took several long breaths like the therapist had taught him.

"You know I can't."

"It's barely a twenty-minute outing. The wind's set to be fair. It would be quiet and respectful, and we'd come right back. You know Dad would have wanted you at the helm."

Alex shook his head. "I'm never stepping aboard a boat again."

Olivia sighed. "Well, will you let Ellie go? All her cousins will be on board."

"*No*. No way."

"She's not always going to do what you tell her. You won't be able to keep her off the water forever. We are fishermen. We own boats. We live by the ocean. The child can't even swim."

"We're moving to Halifax."

"So I heard. And perhaps you didn't notice that Halifax is a port? There are boats and water there, too."

"Not planning to live anywhere near the shore. And I will make sure she gets swimming lessons—in a pool."

Olivia straightened and gave him a glance so reminiscent of their long-gone mother's when he'd done something stupid that it was uncanny. "Well, there is that, I guess. But you know something? You can close the curtains. You can cover your eyes. But you can never get the sea out of your blood—or hers. It's in there, good and deep. You're a Harris. She's a Harris. Remember that." She twisted around. "Now, where did those boys run off to?"

Alex gave a half-laugh. "Being Harrises on their mother's side, they're scrambling toward the water."

Olivia huffed. "Mine can swim. It's their shenanigans I worry about. They're likely to make off with one of Bob's kayaks, when they could do something normal, like cannonballing off the dock."

She cast a glance at him. "What is it with boys? You guys were just like them when you were little, and when your buddy, Thomas, got in the mix, all hell broke loose."

Alex laughed. "Wasn't just the boys. Seems to me you were part of many of our wild exploits, too."

Olivia tapped her chin. "True enough, I guess. And now I'm getting a good dose of what Mom and Dad put up with."

Alex gently fist-punched her upper arm. "Ah, well, couldn't happen to a better sister. Kids, you've got to love them. Even my one can be a handful." He searched the crowd. "You haven't seen Ellie, have you?"

"If she's with your pink lady, then I saw the pink vision eyeing the offerings in the farmers' market."

"Thanks. I'd better get over there before she buys up every pink thing they're selling."

Olivia laughed. "You know, it's kind of cool to have a signature color like that. I'm thinking of choosing camouflage for mine."

"Camouflage?"

"Yeah, that way I could hide in the bushes when the kids become too much to take. I love the little darlings, but some days, turning invisible sounds great."

Alex looked her up and down. "Not sure it would be the most flattering color for you."

"Yah, sure, nothing like wearing eye-blazing pink to draw attention from the guys like your gal over there."

"Huh, that's not why Cat wears pink."

"Isn't it? She captured your eye, and heaven knows you haven't been interested in anything female in three years."

One of Olivia's boys came bounding toward her. "Mommy, Mommy, Teddy and George are in the rowboat, and they won't let me in."

"Whose rowboat?" Olivia grabbed her son's hand. "Got to run, Alex. See you tomorrow. Make sure you bring your pink lady, too."

Alex set off toward the mob of people lined up at the ice cream seller, keeping his eye out for Cat and her pink hat. Was his sister right? Did Cat wear pink as a man-attractor?

He scanned the crowd and spotted her trying on a pink scarf. She was a totally gorgeous woman, curved in all the right places, and with svelte legs not even her assortment of wild leggings could hide. Cat Silva didn't need to wear pink to entice any man.

He headed in her direction. But what about the weirdo T-shirts? Sure, they made people stare at her, think her a bit silly maybe, but attract men? He didn't think so. Those sayings seemed far more likely to warn men away.

He stopped. Was that it? Did she dress so outrageously to keep men away? But why?

"Mr. Harris."

Alex turned.

Ellie's teacher ran toward him. She pulled up short and caught her breath. "I just had to tell you what a wonderful thing that tourist you had with you did. She paid for every child in the whirligig contest to get an ice cream. Claimed their creations were all so imaginative, how could just one win? Such a kind thing for a stranger to do. I have to leave now, but could you thank her for me?"

"Of course, Mia. I'll let her know." He waved goodbye and resumed striding across the town park.

Cat's outrageous clothing hid a tender heart. What else did it hide? She sure didn't seem like someone in hiding.

A quick scan of the market showed Ellie and Cat loaded with bags and standing in line at the ice cream vendor's truck. Alex slipped in behind them.

"Had trouble finding you in this crowd."

"Look, Daddy," Ellie said. She pulled on the chain around her neck. "Cat bought me this necklace. It's a Not-This-A-Day."

Alex made a puzzled face. "Looks like a moon shell to me."

Cat laughed. "Actually, its scientific name is pronounced *naticidae*, but I like Ellie's version better. I'll have to teach that to my students as a way of remembering the family name."

Alex fingered the tiny shell. "The moon snail is a rather nasty little predator. It drills into clams and sucks out their flesh, but it's sure pretty to look at."

"*Ew*, Daddy. That's yucky." Ellie clutched the shell in her fist. "My Not-This-A-Day is going to be a nice one."

He grinned at Cat. "Sure it is. Now, what flavor ice cream do you want?"

Cat studied the pictures on the sign. "The pink one, of course—strawberry. What are you having, Ellie?"

"Moon Mist. That's the one that's all-swirly colors."

Cat tapped her chin. "Yes, indeed, a very appropriate choice. Matches the stripes on your shirt."

Alex glanced down at his brown shirt. "Well, if we are matching our clothes, it looks like I get the best flavor of all—Moose on the Loose."

Cat elbowed him in the ribs. "No way is that the best." She took her cone from the vendor and swiped up a wooden spoon. She dug out a huge glob and held it up to his mouth. "Here, take a taste of mine."

He lowered his face so close to hers that he could barely breathe and licked the spoon. The cold of the ice cream against his lips did nothing to cool the heat he felt.

He made a show of swirling it around on his tongue then shook his head. "Nope. The chocolate is much better."

"Let me taste." She handed him another wooden spoon.

He filled the spoon and offered it to her. Cat stuck out her tongue and licked. He blinked. At that moment, he wanted to clasp her in his arms and kiss that mouth with the slightly crooked upper lip right here in front of the entire population of Tide Harbor. He wondered if she would let him.

A cheer rose from the shore.

"Oh." Cat pulled back and stood on her toes. "What's going on?"

Alex took a lick of his ice cream to keep it from dripping down the side then flicked his hand toward the water. "The kayak races have started."

Cat gave a little jump. "Oh, I love kayaking. Can anybody enter?"

"Thomas organizes the racing. He was a competitive kayaker in college at Dalhousie."

"Was he? Maybe he will let me join in."

Alex choked on his ice cream. "But the race is about to start."

"Then I'd better hurry." Cat set off toward the pier at a brisk pace, leaving him staring after her.

His stomach did a small twist as she wove in and out of the crowd. He loved the way she bounced when she moved, as if the ground beneath her feet was more resilient for her than it was for others. He loved how she licked daintily at her ice cream while moving at a near run. And he hated how he felt the loss of her nearness. It was like she'd taken all the sun and sweetness with her. She was so beautiful, so full of enthusiasm for life, and she'd disappear on Monday.

Somehow, in six days, she'd wormed her way into his darkness and let him see the light again. Despite everything, she made him want to kiss a woman again.

He smiled at his daughter with her moon shell pendant. The pink-crazed New Yorker had added sparkle to Ellie's life, too.

So, even though it was something he'd sworn never to do, he said to Ellie, "Well, shall we go watch the kayak races?"

Ellie's eyes went wide. "Sure, Daddy."

Taking her by the hand, he walked along the shore. On the grassy strip running along the bank, he found a space on a bench and sat. Licking her cone, Ellie plopped down next to him. The press of her body against his grounded him. Kept him from getting up and fleeing.

He stared down at his feet. Surely, Cat couldn't enter the race at the last minute. In a few seconds, she'd be back, and he could take her home to Rosie's.

He sat up straighter. No, he couldn't. He'd promised her dinner. What in the world could he serve her? He was no cook, and there was nothing in the house. Maybe he could pick up some take-out from Huang's.

He felt a tug on his shirt sleeve.

"Daddy, look. Cat's in a boat."

He peered down toward the dock. Cat had shucked the black T-shirt, revealing a form-fitting pink tank top that matched her shorts. And, sure enough, she was sitting in the front of a two-man kayak. Leave it to her to talk her way into the race. What man wouldn't want her sitting in his boat, looking the way she did?

He forcibly relaxed his shoulders to relieve the building tension that was sending tugs of pain through his back. Who had taken her on?

Alex narrowed his eyes. *Oh.*

There was no mistaking the man climbing into the kayak. *Thomas.* The man who had to win at all costs. What could she have said or done that he'd replace his usual bruiser with a New York City tourist?

Cat picked up her paddles and said something to Thomas. Thomas laughed back and gave her his patented sexy wink that said, *I'm all into you, baby.*

Alex stuffed the rest of his cone in his mouth and forced it down. The cold ice cream formed a hard lump in his stomach. Thomas couldn't want Cat. Could he? He already had a girlfriend.

Alex scanned the shore. Yep. There was Gloria, tall, blonde, and dressed in tight-red shorts and a halter top. The poor woman appeared none too happy.

So, why would Thomas come on to Cat? Did his old friend just want to make him squirm? Why now? So what if Helen had chosen him over Thomas? She was gone, and he had nothing left. Only a heavily mortgaged house, a job he hated, and a hole in his heart.

Thomas believed he owned the world. He'd not been born rich, but he was rich now. He had a mansion overlooking the harbor, a rapidly growing fish farming operation spreading up and down the coast—he glanced at the glowering girlfriend—and a new girl every week.

Couldn't Thomas leave him with one good thing? A few days with a crazy New Yorker who made him smile?

There was nothing serious going on between him and Cat. Not at all.

The kayaks entering the race milled around the starting point. Alex stood to get a better view. In Thomas's kayak, Cat turned to answer something Thomas said. His stomach knotted as a shaft of something that felt a lot like jealous anger shot through him.

Straining to see, he left the bench and moved closer to shore. The kayaks took their position at the starting buoy just as some onlookers moved into his field of vision. Alex worked his way around them. This was one race he wouldn't miss. Thomas had been having a winning streak these last three years.

But why take on Cat? Even if Thomas were paying him back for his marrying Helen, the man was too cutthroat to risk losing a race by taking on a stranger. It made no sense.

Or wait. He wouldn't put it past Thomas to try to find out why Cat was here by being nice to her.

Alex rubbed a hand across his forehead. It would be like Thomas not to trust his reports.

Flags flapped in the wind. Waves kicked up along the shore. Steering the kayaks straight would take a lot of effort.

Bang.

The starting gun went off. Alex held his breath. For a moment, the water churned as all the paddles dug in, and then Thomas's bright, orange-striped Skipjack nosed forward. In the front seat, Cat, her hat dangling by its cord from her neck, her wild pink hair flying out behind her, dug in her paddle, and the kayak pulled farther ahead.

Alex whistled through his teeth. Man, she was good. Thomas and she worked in total unison as if they'd raced together for years.

From the past came a vision of him and Helen doing the same. Gliding over the water like the wind. Her back flexing. Her smile loving. The complete joy of winning the trophy that summer before she had drowned.

Drowned.

Alex dropped back into the crowd. He had to get away. Stop the image of dark water and tangled branches shooting through his head. He turned and crashed into a hard body.

He jerked back then smiled. "Logan."

His younger brother shook his head. "Never thought to find you here, at the kayak races of all things. Got to bring back bad memories."

Alex shoved his hands into his jeans pockets to keep from pushing his brother away and fleeing as far as he could from his memories. "Well, I'm here. So, you decided to show up for the weekend?"

"Came for the barbeque and the sailing of the sloop in Dad's memory."

"How's grad school going?"

"It's going. Can't wait until I'm out of there. I hate living in a city. Hear you're moving to Halifax."

"Yeah, who hasn't heard?"

"What's Ellie think about that?"

"She's fine with it. Going to get her a puppy."

"Right. Bribes *always* work."

From the shoreline came a scream, then another.

No. Cat.

Heedless of the curses, he shoved his way to the water's edge. One of the kayaks had capsized. Cat was bringing a man onto the beach using a lifeguard's underarm hold. Thomas, in his dead -in-the-water kayak, was looking daggers at Cat.

Alex ran down to where she was coming in and, with Logan's help, lifted the man up over the stone breaker wall. Cat scrambled up, kneeled beside him, and began compressions.

She spit a wet lock of hair out of her mouth. "I think he had a heart attack out there. Gave a cry and just toppled out of his kayak."

A siren echoed off the harborside buildings. At last. Alex blew out a breath.

The crowd parted, and Tide Harbor's EMR squad came through.

The crew took over, and Cat sat back on her knees. She pushed her dripping hair behind her ears. "That slimeball,

Cowling, wasn't even going to stop. Wanted to win so much he'd let a man die." She peered up at him. "I don't think I won any points for you with your boss." She gave a shiver and crossed her arms in front of her. "Forgot how cold the water is up here. Need my wet suit."

Alex took off his shirt and threw it over her shoulders.

She tugged it on. "Thanks." Then she raised her chin. "And who's this big guy who looks like a movie star?"

"Logan, my little brother."

Cat grinned. "Not so little."

Logan grinned back. "Tallest in the family. By the way, Alex, where's Ellie? Didn't see her with Olivia's kids. Not that I'd expect her to be on the dock. I bought her a new charm for her bracelet."

Alex spun around, his breath stuck in his throat. He'd completely forgotten Ellie. She'd been sitting at his side just seconds ago. Or was it minutes? In his desperation to help Cat, he'd gotten up from the bench and walked away from the most precious thing in his life.

He'd left her alone by the water.

His heart pounded. His blood thrummed. He spun around and around and didn't see her.

Her name tore from his throat. "Ellie."

Everything he ever feared raced through his head. She'd fallen in. She was going under. He wouldn't be able to save her.

"Ellie," he shouted again.

Cat put a wet hand on his bare arm. It should have felt as cold as ice. Instead, heat zinged through him.

"I know what you're thinking. Don't go there." Cat's voice cut through his recriminations. "She woudn't go far We'll find her."

He froze. *Fool.* He was one of those terrible dads who completely forgot about their child then jumped to the worst conclusion.

Alex forced himself to breathe. Cat was right. Ellie was here. They'd find her.

Chapter 16
CAT

Saturday Afternoon

Cat fought to control her rising worry. Alex must be going out of his mind. He never let Ellie out of his sight.

Standing on her toes, Cat surveyed the festival grounds. Now, where would she go if she were a little girl fascinated by the water, but who knew going near it was off limits? She scanned the shoreline and street again.

"*There.*" She pointed toward the boatbuilder's shop where he had an old-fashioned dory boat on display. "Over by that workshop, I think I see her striped shirt."

Cat gazed at Alex's face. His cheeks were red, and his mouth was set in a hard-ridged line, as if he could keep all that worry and fear inside him.

She remembered her own father's face when he'd found her hiding under the boardwalk after being teased by the neighborhood kids. He'd felt like he was a bad dad not to have protected her. But instead of hugging her, he'd yelled, telling her to never go on the beach again. An impossible rule they both knew she was never going to obey.

Alex was sure to say something he would regret. Perhaps even make the child more upset. Better she get there first and give Alex a chance to cool down and soften the blow for Ellie. So, Cat took off at a run, leaving him behind.

She stopped in front of what turned out to be a boat maker's display of his wares.

Ellie sat in a small rowboat, facing the sea, struggling to move the heavy oars. The child hadn't seen her approach.

Trying not to startle her, Cat came around the side and caught her eye. The look of determination on her face surprised her.

"Ellie, that looks like such fun. Where are you going?"

The little girl smiled up at her. "To find my mommy."

Cat's heart skipped a beat. She might get annoyed with her mother, but imagining growing up without one broke her heart.

She leaned against the side of the boat. "Where do you think she is?"

Ellie frowned. "You know, out there by Whaleback Island, playing with the mermaids. So, come. Get in and help me row. These oar things weigh a ton."

Cat peered back into the crowd. Alex was just yards away, coming fast. She smiled to let him know Ellie was okay then signaled him to slow down. She prayed he did. It would cool his anger somewhat.

"Your daddy will be here in a second. He's very upset. He didn't know where you were."

Ellie dropped the oars and stuck out her lower lip. "I didn't know where he was, either. He just disappeared, like Mommy."

The pain and confusion in the child's voice drilled into her.

Cat laid her hand lightly on the child's head. "I bet you were scared, but he was scared, too, when he couldn't find you. He might yell. Sometimes, grown-ups sound angry when they are really just very, very worried."

Alex came to a halt beside Cat. True to prediction, his normally steady voice came out as a growl. "Ellie, get out of that boat this minute."

"Sorry, Daddy." Ellie jumped up, stumbled on the inside ribbing, and fell. Tears welled in her eyes. She rubbed her banged knee. "Owie."

Alex swooped in and picked her up. "Oh, sweetheart, sorry I yelled."

Ellie buried her head against his shoulder. "I couldn't find you, Daddy."

He cupped a hand behind her head and nestled her under his chin. "I couldn't find you, either. I'm glad you found a safe place to wait."

Cat moved away. They didn't need her. Alex was such a good father. Though, later, she'd have to tell Alex what his daughter had said. The child knew her mother was dead and not a mermaid, *right?*

Something sharp cut into the sole of her bare foot. Balancing on one leg, she lifted her foot up to examine the spot. No damage. Must have stepped on a rock or a broken shell.

She wobbled, and a hand came under her arm. She gazed into brown eyes so like Alex's she did a double-take.

"Logan, thank you." She pulled free. "No harm done. I have tough feet." She peered up at the towering Harris who had to be at least six-foot-six. "Sorry I didn't get to say a proper hello."

The guy winked at her. "And you're the Pink Lady from New York who's been dating my stubborn brother."

Cat opened her mouth to correct him then closed it. For heaven's sake, she *was* Alex's date. Even if the stubborn Fish Cop didn't think so. So, there.

Ellie's little head popped up. She wiped the tears from her eyes. "She's a mermaid, Uncle Logan. She's got a seahorse."

Cat laughed. "Actually, seahorses. A whole tankful in my lab."

Logan's eyes widened. "Lab? What work do you do?"

Oops. Cat peered over at Alex. Surely, she could be honest with his brother? But his mouth was pinched in that hard line again. Better to give the safe answer.

"I teach biology."

Alex set Ellie on the ground but kept hold of her hand. "See? You two have something in common. Logan is studying marine biology at Dalhousie. Working on his degree."

Cat gave a huff. She hated this need for dishonesty. She would have loved to talk to Logan about his work. He might even be able to help her in her research. But she'd promised Alex not to let anyone know about her scuba diving, and she didn't want him to get in trouble at his job. Thomas Cowling had a mean streak to him.

Still, she had to ask, "So, what are you studying?"

"I have a great professor, Gil Moses. He's asked me to work on a major project focusing on the new tidal energy turbines they just installed here in Tide Harbor."

"Wow. That sounds fascinating. What will your focus be?"

He dipped his head toward the fish pens. "Any time you introduce something new into the ecosystem, you get problems. I want to monitor the effect on the invertebrates. So often they are forgotten. Studying lobsters and haddock sounds more exciting."

Cat opened her mouth to ask him what he thought of fish farming when a loud voice interrupted.

"Miss Silva, you left these over on the dock. Your phone has been ringing constantly."

She whirled around and came face-to-face with Thomas Cowling. He stood there, holding her sandals on his pinky finger as if they were covered in garbage or something. Her phone and knapsack strap rested in his other hand. The fish farm owner hadn't been happy about her jumping out of the kayak in the middle of the race. Not that she cared what he thought. That man who'd passed out could have died. And their kayak had been the closest.

"How is the accident victim?" she asked.

Thomas flipped a hand. "Old Doughtery will be fine. Guy's too old for this boat racing. Paramedics said high blood pressure probably caused him to black out." He gave her a hard look. "We could have won." The phone he was holding rang. He tossed it at her. "Here. Get this thing to stop ringing, will you?"

Cat caught it and stepped aside. Momma. Again. With one ear, she half-listened to her mother's latest complaint. With the other, she took in the conversation among the men. The tension between Thomas and the Harris brothers was sharper than when her brothers used to fight over who got the car.

Thomas took a step back. "Logan, good to see you. Must be having one of those family get-togethers to get your nose out of the books. Not like your brother here. Bet he hasn't read a book in years. Oh, wait, that's right. He did go see the Shakespeare play." He turned to Alex. "Bring back any memories of your college days?" He took another step back. "Well, Miss Silva, bon voyage. I wish you better luck in your next race."

Cat stuffed the phone into her shorts pocket, glad they were mostly dry by now, and dipped her head. "You, too. Been a pleasure meeting you." *Sure.* And it was going to be a pleasure publishing her data on his filthy fish operation.

With a nod, Thomas strode off, stopping to insert his arm into some well-endowed woman's arm, then continued down the street.

Alex turned to her. "Apparently, you're an experienced kayak racer?"

"Sort of."

"What's that mean?"

"Remember, I have three brothers. Well, they're sports crazy. There isn't a sport they don't compete in. Mostly, they are into mixed martial arts. My brothers, Frank and Angelo, run a gym in Manhattan. My older brother, Rob, is a sports agent—just starting out, but he has signed two NBA players, and some wrestler, whom I suppose is good, but I really haven't paid too much attention.

"Anyway, they used to do kayak tandem races every year, and they needed me to complete the second kayak. Angelo and Frank against me and Rob. Rob's the biggest, so it kind of evened out having little old me in the front. We won once."

Alex gave her a puzzled look. "How do city kids get into kayaking?"

Cat laughed. "In case you haven't seen a map recently, New York City is surrounded by water. The Hudson River on the west, Long Island Sound on the northeast, and the Atlantic Ocean on the south. But you do know that. Didn't you dream of sailing your sloop up New York Harbor? Anyway, I actually grew up in Far Rockaway, a few blocks from the ocean. Spent my childhood on the beach."

But enough about her. If she spilled any more about herself, Logan would put together her background and her name and discover he had read some of her papers on marine invertebrates, or worse . . . knew of her award-winning grant proposal. Time to change the subject.

"So, Alex, what did Thomas mean about the Shakespeare dig?"

Logan grinned. "Didn't my brother tell you? He has a degree in English literature. Was going to be a poet, as I remember." He shoulder-bumped Alex. "You sure got teased about that, old boy."

"Yah, sure, and you were always the worst."

"Remember that time I tore up the poem you had written for that sophomore you were so head-over-heels for?"

"All guys are stupid about girls at fifteen." Alex lifted Ellie up onto his hip. "Enough reminiscing. I promised Cat dinner. You can tell her more family secrets tomorrow at the barbecue."

"Don't worry, I will. See you there." With a wave, Logan disappeared into the crowd.

Cat slipped on her sandals. "So, where are we going to eat tonight?"

Alex hefted Ellie higher. "It's been a long, exciting day. Ellie's half-asleep now. I think she needs to get to bed early."

Ellie lifted her head off his shoulder. "I'm not tired, Daddy."

Alex rubbed her back and winked at Cat. "Not much." His mouth turned up in the corner. "I was thinking of Chinese takeout, if you don't mind. But we can cancel if that's not something that appeals."

"I'd love Chinese food." Cat settled her hat on her head. "Especially if I can share it with you and Ellie."

Alex's face burst into the brightest smile he'd yet worn. "Terrific. We'll pick some up on the way home."

Oh my. He was inviting her to his house, and he sounded happy about it. Her stay in Tide Harbor was coming to an end, and any chance to spend more time with this less-gray Alex sounded wonderful.

She gazed at his smiling lips. Maybe she'd even get a goodnight kiss to take back to New York with her—a kiss to cherish on long, lonely nights.

Chapter 17
ALEX

Saturday Night

It had been a long time since a woman sat at his kitchen table. Alex put a forkful of lo mein in his mouth, but he could barely taste it. Not with Cat sitting across from him. He could no longer deny his attraction to the Pink-Haired Lady nor his desire to get closer, maybe even kiss her.

Cat nibbled on an egg roll then bent over to give Ellie a bite of her crispy chicken. A length of her hair fell forward, and she brushed it behind her ear. It wasn't as pink as when he'd first seen it, more a pale rosy blonde. Long and straight, he wondered if it felt as silky as it looked.

He laid down his fork. *Idiot.* What had he been thinking? He should never have brought Cat Silva to his house. A brassy girl in a marine supply store. A mud-covered waif on the beach. A superhero saving a man's life. A moment, tasting her cone and her tasting his. Those memories, he could have put away in a secret place in his heart and slowly let fade.

But having Cat here, sitting at the table where Helen had sat and looking like she belonged. Having her walk through his house, admiring his carpentry. Letting her throw open the drapes so light and sea filled the room. Seeing her caring for Ellie as if she were part of the family.

Those images were ones he could never wipe from his mind. He wanted her to be here forever, helping Ellie and driving away his loneliness. And she was leaving. If that said he was a fool to think of a future with her, then he was a fool.

Forget eating.

He slid his plate away. Somehow, in the last six days, he'd fallen for a brassy New Yorker with pink hair and a tattoo of a fish on her collarbone. Well, he thought it might be a fish. He could see a fish-looking tail peeking above the neckline of her tank top when she moved. Though, knowing Cat, it could be something totally bizarre.

She peered up from her almost empty plate. "Didn't you like what you ordered? You can have some of my chicken if you'd like. I've eaten a lot of Chinese cuisine in my life, but this is definitely the best I've ever tasted."

"The Huangs use all fresh local produce. Nothing canned."

She wiped her plate with her last piece of her chicken. "Amazing. Can't believe you have such a treasure in Tide Harbor. In fact, all of Tide Harbor is a treasure. Might just steal the whole place. Take it home with me on Monday." She batted her eyes at him. "How about it, Fog Man?"

Ellie giggled. "Silly Cat."

Fog Man. Home. Monday. That sounded a lot like an invitation. Alex knew he was in trouble because, at that moment, he wanted to put his arms around this incredible woman and go wherever she was going, even to New York City.

He gave himself a shake. Now he was being the silly one.

"You can't take a whole town home. Besides, it would be too wet for everybody," Ellie said.

Cat laughed. "Wet?"

"Uh-huh. Under the ocean, swimming with the mermaids." She raised her eyes. "But you can take me. I'd go."

What? Alex sat up in his chair. This had to stop.

"I've told you before: mermaids are imaginary, Ellie."

She crossed her arms over her chest. "No, they're not. They're real."

He firmed his voice. "Ellie, mermaids are make-believe."

"No. No. No." She shook her head. "Cat's real, and she's a mermaid."

Alex caught a movement out of the corner of his eye—Cat held up her palm as if to stop him—but he couldn't let his daughter go on living in a pretend world. The real world was hard and cruel.

"Miss Silva lives in New York City. She's a teacher, like Miss Paquette."

Ellie sniffed away tears. "You're lying, Daddy. Cat came out of the ocean. I saw her."

He raised his voice. "Now, see here, young lady. That's enough. Cat was scuba diving. That's all, right?" He looked to Cat for confirmation.

"Yes, Ellie. I was swimming, using the gear I showed you the other day."

"But . . ." Ellie's chin quivered.

Alex stood. "Time for bed."

"Yes." Cat stood up and held out her hand toward Ellie. "How about you show me your bedroom? Maybe I could tell you a story about mermaids?" She smiled at Alex. "If that's okay with your daddy?"

Alex started. "I don't think—"

Cat leaned over and whispered in his ear, "She doesn't know her mother is dead, does she?"

She touched his arm. "Let me try." She turned back to Ellie. "Show me the way."

"Okay." Ellie took Cat's hand and led her down the hall.

Maybe I could tell you a story about mermaids?"

Alex trailed after them, feeling abandoned in his own home. He peered through the doorway as Ellie got on her pajamas and climbed into bed.

Cat tucked the covers up to Ellie's chin, made sure Dorchester was comfortable, then gazed over at him. "Come on in. You can hear the story, too."

He slipped into the room and folded his large body into Ellie's small desk chair.

At that moment, Cat's phone rang. How unfortunate. He expected her to jump to answer it. Instead, she flicked it off and put it on the nightstand.

"Was that your mother?"

"Yeah. But she can wait a few minutes. My story can't. So, Ellie, the story begins as all good stories do—with once upon a time . . ."

Ellie nodded. "Of course, it does." She rolled to her side and twisted a curl around her finger.

Cat smiled. "So, once upon a time, mermaids played beneath the sea. They had hair like seaweed and eyes like stars. Down in the dark, they made their beds in the sand

and their houses of seashells. And they played. Sometimes, they floated with the fishes. Sometimes, they explored a shipwreck sitting on the sea bottom. And sometimes, they watched the people on the shore."

Alex rested his elbows on his knees and felt the tension lift. Cat's voice was low, rich, and enticing. The cream-colored shade of the table lamp on the nightstand cast a golden glow over her profile. Outside, the soft lapping of the waves in the cove provided a lullaby rhythm that matched the soft lilt of her voice. He wanted this moment to last forever.

Cat tousled Ellie's curls. "When the people on the shore went out in boats, the mermaids watched them sail. Sometimes, they worried about the sea creatures the fishermen caught. But they knew people had to eat, too. Sometimes, when a boat sank, they'd help the people who disappeared under the water. They'd kiss them and lay them on the seafloor.

But now the mermaids are all gone to the kingdom under the sea, far away from noisy motor boats and giant ships and polluted water. Today, when someone drowns, all the fish, and lobsters, and seals, and sea cucumbers come and say goodbye. And each leaves a shell or a stone until the dead person is covered and part of the sea. And sometimes, people who miss someone they love, who disappeared beneath the water, can find a special shell or a stone and put it in their pocket so they can have that person close whenever they remember them."

Cat reached into the side pocket of her shorts and took out a tiny shell. "See? This is my special shell. When I hold it, I think of my father. He died last year when I was far away. I miss him very much."

Ellie, her eyes closed, nodded. "I miss Mommy."

"Of course, you do. You can be sure that when she died, the creatures under the sea buried her with great care and love. And tomorrow, how about your dad, you, and I search for a special shell to remember her by?"

Her voice soft with sleep, Ellie whispered, "Okay."

Cat rested her hand on the little girl's head then clicked off the lamp.

Alex met her outside the door. "Thank you. I couldn't have done that. I couldn't—this sounds crazy—find the words to tell her Helen was dead."

"That's natural. Our deepest hurts are the hardest to bare to the world."

He put a hand on her wrist. "I'm sorry about your father. It was beyond kind to open yourself up like that for my daughter."

She drew her hand away. "Sharing stories of the one you love is a way to heal. If you keep them all inside, they turn into twisted memories that can strangle you."

Her words froze him in place. She knew. She knew just how he felt. She'd lost someone she'd loved, too.

Cat tiptoed to the kitchen and gathered up the plates from the table. "I should be going."

"No. Not yet." He couldn't bear to see her go. She'd just performed magic with his daughter. Just reached far into his heart.

Alex took the dishes from her hands and dumped them in the sink. "Leave those. Come with me." He took her hand and led her out onto the deck that wrapped around the house. The air held a pleasant chill after the heat of the day. The tangy scent of the pines surrounded them. Above them, the Milky Way splashed across the heavens, and Polaris, the sailor's star, shone down, centering them in the universe.

Cat walked along the deck, her sandals barely making a sound, and put her hands on the railing. She peered out toward the cove. "I really do wish I could take all this home with me."

Alex shifted his weight. "But you said you live by the ocean."

"It's not like this. Far Rockaway is crowded and noisy with people. The sky above is murky. The stars invisible. The shore is littered with rubbish. I love it, anyway. But this is heaven."

Alex moved to stand beside her, so close he could feel the heat of her skin on his own. She smelled toasty, sunbaked, real. He resisted pressing against her or taking her in his arms and kissing her. He didn't want to scare her away. He wanted her to stay. To stay the night. To stay forever. To fill the emptiness that Helen had left inside him. To be the mother Ellie needed.

The words came unbidden. "You could stay."

She turned toward him, confusion on her face. "Are you asking me to stay longer in Tide Harbor?"

"Well, yes." He moved nearer.

Cat ran her hands along the railing. "I could."

Hope bubbled through his veins. She could stay here. They could become friends. She could learn to love him.

Alex licked his lips, swallowed, and the weight of the future pressed down. Who was he to ask her to stay? He had nothing to offer a woman like her, no matter how attracted he was or how amazing she was with Ellie.

In a few weeks, he and Ellie would be in Halifax, not here in Tide Harbor.

He stumbled over his words, trying to pull them back. "If you liked—if you wanted—you could buy a place here in Tide Harbor. Live here. In fact, I'm selling this house."

Her hands tightened on the railing. "Oh." She peeked at him sideways. "You're selling this house? Why?"

"Ellie and I are moving to Halifax at the end of the month. I'm going to be head of security at Cowling's warehouse there."

"I see." She rubbed her hands up and down her arms. "Well, as much as I love Tide Harbor, I'm not in the market for a summer place. I have my work and my research back in the city. I have my mother to care for."

He sank back. "Of course."

Cat turned and gave him her signature crooked smile. "But maybe someday."

He could have kissed her at that moment. They were so close. Her eyes reflected the thin curve of the rising quarter moon. Her lips looked moist and wet. Her hair floated around her like wisps of silver.

He leaned forward slightly, drawn to that warmth.

She stepped away.

"Well, thank you for the lovely day, and the dinner, and the time with your daughter. She is a marvelous child. But it's late. I must get going." She headed down the steps, stood for a minute at the bottom, gazing up at him as if waiting for something, and then she was gone into the dark.

Alex cupped his hands over his face. He should have taken her in his arms and given her that kiss.

He shook his head. No. It was better this way. Cat Silva had a whole other life that didn't include him and a five-year-old. Better to quash his feelings now, no matter how much it hurt.

"Oh, I forgot."

Alex jerked his head in the direction of her voice. She'd come back. He moved toward the steps.

She peered up at him, her hand patting the side of her thigh. "We have to take Ellie to the beach to find her shell. Do you want to do that before or after we get together with your family tomorrow?"

His blood buzzed through him. How had he forgotten? She'd still be here tomorrow. He had another day to spend with her. Another chance to kiss her, even if it was to say goodbye.

"Oh, after, I think."

"Great. See you." She gave a wave then disappeared into the night, taking all the warmth with her.

Chapter 18
CAT

Sunday Morning

Cat worked at combing out the sleep tangles from her hair. Getting up at four in the morning to go diving was tiring her out. She yawned and peered into the mirror. Flamingo pink was starting to look a lot like her natural blonde. Well, that should make Alex and the rest of Tide Harbor happy.

The phone rang, and Cat jumped. Heavens. What was Momma doing up so early? With the time zone difference, it would be near three a.m. in New York. She sure hoped it wasn't an emergency.

She swiped the phone off the nightstand and flicked it on.

"Catalina, when are you coming home?"

Cat let out the breath she hadn't known she'd been holding. Okay, not an emergency call.

"It's Cat. Why are you up so early?"

"Cat is no name for a girl. Don't get why you won't use the beautiful name we gave you."

Cat looked at the phone. There wasn't time for this. She had to get out to the pens. Get her samples before Fish Cop Alex was awake. Then be ready for the Harris barbecue.

"Mom, I'm on my way out to get samples. Can we talk later?"

"In the middle of the night, you're diving?"

"It's later here." *Oops*. That slip of her tongue was going to set her mother off. She'd never get her off the phone now.

"Wait a minute, Catalina Maria Silva. Have you been lying to me about where you are? Tell me the truth. You on the other side of the ocean again like when your dad died?"

Cat let out a long, hard breath. Why did her mother always throw that in her face? It wasn't as if she could have made it back in time no matter where she had been. The head injury from his fall from the ladder had only taken minutes to steal her father away.

She planted her feet. Okay, no more being a jellyfish. "No, Momma. I promised never to go that far away again. Now, you go back to sleep. I'll be home Monday night."

"Why can't you leave today?"

Cat tossed the phone from one hand to the other. Her brother was wrong. Ultimatums didn't work. Only one thing would settle her mother down.

"I've met a man. Someone I like. I have a date today." And if saying that made her heart beat a little faster, as if it were true, then so be it. There was no denying that, for the first time in her life, she felt a spark of interest in a man, even if his heart was fixated on his dead wife.

Her mother's voice turned all perky. "A date. That's wonderful. Now, don't you wear those ugly tight leggy things you teach in."

"He likes them." Phone to her ear, Cat stuffed her feet in her sandals and shuffled to the door. Did Alex like them? He hadn't said. But her legs *were* her best feature. She shook her head and let the screen door slap behind her. She liked her wild leggings, and that was all that mattered.

"You have to tell me all about him."

She picked up her jacket and sample case. "I will when I get home. I'll try to send you pictures later today."

"You have fun on your date, and don't you dare mention your scar."

Her stomach did a nosedive. *Oh, Momma.*

Cat ran a finger across her top lip. She didn't have to mention her scar. It was there for the world to see.

The bubbles of lightness she'd been feeling popped.

Sure, Alex had been kind to her. Sure, he'd been grateful for her helping his daughter. But it was his brother who'd invited her to the family get-together, not Alex.

She'd be a fool to think he cared for her. He had the chance to kiss her last night and merely stared at her. Offered to sell her his house. She touched her lip again. No one wanted to hook up with someone who'd been born with a cleft palate. The few men she'd dated before had acted like it was contagious or something.

She headed outside into the foggy dark. Static from the phone filled her ear.

"You heard me, didn't you?"

"Yes, Momma. Goodbye, Momma. See you soon, Momma." She clicked off the phone. Those boxes for marriage and family on her Happiness List? Well, they could just stay unchecked.

She was going to enjoy her last day in Tide Harbor. Then she'd leave with no regrets.

Crunch.

Cat spun around and gasped. The man approaching the dock wore a gray baseball cap with Cowling Fish Farms printed across the front in large green letters. A Cowling security man, for sure. Unfortunately, he wasn't Alex.

This man wore a sour expression as he toyed with the keys on his belt. "What'ch doing, lady?"

Cat forced her trembling lips into a giant smile. "Just went for an early morning swim. It's my last day here."

"A swim, eh? In all that gear? So, explain what you plan to do with that." He pointed to the open bag of samples at her feet.

If Thomas Cowling was as anti-ecological science as Alex said, it would best to be less than truthful.

"I'm doing saltwater tests for a school research project." No way anyone could prove different. That was all they were—water samples. And it wasn't even much of a lie. More like misdirection. They were for school, in a way. New York University was a school, right?

Mr. Overeager Fish Cop shifted from one foot to the other, considering her answer. "Why do you have to go out there to get seawater? There's plenty of water right here." He pointed at the swells slapping the pilings of the old dock.

She rubbed her forehead. "It's saltier out there."

"All tastes salty to me. Don't know why a tourist would want to test the stuff." He cleared his throat. "You a scientist type?"

Cat bit the inside of her cheek and wished he'd at least shown up *after* she'd gotten out of her scuba gear. With the sun coming up, she was starting to sweat.

"I teach biology."

He took out a pad and paper. "And your name is?"

Well, she couldn't lie about that. "Cat Silva."

"Well, Miss Silva, I will have to report this to my boss. Where are you staying?"

"Fletcher's." She plucked at the neck of her wet suit.

"Yah, sure, Rosie's place." The man stuck the pencil behind his ear, bent down, and hefted her satchel.

"Wait. What are you doing?"

"I'll be confiscating these samples. Mr. Cowling, he don't like people busy-bodying around the pens."

If she hadn't been a mature woman with a degree in marine biology, Cat would have stamped her foot and screamed like some cartoon character. Those samples were essential. They completed the series of daily readings she'd been taking. Without them, she'd have to start the whole sequence over again. Her research would be set back another week, and she couldn't afford to stay any longer. Momma would go bananas if she didn't show up tomorrow, and another week with Alex and Ellie would make leaving seven days later harder.

She couldn't keep the irritation from her voice. "So, when can I have them back?"

"Dunno. My boss has the day off. No telling when he'll be back." He swung the bag over his shoulder. "Come down to the offices tomorrow and ask."

Cat gnawed at her lip. *Tomorrow.* She had to leave before dawn. Momma expected her for dinner.

"I can't. Today's my last day here. Give me my case, please." She reached for it.

He jerked it away. "No way, lady. Want me to call the police?"

She let her hand fall. She didn't need the police involved. Alex would just have to retrieve them for her tonight. She nodded. "Okay."

As the man turned to go, she caught a glimpse of the zippered case of vials. There was nothing to identify that it belonged to her except that it was pink with tiny white polka dots. She might need written proof to claim it.

"Wait. Can you give me a receipt?"

The guy scratched his belly. "Guess so."

Mr. Security's pencil scratches on a torn-edge paper scrap wasn't much of a receipt, but it would have to do. Holding it in her teeth, Cat hurried to zip out of her wet suit.

She shoved everything into the car trunk and slammed the hood. Despite the warmth of the sun, a chill swept over her. Surely, Alex would get her samples back.

She came around to the driver's side and slid in. Who was she kidding? He'd be furious when he heard. She'd kind of agreed to stop diving out by the pens. He'd trusted her not to. He'd feel betrayed to know she'd been going behind his back. It was why she still hadn't reported the dangerous debris tangle when she knew better.

Cat curled her fingers. She didn't have a choice. She'd just have to hope he'd forgive her.

By the time, Cat was back at the cottage, she barely had time to shower and dress. She wrinkled her nose at her suitcase. Rarely did she worry about what people thought of her. Loud and in-your-face, that was Cat Silva. But maybe she ought to wear something more conservative for the family gathering so as not to embarrass Alex? Not that she had much choice. But she had packed a pair of jeans, and she hadn't worn the dull gray tee she'd bought at Labranche Marine.

Cat glanced in the mirror and focused on the little scar bisecting her upper lip. No. Dull hair was enough concession to Tide Harbor's sensibilities. She'd stick with pink.

Just her luck, her last pink tee happened to be a direct affront to sword fishermen. Might as well give the Harris family something else to gossip about.

Grabbing a bandana, she swept her hair into a ponytail and tied it behind her neck. She hurried to the door.

Before stepping out, she glanced down and gave herself a once-over, hoping she hadn't gone too far. The leggings were okay. Pink jellyfish floated against a deeper pink background, looking more abstract than slimy. The pink crop top with the swordfish joke wasn't too off-the wall. It was the hat.

She took it off and studied it. The pink baseball cap featured a picture of a large fish hook and read, "*I'm a Hooker.*" She'd avoided wearing it in Tide Harbor after the shopping cart incident. But it seemed a shame not to wear it at least once while she was here. She hoped Alex's family didn't take it the wrong way.

She slapped it back on her head. Even if they did, what did it matter? When Alex found out she'd continued diving and hadn't reported a deadly hazard, she'd be in the Harrises' bad graces, anyway.

Chapter 19
ALEX
Sunday Morning

Alex traipsed along the cliff above the shoreline, keeping an eye out for the missing kayak. He sure hoped Zack Wilson, the fill-in guy, was up to taking his place for the day. But he'd put off the search for the kayak for too long, and he had that annoying family barbecue later in the day to get through.

He groaned under his breath. Cat probably never wanted to see him again after that almost kiss. How would he face her surrounded by his interfering siblings?

Shoving a pine bough out of his way, he scanned the pebble beach below. If the RCMP couldn't find the boy's kayak, why in the world should he be able to?

Alex climbed over a protruding boulder. And what was he going to do if he did find it? Destroy it like Thomas wanted? Or throw his future away and do the right thing—call the police?

Alex gazed out across the harbor. The fish pens lay to the northeast of where he was standing. With the tide coming in, as it had that horrid night, the body would have washed up to the fish pens. But so would the kayak.

He gave a quick shake of his head. No, it wouldn't. The kayak had been one of those molded plastic ones. It wouldn't have sunk like the body had. With the wind blowing from the southeast that night, and the kayak floating above the surface of the water, it would have been blown against this shoreline, for sure.

He pushed back his Cowling ball cap. It had to have washed ashore or be trapped in the rocks some place around here. There were plenty of semi-submerged boulders that could snag a kayak. Still, why hadn't the police found it?

Alex drew his binoculars from his pack and scanned the shore and close-in rocks for anything that didn't belong. He wished he knew what color it was. But that piece of information hadn't been in the report.

Most people, especially younger ones like the victim, loved the brightly colored sit-on-top ones—flaming orange, neon green, fiery red. They were easier to find if they floated off.

He lowered the glasses and hiked along the cliff path, eyes peeled. Maybe, with luck, he'd find the darn thing. Or maybe not. But he had to try.

Two hours later, Alex was ready to give up. He'd walked the cliff face twice and sighted nothing. He checked the time on his phone. Eleven o'clock. Time to head back if he planned to get to the barbecue in time.

"Hallou."

Alex spun around.

A tall, lanky man with a crow on his shoulder and wild chestnut hair that demanded a good combing, stood farther down the path. A mangy, tannish-gray dog leaned against his leg, If someone had seen a wayward kayak, it would be this man, Will Young, Tide Harbor's world log-rolling champ, turned resident recluse. He had a cabin up in the woods and knew this part of the peninsula better than anyone.

"You lost, stranger?" Will called.

Alex hurried toward him but stopped a few steps away, not trusting the foul-eyed crow nor the growling dog. "Not a stranger. I'm Alex Harris. Went to school with you. And not lost. Looking for something lost, though."

"I remember you. Built that lovely schooner." Will tickled the crow under the neck. "So, what did you lose?"

"A sea kayak. Might have washed up two weeks ago?"

"Police came through looking for one the other day." Will squinted at him. "Same one?"

Will might be weird and antisocial, but he wasn't stupid nor uninformed. He'd need to be honest with him.

Alex nodded. "That would be right. It's tied to the death of that young man whose body turned up at the Cowling fish pens. Did they find it?"

"No." Will petted the crow again. "Neither will you."

Alex rubbed his temples. "You know where it is?"

"Gone." Will shrugged. "The kayak got hung up on those rocks below. I saw it last Monday morning when I was checking my wildlife cameras. I planned to go down and secure it after I finished, but it must have rocked loose and floated out to sea or onto rocks farther out."

Alex unclenched his jaw. That was good news for Thomas and good news for him. With luck the kayak would be found by someone who really needed it.

He waved goodbye and hurried back along the cliff path. Now all he had to do was get to the barbecue on time.

Chapter 20
CAT

Sunday Afternoon

Cat pulled into the gravel drive and turned off her GPS. From the outside, the weathered, cedar-shake sea captain's house looked a lot like Rose Madsen's fake captain's house, except this one was truly old. It was also a lot more active as the scent of a charcoal fire and the sound of shouting children came from around back.

Cat grabbed the box of mini-cupcakes she'd picked up at Kate's and approached the house.

"Miss Silva," a woman yelled from the half-open screen door. "Come on in. I can't wait to meet you."

In minutes, Cat found herself relaxing in a chaise lounge on the back deck and sipping an iced coffee while Alex's sister pried her with questions. In the yard, the Harris men played some weird version of ice hockey with Olivia's three little boys and Ellie. There were two nets and hockey sticks, but the puck was a large beanbag, and instead of ice, they were playing on sandy grass.

Alex, dressed in jeans and a bright red, close-fitting T-shirt, looked tan and fit and, as powerful as his equally well-built brothers. Why had she ever thought Alex Harris ordinary? Muscles he'd kept hidden under those baggy gray shirts bulged as he lobbed the beanbag to Olivia's youngest. The tyke picked it up with his hands and ran toward the goal.

Olivia gave her a wide grin. "Can't keep your eyes off him."

"Who? Alex?" Cat slapped her forehead. "Sorry, that was a dead giveaway, wasn't it?"

Alex's sister had the same black curly hair and crinkle lines at the corners of her eyes that Alex had. The difference was Olivia laughed and smiled constantly.

She was laughing now.

"That brother of mine hasn't looked that happy in a long time. Not since his wife died. He's told you about that, right?"

Cat gnawed on her lip. "A bit. I know she died. I assume something to do with a boat, seeing his aversion to anything having to do with them and the sea."

"They were kayaking in the harbor. Somehow, despite being an expert swimmer, she ended up in the water and drowned, and that's about as much as any of us know." Olivia shrugged. "Only Alex and the police know exactly what happened. Nothing specific was ever made public. And Alex won't talk about it."

At that moment, Olivia jumped up and cheered as her little one ran into the goal cage and flopped down on the beanbag. "Yay, Teddy. Way to end the game."

Matt cupped his hand around his mouth and yelled back, "Don't encourage him, sis."

Olivia laughed again. "You guys get over here and put the steaks on the grill. It's past noon."

She turned to Cat. "How about you come inside and help me get the salad ready? The crew will be hungry after all that running. If we set the salad out first, the kids might actually get some vegetables inside them for a change."

Cat followed Alex's sister into the kitchen.

Olivia took a head of lettuce and three tomatoes from the fridge. She gave Cat a knife and a cutting board. "Here, you dice the tomatoes while I prep the lettuce."

Cat cut the first tomato in half. She peered down at the tomato halves. That was just how she felt—cut in half. On the one hand, she wanted to run away and hide so Alex wouldn't know she'd been lying to him once he found out she'd kept diving. On the other hand, she wanted to tell him how much he meant to her and that she wanted to stay here forever. She loved Tide Harbor. She loved his family. She loved . . .

She sliced the knife down again. No. People didn't fall in love in seven days. Besides, he was in love with his wife—his dead wife.

She touched her tongue to her lip. And she had something else to feel ashamed of. She ought to tell him how she had gotten this scar.

Olivia dumped the clean lettuce leaves into a wooden salad bowl then peered out into the yard. "He's a good man, our Alex. But he doesn't deal well with loss. After our dad died, Alex took up kayaking. Said he liked the solitude. Just him and the water and nature. I think it was his way of working out his grief. He was the closest to our dad. The two of them built that sloop together. Anyway, one thing led to another. Then he met Helen at the Annapolis River kayak championships, and they just clicked. Started racing as a tandem team, which sent them racing to the altar."

Olivia held out the bowl. "Hand over those tomatoes before you chop them into sauce."

Cat looked down at the dripping cutting board. "Oh, I guess I got overly enthusiastic there. Sorry."

"Don't get your hair in knots. Those guys won't care. Probably think it's a new kind of dressing. Chopping is great therapy. Things can get pretty dicey 'round here sometimes. That's when I take out a head of cabbage or a bunch of potatoes. Better than chopping off some little guy's head." She wagged her hand at her. "You can clean up at the sink."

Cat carried the board and knife over to the sink and ran them under the water. It was her head that needed chopping. Yesterday, her crazy enthusiasm for anything to do with water and boats had sent her hurtling into Cowling's kayak without a care for Alex's and Ellie's feelings.

She turned to Olivia. "I feel terrible. I shouldn't have entered the race yesterday."

"Hey, don't sweat it. Logan said Alex was down on the shore, watching you race. That's a milestone for him. Every other year, he's left before the races start."

"But it brought back bad memories for Ellie." A sudden thought pierced through her. "Was she there—when her mother died? Ellie mentioned something about Whaleback Island." And mermaids. But Olivia didn't need to know about that.

"Yeah, it's where the three of them capsized. Whaleback is the small island that sits out at the head of the harbor. At low tide, there's a charming beach many couples like to picnic at. *Very private*, if you know what I mean?" She gave her a wink. "Ellie was only three. I doubt she remembers much. But it's not my story to tell. You'll have to ask Alex."

Olivia shook the bottle of salad dressing and poured it over the lettuce and tomatoes. "You're good for him, you know. You're so different from Helen. You're . . ." She gave her a measuring gaze. "Uh, don't take this the wrong way, but everything about you, from the way you talk to the way you dress, is like the pop of a firecracker going off. Helen was real quiet."

Cat set the knife and cutting board in the dish rack. "She was so beautiful. All those golden curls."

"How do you know what Helen looked like?"

"Alex has her picture on his mantel."

Olivia looked up from tossing the salad. Her eyes twinkled. "So, you've been in his house, have you?"

Cat wished she wasn't wearing the stupid hat. It was giving Alex's sister the wrong idea about her.

"Uh, last night, for Chinese takeout."

Olivia handed her the bowl. "Listen, Alex was swept up by that woman beyond all commonsense. She was a nice enough person. A wonderful mother. But he was over in love with her, if you know what I mean. Treated her like a queen or something. Built that crazy fancy house for her. Had to have the best of everything in it. A kitchen copied out of a magazine spread. A full wrap-around deck." Olivia wiped her hands on a towel. "Well, you've seen the place. Anyway, he saddled himself with a mortgage from Thomas Cowling that he's still working to pay off."

Cat let out a breath. So that was the hold Cowling had over Alex.

"But your brother's selling the house."

"If wishes were lobsters at fifty dollars a pound, then maybe. He'll have a hard time getting enough from the sale to make good on that debt. Real estate is not a hot item around here. The locals can't afford the price he needs to get to cover the mortgage, and the summer people want something bigger. Two bedrooms and one bath just don't cut it." Olivia picked up the ketchup and steak sauce and swept past her.

Cat hurried after her. "But the view from his living room is breathtaking. Fletcher's Cove is surely one of the most beautiful spots in Nova Scotia."

"Ask him why he's moving to Halifax."

"What? Isn't it because he thinks fish farming is the way of the future?"

Olivia looked over her shoulder as she pushed out the back door to the deck. "If you think that, you don't know my brother at all."

Cat trailed after her, a lump of guilt stuck in her throat. Here, she'd been wishing she was part of Alex's life, yet she knew absolutely nothing about how he felt about fish farming or her.

Matt dashed up the steps and swooped the salad bowl out of Cat's hands. "Of course, she doesn't. Nobody knows what Alex has going on in that seaweed he calls a brain." He looked down at her tee. "So, what does your shirt say today, Pink Lady?"

"Oh, this one is for you." Cat turned one way then the other, showing off the cartoon of a swordfish spearing a fisherman that read, "*Swordfish don't get mad they get even.*" "You like it?"

Alex came up behind her and put a hand on her shoulder. "Since I don't hunt swordfish, I think it's just fine. Matt might disagree, but he's always disagreeable." His fingers brushed the exposed skin beneath her midi.

Cat took in a breath and forced herself to focus on his brother. She gave Matt a wink. "I think it was quite gentlemanly of your brother to invite me."

Alex snorted. "He's just acting nice to you to bug me."

"*Bug you*? Who? Me?" Matt hooked his arm through Cat's and shook a finger at Alex. "Just for that, dear brother, I'm going to steal her away." He tugged her toward the battered picnic table in the corner of the yard. "Come sit by me. Let's see if I can convince you to ditch that shirt and get one that reads, '*Matt's Fish is Bigger.*'"

Olivia gave him a shove. "The children."

Matt grinned at her. "I said fish—F.I.S.H."

Ellie bounced over to them. "Cat's got a T-shirt with a policeman fish on it, Uncle Matt. He's got a cop hat and a badge, just like Daddy."

Matt slapped Alex on the back. "Crickets. The woman already owns an Alex shirt. Guess I'm out of luck." He turned his hand palm up, then with a bow, invited her to the picnic bench with the aplomb of a waiter in an elegant resort. "Be my guests."

Cat slipped into the middle. Alex joined her on one side. Ellie, on the other. Everyone else squeezed in around and across from them. It was like being part of a big, happy, laughing sandwich.

Cat looked up and down the table. This was where she wanted to be. Part of Alex's big happy family. Living in this beautiful place. Not back in New York, dodging traffic, grading student papers, and vying to be as cutthroat as her fellow faculty members.

Her phone buzzed in her pocket. Momma.

No matter what her heart said, it wouldn't work. She had a mother who relied on her. Alex had a dead wife he still loved and a fear of the ocean that would always divide them. She spent half her life out on the water. It was her career, her life's work.

Cat gave herself a mental shake. *Stop being foolish.* She was quirky, perky Cat Silva. She'd enjoy this last day in Tide Harbor with these delightful people. Tonight, she'd confess to Alex, watch the smile leave his face, hope he cared enough to rescue her last batch of samples, and go home.

The salad bowl came tipping and tottering around the table, passing from small hands to big hands, then back to small. Cat took a serving and passed it on.

Logan, wearing a faded frilly apron, forked a steak onto Cat's plate.

She grinned up at him. "You the cook today?"

"Luck of the draw," Logan said as he moved down the row, dishing out the sizzling T-bones. "Whoever is slowest cleaning fish gets to wear our mom's apron and sweat over the grill."

Cat peered down at her steak. "Say, why aren't we eating fish? I thought we were celebrating Matt's great haul?"

"Exactly. That great haul paid for us to eat steak instead of fish."

She raised an eyebrow. "So, you're not big fish eaters?"

Everyone laughed.

"We eat plenty of fish—fried fish, broiled fish, smoked fish, fish chowder, fish cakes, finnan haddie. Even tongues and cheeks." Olivia took a bite of her steak. "Everything but farmed salmon."

Now that was interesting.

Cat peered around the table. "Why not salmon?"

Matt waved his fork at her. "Those farms threaten the small fishermen's livelihood. It's much harder to longline fish on hooks and reel them in out in the open water, exposed to the elements, than to net them out of a pen sitting a few hundred yards offshore. When we go out, there's no guarantee we'll make a profit." He cast an eye at Alex. "Or that we'll make it back in." He thumbed his finger up and down the table. "And we rely on that income. Our longliner, good old *Emma Mae,* supports Olivia and her brood, supports me, pays for Logan's university fees, even supports our Cowling traitor over there."

"I'm not a traitor." Alex swung his leg over the bench and stood. "I'm doing what I think is best for me and for Ellie."

Matt laid down his fork then straightened his napkin. "Fine. Go to Halifax. Turn your back on us. Work for Thomas. But make it a clean break. Sell me the sloop. You know you could use the money to help pay off your ridiculous mortgage."

Alex swung his hands out. "No. Never. The sloop is all I have left of Dad." He spun around and stormed off down a path that disappeared into the piney woods behind the house.

Cat rose.

Olivia waved her back down. "Sit. Let him stew. He's good at that."

Cat turned to Matt. "I don't understand. The sloop is Alex's?"

"Dad left it to him but gave us user rights. At the time, it was fair. Alex built most of it on his own. I was out sowing my wild oats in Toronto, and Logan and Nick were just dopey school kids. But now he won't even go out on her. Seems a waste."

Olivia wiped ketchup off the mouth of her youngest then turned to face her. "Speaking of which—we are planning a family outing on the sloop after we are done here. Want to join us?"

"Uh . . ." Cat peeked toward the woods.

Olivia threw down the napkin. "He and Ellie are not coming. We already asked."

Ellie stopped poking her cousin and tilted her face up at her aunt. "But Dorchester and I want to go on the boat."

"Your daddy said no, honey."

Her mouth formed into a giant pout. Her eyes filled with tears.

Cat patted her on the shoulder. "Tell you what. Remember that special shell we talked about? How about as soon as the food is cleared away, we go to the cove and do some beachcombing?"

Ellie nodded.

"So, let's get chugging." Seizing her dish, Cat stood and began collecting the rest of the plates and utensils. Heading toward the kitchen, she couldn't resist looking at the well-worn path into the woods.

"Olivia," she called. "Where does that trail Alex took go?"

Olivia laughed. "Worried about him getting lost? Don't be. This was our childhood home. That path goes back to a small pond where we used to build rather pitiful rafts. There's a treehouse, too. My two older boys mess around back there, so I can't say what condition it's in. Say, if you want to go find him and drag him back, I'll keep an eye on Ellie."

Here was her chance to talk with him in private. She might not get another.

"I think I will."

She called over to Ellie, "I'll fetch your dad. Then we can go pick out your shell. Stay here with your aunt."

"Wait." Olivia ran into the house then came out with a bottle of insect repellent. "The mosquitoes and black flies will be fierce back there. Surprised Alex hasn't come back swatting by now." She tossed her the bottle. "Just in case you're thinking of engaging in some hanky-panky."

Enough.

Cat took off the hat. "It's just a joke. We barely know each other."

Olivia winked, setting the hat back on her head. "So, go on, girl. Here's your chance to get better acquainted."

Chapter 21
ALEX
Sunday Afternoon

Alex lay flat on his back, staring at the blue bowl of the sky. Mosquitoes droned around him, biting at will. He had to go back. And he would, when his heart stopped racing and his head stopped pounding. How could he ever sell the sloop? Matt's offer was completely unexpected, though he should have known it was coming. It had been three years since he'd sailed it.

Above, a raven cawed. A twig snapped. A familiar voice grumbled.

He rose onto his elbows. A vision in wild pink jostled through the pines.

He shook his head. "Cat, what are you doing here?"

"Getting bitten by mosquitoes." She plopped down on the grassy bank next to him and scratched the back of her neck. "Give me the ocean any day. How can you stand it?"

"My skin's a lot tougher than yours." He side-eyed her bare midriff. "And I'm exposing a lot less of it."

Cat tugged at the hem of her shirt. "Bad fashion choice. Don't happen to have one of those boring gray, long-sleeved dress shirts you usually wear with you, do you?"

"Nah. Sorry."

A mosquito buzzed around her head. Cat swatted at it and missed. "These blood-sucking machines are sure hungry, and they're using me for dinner. Your sister gave me some bug repellent." She pulled the bottle out of the waistband of her leggings.

Alex perused the label. "'*Totally Organic?*' '*As Seen On TV?*' That stuff doesn't work. My sister's gullible as anything."

"Well, I'm to the point where I'm willing to be gullible, too." Cat twisted off the cap and poured some on her palm. She slathered the white cream up and down her arms then sniffed. "Smells too nice to chase away the bugs."

Alex stifled a groan. The tangy lemon combined with Cat's own enticing scent made him want to take her in his arms and kiss her the way he should have last night. Bad idea. His whole family was only a couple hundred yards away. In fact, his brothers were probably spying on them right now.

Alex sat up and looked back toward the trail. "So, is everybody else tagging along behind you?"

"Just me." She rubbed the cream on the back of her upper arm. "Olivia is watching Ellie. I have to talk with you about a problem I'm having."

His pulse rose. Had Thomas found out why she was here? The last thing he wanted was for Cat to be in trouble.

He forced lightness into his voice and tried a joke. "Your mother stopped calling you? I haven't heard your phone for hours."

"Huh? No. I turned the ringer off so we could eat in peace. This problem has to do with you . . . and me."

Alex sat up straighter. That sounded ominous.

"*We* have a problem?"

"Uh, sort of. Well . . ."

All kinds of wild thoughts whirled through his head. What could he have done to cause his sassy-mouthed Cat to become tongue-tied?

"Well, you see . . . I . . . I was . . . "

Cat Silva nervous? Alex couldn't believe it.

He tried again. "What's up?"

She squirted the bug lotion on her palms, rubbing them together. She sniffed it. "Uh, I have no idea what's in this repellant stuff, but it seems to work. Only got two bites in the last second. Here, have some." She turned and ran her palm down his arm.

Oh. Alex let out a long, slow breath. They had a problem all right. Her touch felt like heaven, and he wanted more. Much more.

Cat's hand moved down over his biceps, across his lower arm, and settled on the sensitive skin of the inside of his wrist. The warmth of her touch penetrated right to his inner core.

She did it again. Then again. Every stroke of those magic fingers loosened the tension in his muscles. Slightly nibbled nails, polished cotton-candy pink, danced over his bare arm.

He didn't want to be thinking about the color of Cat's nail polish, or Cat's anything, but he had no will to stop.

Alex squeezed his eyes closed and wished that satin-skinned hand was touching him all over, not just his arm.

"So, about this little problem of mine . . ." Cat's fingers skimmed across his palm. "You still listening?"

He snapped his eyes open. "Uh, sure." He'd listen forever if she kept her hand right there on his pulse. It had been a long time since a woman had touched him.

"Now, about my problem." Still stroking his palm, she moved around him until she was facing him, took a sibilant breath, and peered into his eyes. "Okay. Remember when you asked me to stop scuba diving out by the pens, and I kind of said okay? Well, I thought since . . . well, since I didn't actually promise I'd stop, and since you didn't start work till eight, and if I dived very early in the morning . . . well, I'd get my samples and no one would know any better."

That was her problem? Alex tried not to laugh.

"I know."

Her hand flew up like a startled sandpiper. "*You know?* What? How?"

He recaptured her hand and gave it a squeeze. "This is Tide Harbor, where everyone knows everything. At least three people mentioned seeing a 'seal' out by the pens. Which, as a fish policeman, I dutifully checked out."

"And you didn't stop me?"

"I decided you weren't doing anything wrong testing the water. Thomas might bluster and make a big to-do about protecting his pens, but he doesn't own the ocean or have the right to pollute it. Tide Harbor folks need to know the state of their harbor. Besides, you're leaving tomorrow. So, see? No harm done."

She sat back. "Oh, well. Only, today, I got caught."

He frowned. "Caught? By whom?"

"A bald grouch wearing a Cowling hat."

"Oh, that sounds like Zack-a-Mac."

"Who?"

"Zack MacDonald, my fill-in man. Does the security circuit on my days off. He reports to me. I'll take care of it." He patted the hand he held. "So, see? No worries."

She lifted her hand away. "Yes, worries. He took today's samples. I have to get them back or all my work here will be for nothing. I need a full seven-day set of samples to complete my research."

Small lines marred her brow. He hated seeing those lines there. He wanted her quirky smile back.

"No problem. I'm sure he dumped them in my office. I'll fetch them later. I promise you'll have them before you leave in the morning."

She rubbed the back of her neck. "I feel so guilty putting you in this position. I don't want you to do anything that risks your job." The creases deepened.

He brushed a finger across her brow. "Trust me."

She shifted a little nearer, so close he could see the flecks of green in the sandy-bottom blue of her eyes. "I do, Alex, I do." She closed in until her lips were mere inches from his.

Long-forgotten desire rushed through him. He cupped his hand under her chin. Her skin was so soft. So kissable.

He moved in, as wary as a fish circling a baited hook, drawn by the need to drive out the cold inside him. To live again. To feel joy again. To maybe love a woman again.

The brim of her cap blocked the way.

"This crazy hat has to go." He lifted the hat off her head and picked up a lock of her hair, surprised at how thick and silky it was. Was it pink? Was it blonde?

He wove his fingers into the strands and pulled her closer. Her hair color no longer mattered. Only her. This bright, sparkly woman who'd brought laughter back into his home and heart.

"Cat, I want—"

"I know." Her hand slipped over his shoulder. "To kiss me." The words were a whisper, a caress, an invitation he could not resist. "Alex."

How he loved hearing her say his name with that twangy New York accent of hers.

She ran her tongue over her top lip. "There's something . . ."

That small movement drew his attention. There was something about her mouth. The imperfection of it. How it looked so enticing and vulnerable.

His need to become one with her brightness was suddenly as strong as his need for air to breathe. One kiss. Just one. There was no harm in that.

"May I?" He brought his lips nearer.

"Oh, Alex. Please . . ." Cat came within inches. Her hands cupped his cheeks. Their mouths aligned, met, touched, and melded.

Her lips were like some fine exotic silk. He kissed her as gently as he could. Skin met skin. Breath met breath. Fire met fire. He ran his tongue along the seam, seeking entrance. There was a hint of warmth, and she welcomed him in.

Heat rushed through him. He drew her into his lap and turned to deepen the kiss.

She pulled back and covered her mouth. "Wow, I didn't expect—" For a moment, she sat there, staring at him. Then she peered out over the pond. "Alex—" There was something hesitant in her voice.

The warmth he'd felt fled. Of course, she would be disconcerted. He had no right to kiss her. None. She was leaving tomorrow, and he had nothing to offer her that would make her stay. He had no way to keep her here.

"Sorry. I . . . uh, lost control."

"No." She turned to face him. "Don't apologize. The kiss was lovely. More than lovely. It's just . . . well, I'm getting very attached to you, and maybe I shouldn't? I'm leaving soon, and there's your family, and your . . . wife."

She gathered her hands together. "She must have been very special. Maybe you could me about her? What happened? Why are you so afraid of the water?"

Alex froze in place. He didn't want to talk about Helen. Not with Cat. Not now when he'd finally found a reason to love again.

Cat twisted her fingers. "Please. I know she isn't a mermaid. I know she drowned. I know you still love her."

Alex licked his lips. He could still taste her. He still wanted her. But she deserved a better man than him. She deserved to know what had happened.

He turned to stare out at the water. "We went kayaking out in the harbor, by Whaleback Island. We had Ellie with us. A three-year-old in a kayak, none of us wearing life vests. It was a stupid thing to do, but we just didn't think. We lived on the water. We were strong swimmers. Competitive kayak racers. We trusted we could handle anything. So, we paddled close to the shoreline, looking for a spot to eat our picnic lunch."

His vision blurred. "I still remember Helen making the sandwiches that morning. How she spread the mayo, layered the ham, cut the bread like she'd done a thousand times before, never thinking it would be her last time."

Cat's hand slipped into his. He clasped on.

"So, the kayak got stuck on something, and Helen bent over the side to untangle it, and the boat flipped almost over. I was in the front. I heard Helen scream, spun around to see what was happening, and saw Ellie sinking into the water. For such a little thing, she sank like a stone.

"I jumped in, but the water was thick with a tangle of seaweed and deadfalls, and old fishing nets and tackle. I kept getting caught and having to fight free. Just when I was running out of air, my fingers brushed against Ellie's little body. The deadfall had kept her from sinking all the way to the bottom. I seized her in my arms and rose to the surface.

"She wasn't breathing, but I didn't panic. All my training kicked in, and I made for the island, climbed the rocks, and began compressions. When Ellie choked up the water and struggled in my arms, I knew I had saved her like one of those heroes you read about. Smiling, I looked up to tell Helen, and she wasn't there."

He let out a slow exhale. "We never found her body. She must have jumped in at the same time I did but gotten caught farther down in the tangle and been unable to free herself. But we will never know." He closed his eyes and bent his head. "She was just . . . gone."

Cat squeezed his hand. "Mermaid kissed."

He pictured Helen cradled in the arms of a mermaid, being laid to rest at the bottom of the sea, and felt more peace than he had for a long time.

"You are a miracle come into our lives. Thank you for giving Ellie, and me, that image to carry with us."

Cat kissed him lightly on his cheek. "I've helped with sea rescues. There's a place for truth, and a place for prayer, and a place for peace." She unfolded her legs from under her and rose. "I think we'd better get back."

"Of course." He picked up her hat, stood, and set it on her head. He brushed his lips to hers. "And we'd better hurry. They're going to be sure that you hooked me."

Cat gave him a smile so full of wariness and confusion that it shot through him. Then she laughed. "Maybe I did." She slapped at a mosquito. "But I've had enough of the bugs. And Ellie is waiting." She spun around and straight-arrowed down the path.

Alex moved to follow her then stopped. He pressed his hands to his face. What was wrong with him? How could he even think of loving a woman like Cat Silva? Someone full of life and joy. She didn't need a sorry fool like him, who'd let the first woman he loved drown. He didn't deserve love or forgiveness.

Alex turned back to the pond, squatted down, and poked the surface with a stick. Ripples spread out across the water, marring the perfect reflection. His whole life was like those ripples—unclear, spreading in directions he never intended, destroying everything he loved and dreamed.

He broke the stick in half, tossed the pieces in, and watched them float away. Thomas was right. He was a broken man. He couldn't even keep his hands off a woman who wasn't for him. A woman whose world was focused on the sea that he couldn't face.

He should sell Logan and Matt the sloop. He'd never sail it again.

Alex gazed at the pond. The water was cedar dark, no more than ten feet deep in the middle, the bottom smooth mud and snag-free. He and his brothers had splashed in it as children, practiced their cannonballs, played pirates, and sank a thousand homemade rafts. It had been one of the joys of his childhood.

Memories rippling through the water pulled him toward the water.

He kicked off his sneakers. He could do this. He could face a small pond. There were no waves to draw him under. No seaweed to tangle his legs. No undertow to fight.

Taking in a breath, he waded in up to his knees. For a moment, all was fine. Birds sang. A breeze whispered through the pines. Mosquitos buzzed.

He waded in farther. Cold water sucked at his thighs like icy fingers.

He took another step. Water sloshed around his waist. Pinpricks of fear raced upward, followed by shivers, then shaking.

The last remaining warmth of Cat's kiss fled. Gravel, sand, and muck oozed between his toes, loosening his footing, and he tripped forward. Water splashed over him. He flailed and gasped, panic stealing away his breath. For a moment, he couldn't inhale, or see, or hear as the memory of that day washed over him. Colder than any pond water. Clearer, harsher, and crueler.

With a moan, he clawed his way back to the shore and flopped down on the bank. Above, a raven cawed. His mother had always said that when you heard a raven cry and its mate answered, you knew that all was right in the world.

He followed the black flap of wings. Waited for the answering cry. It never came.

Of course not. Nothing was right. He had the chance to love again, but there was a storm of reasons why it wasn't going to happen. The first being the need to conquer his fear of water.

Alex glared out at the pond. If he wanted her, he'd have to change or stay stuck in the mud, going nowhere. He took a series of deep breaths, like he'd been taught in therapy, and then jumped back in. This time, he lasted longer before the black panic set in.

Alex crawled out and plucked the wet T-shirt away from his skin. He flopped down on the bank and lay there until the shadows turned dark and the sky above changed from blue to lavender. He could change, too. It would just take time.

He sat up. Time he didn't have. Cat would be gone tomorrow morning.

Alex stumbled his way to his feet and followed the well-trodden trail back to the house.

He couldn't let her leave without telling her how she made him feel. How kissing her had shaken him awake.

Chapter 22
CAT
Sunday Evening

Cat stared out the windshield as she drove away from Olivia's. The Harrises would think her crazy for leaving so abruptly. But she couldn't face Alex again. Not after that kiss. A kiss that, like him, had been gentle, caring. He'd asked permission, for heaven's sake!

She took a calming breath. Or, at least she tried to.

But how could she ignore her first true kiss? Not a perfunctory end-of-a-date kiss. Not a lusty kiss to convince her to put out. No, Alex's kiss had been a wow of a kiss. One that curled her toes and turned her analytical mind to mush.

And if that meeting of lips made her pulse speed up and her body feel so light she felt like dancing across the white sand of Fletcher's Cove, that was pure foolishness. But she couldn't stop herself from touching him, caressing his tender skin, and running her fingers along his taut back and broad shoulders.

She'd let her enchantment with Alex go too far.

Shaking off the lingering regret, she pulled into Cowling's and parked near the main entrance. She hated acting like a coward, but no way could she face Alex and not fall into his arms again. So, she'd pick up her sample case herself and leave tonight instead of tomorrow morning. She'd stay overnight at the airport hotel.

Cat got out of her car and slammed the door. As much as she detested the idea, at least Momma would be happy. She checked her watch. Almost six. This should just take a minute or two, and then she'd call her and give her the good news. She was coming home.

Inside the building, Cat followed the signs to the security office. Alex's door stood open. The room empty. She peered up and down the hall. Nobody seemed to be around. Maybe this would be easier than she had imagined.

She slipped inside and scanned the room for her cute case of vials. But it was the photo, sitting on what must be Alex's desk, that drew her attention.

Helen stood, holding a tiny Ellie and giving Alex a huge smile.

Cat covered her lips with her hand. She should never have kissed him. She could never give him that perfect smile, nor a perfect child.

"What are you doing?"

Cat spun around. The bald-headed man stood in the doorway. What had Alex called him? Zack-a-Doodle? No, that wasn't right. Zack-a-Mac . . . uh . . . *MacDonald*. Yes, that was his name.

She straightened up and used her most no-nonsense voice, the one she usually reserved for the chair of her department. "Oh, Mr. McDonald, so good to see you again. I'm here to pick up the water samples you confiscated this morning. They were in that pink case. Remember?"

The security man shrugged. "Turned them over to the boss."

"Mr. Cowling?" Cat's stomach knotted. She'd hoped to avoid Thomas, but it was not to be. She pasted on a smile. "Is he in his office?"

"Yah, sure. At the end of the hall."

Cat slipped past him and walked the few steps to the door with the large bronze nameplate, *"Thomas Cowling."* Cat gave herself a shake to loosen the tightness that had crept into her muscles, raised her chin, and knocked.

There was a loud smack, a cry of pain, and the door snapped open. Thomas stood, half-in and half-out of a dress jacket. Head down, he rubbed his elbow. "Sorry I'm late, Gloria. Caught the end of the file." He looked up. "Oh, it's you, Miss Silva. I wasn't expecting you. But please, come in. We need to talk." He stepped back to let her enter.

There was something off about his voice, but he *had* just whacked his elbow.

Cat stared at the outsized desk in the middle of the messy office and looked for a place to sit.

Thomas hurried to clear papers off a folding chair. "Sorry for the mess."

She sat and peered around, searching for her sample case but not seeing it. Her gaze came back to the huge ugly desk. Was it stashed behind it?

Thomas pushed away a stack of files and sat on a corner of the polished mahogany top. "You admiring my desk? It was a gift from my mother. She always had great aspirations for me. Bought the desk when I built this place. But I am afraid she had no idea what a messy business fish farming is." He crooked his finger at her. "Neither do you. Testing the water in my pens requires my permission."

"I was testing the harbor water, not the water in your pens. And that's legal. I checked."

"Can you prove that you weren't sampling my pens?"

Cat wanted to give the man a shake. They both knew he was trying to keep the extreme level of pollution his operation was causing from becoming public. "Can you prove I was?"

"You've been watched quite closely by Alex Harris. He's kept me well-informed. And, as my employee, he'd be called to testify to your actions."

A chill, colder than the water in Tide Harbor, wrapped around her. No matter what, Alex, with that mortgage hanging over him and his job on the line, would say whatever Thomas wanted, and with his testimony, Cowling could bring suit against her. Whatever the outcome, her professional reputation would be ruined. Forget a promotion. She'd never teach again. Never do the research she loved.

"Miss Silva?" Thomas's voice cut through her whirling thoughts. "I think the authorities would believe me over a sneaky eco-freak from out of the country, don't you?"

He was probably right about that, but she couldn't let him get away with his threat. She had a weapon of her own.

"You try to charge me, and I will tell everyone about the ball of debris you have planted at your pens. Deadly thing. And I heard a body had been found near that spot."

"*Planted*?" Thomas's eyebrows rose, giving him an innocent appearance that probably worked on most people. But not on her.

"*Planted,* as in attached to the sea bottom. I tried to remove it and nearly got killed."

"The sea and negligent fishermen are responsible for whatever you found." He steepled his hands. "I am so sorry that happened to you, but fishing debris is a hazard everywhere. And I resent your accusation that I would do anything so callous—deeply." He stood and gave her a crooked grin. "However, seeing as Alex seems to have some feelings for you, let's settle this amicably. All you need do is sign an affidavit stating you will not use my name, or my company's name, in your reports."

The man was clever, but he hadn't said she couldn't mention Tide Harbor. That worked for her. Anyone could find out whose fish farm occupied the harbor. And as soon as she could, she'd report the death ball to the police.

"I can agree to that."

He sat at his computer, typed up the agreement, and printed it out. He cleared a space on his desk, set it before her, and put a pen in her hand.

She read it through then looked the man in the eye. "And I can have my samples back?"

He shrugged. "I'm afraid I dumped them. MacDonald said they were just seawater."

"Really?" Cat stood. Without her samples, she required nothing from this man. With her research destroyed, her promotion was toast, but at least she'd still have her reputation. "Then I don't need to sign this, do I?"

Thomas shrugged and gave her that fake grin again. "Please do. I'd feel better."

She picked up the pen. "I'm not here to make you feel better. Your fish farm is one of the most polluting I've ever seen. But rest easy, I will not be reporting it." She signed the paper with a flourish then threw it at him. "But that death trap of debris you have out there, that, I will report."

"*Death trap?*" Thomas's face turned stone-hard. "Enough. I refuse to let you leave thinking I would do something so criminal. Come. Show me where it is so I can remove it."

Cat recoiled. "Now? It's near dark."

"Our aluminum outboard is right out there at the dock. It will take only a few minutes to circle the pens and point out any *deadly* flotsam you see. Then you can go back to wherever you came from and never be heard from again."

She couldn't risk some swimmer or diver getting caught just because she was in a hurry.

She studied Thomas's face. He definitely looked concerned.

"Fine. But I don't have long."

"Of course." Shucking the dress coat, he grabbed a gray Cowling jacket off the hook behind the door, shrugged it on, and then led the way out.

Cat avoided looking at the jacket—it brought back too many memories of Alex and his too-tempting kiss—and hurried after him. She surely hoped Thomas was right, and it was some freak of nature that the deadly debris had rooted itself right where she had been diving and the body had been found.

In minutes, she was on the rocking open-back motor boat and wishing she hadn't agreed to this expedition. If she hadn't mentioned the tangle, she'd be on the road right now.

Later, once she was away from Tide Harbor, she could easily have called it in.

She considered jumping back onto the wharf, but the twenty-five-foot aluminum boat Cowling used to transport personnel to and from the pens was already pulling away.

Cat gripped the low rail running along the gunwale and gazed out at the harbor. Despite everything, she loved it here. Purple-green hills ran down to the water. Sea-carved cliffs rose from white-sand beaches. The sun hovered near the horizon, a pale red disk sitting on a liquid indigo sea. Heavy dark clouds darkened the sky to maroon with streaks of mauve to the west. Everywhere she looked would make an award-winning photograph.

She reached into her pocket for her cell phone. Drat. She'd been in such a hurry to get her samples that she'd left it in her pack in the car. That didn't bode well. It had to be well past six. Momma would be going crazy.

She glared at Thomas, sitting in the stern, steering the outboard. "This won't take long, you said?"

"Not at all. But I hate the idea someone else might get hurt."

She didn't like Cowling, but she admired him for making this effort to remove the debris.

"The weather sure changed fast. Looks like a storm coming."

Thomas squinted against the dimming sun rays. "Heard they're predicting a big one. Won't be fun being out on the sea tonight." He wagged his hand. "So, where's this death trap?"

"On the west side of the third pen, opposite Fletcher Cove."

He steered in that direction. "There's a gaff clipped to the other side of the gunwale. When we near the spot, try to hook on to it. If it's stuck, the pull of the engine might release it."

Cat unhooked the sharp-ended pole from its clips and peered down into the water. The boat had stirred up the sediment, but she could make out the dark mass shadowing the water.

She checked the position and called over her shoulder, "See it. Just ahead on the right."

Thomas cut the motor. The boat rocked.

Cat bent over and stretched as far as she could. The gaff skimmed the mess of ropes and netting but didn't catch hold.

She regained her footing. "Sorry. Missed."

"No biggie. I know where it is now." The boat leaped forward, cutting through the choppy waves being kicked up by the increasing wind.

Cat brushed her hair from her eyes and peered back at the rapidly diminishing Cowling fish pens. "Where are you going?"

"Thought we'd take a quick spin around the harbor. Seems a shame you've only seen the pens. Alex's fault. A man afraid of the sea just doesn't seem your type."

She turned to face him. "I told you I must leave. With the storm coming and all—"

He laughed. "Admit you like being out here on the water. This will only take a few minutes. Consider it a goodbye to your Tide Harbor trip." He gunned the engine and headed south, toward the mouth of the harbor. "You haven't seen Whaleback, have you?"

"Whaleback? The island where Alex's wife drowned?"

"Was murdered."

Cat grasped the rail as the boat slapped over the increasingly rough sea. "*Murdered*?"

"Did Alex trick you with his oh-so-nice manners? He tricked Helen, too. Of course, he murdered her. She loved me. She was going to leave him."

A twinge of unease ran through her. Could the Alex she knew with his cherished daughter and his loving family do such a thing? She'd known him only a week, but she could not be that poor of a judge of character. The woman in the photograph on Alex's desk hadn't been planning to leave her husband. She'd loved him. She was sure of that.

Cat turned to look at the man at the helm. His jaw was clenched, and his hands gripped tight to the wheel. Thomas Cowling was no upstanding businessman. He would have willingly allowed a fellow community member to die just to win a race. And he might just be cutthroat enough to set deadly debris traps to protect his underhanded fish farm operation.

Every muscle tensed. What was she doing alone with this man, in a boat, speeding farther and farther away from the shore and safety?

Thomas glanced over at her. "Enjoying the view? That little speck ahead, where the surf is kicking up, is Whaleback."

Cat squinted into the deepening dusk. "I didn't realize it was so small. Alex said they'd planned a picnic."

"I'm surprised he told you about that day. But yeah. There's a small pebble beach between the rocks at low tide, but most of it is underwater at high tide, like now." He wagged his fingers at her. "Come here by me, and I'll show you the exact spot where Helen drowned."

Cat shook her head. "I really need to get back."

"No, you don't, you interfering eco-nut." Thomas let go of the wheel and lurched forward. He shoved her hard just as the boat slapped down into a trough, and over she went.

For a moment, Cat clung to the rail. But like a man possessed by a demon, Thomas whacked at her hands with the gaff until she let go. The boat dipped. Then she was in the water and struggling for her life.

Without her wet suit, cold water penetrated to her skin. Without her special earplugs, water filled her ears and set her head to throbbing. Shock froze her muscles.

Even though panic clawed through her, a level of self-preservation took over, and she dived away from the boat in time to avoid the outboard's propeller passing over her.

Thomas gunned the motor, and the boat shot away.

Gasping, she broke the surface and blinked the water from her eyes. She stiffened.

The boat had turned and now raced directly at her.

Thomas stood, the gaff in his hand. "I knew you wouldn't be easy to drown. Not like that stupid college kid who thought to mess with my pens." With one hand on the wheel, he leaned over the side and thrust the gaff at her.

Cat kicked back. She was a capable swimmer, but she couldn't outrace a boat manned by a killer.

He maneuvered the vessel closer. She backed up again. He swung the gaff.

"You won't get away, you know. And won't poor Alex be sad to know you'd gone without saying goodbye." He zoomed back out and circled the boat again.

Cat squinted to her right. From the corner of her eye, she could see the rounded top of Whaleback and the scrubby tidal vegetation covering the barely there island. Fear pulsed through her. As a refuge, it did not inspire much hope.

She fought for the calming skills that had seen her through all those surgeries and several hairy moments at sea. She'd been in worse situations. Been on a sinking raft in New York Harbor. Faced a shark off the coast of Florida. And had survived.

She'd survive again. She had to.

Rrrooom. The roar of the engine got louder.

Cat spun around. And was instantly blinded. Thomas had flicked on the masthead light, the boat storming right at her.

She had no choice. She dived under and swam toward the near-invisible rocks. But she never reached the island. Instead, she found herself entangled in a far larger and more twisted mass of fishing gear, storm-torn fish pen netting, and splintered driftwood, lodged at the foot of the rocky outcrop.

Cat flailed in an attempt to rise above the debris. Something sharp tore into her leg. Pain radiated through her. She stilled in the water and fought back tears. Her mother had been right. She wasn't invincible.

"Gotcha," Thomas called out to her. "Say hi to Helen when you join her in her watery grave. She went down in that exact spot."

Chapter 23
ALEX

Sunday Evening

Alex scanned his sister's backyard. His brothers were playing a wild game of wiffle ball with the little ones. Olivia lay on the divan with her feet up, a wide-brimmed straw hat covering her face. It was a typical Harris-after-the-barbeque scene.

He lifted the hat. "Where's Cat?"

"She left." She squinted up at him. "Something you said?"

Alex's chest compressed. No, it was what he hadn't said.

Ellie tugged on his shirt. "Cat said you have to take me to find my special shell without her. She had to go home. Can we go with her?"

He bent over and kissed her on her nose. "Don't worry. We'll get your special shell. But first, I have to see Cat before she leaves. I have something to tell her. You wait here with Aunt Olivia."

Ellie's brow wrinkled. "But everyone's going out on the sloop."

He studied her earnest face. "If you promise to wear a life jacket and stay next to Aunt Olivia, I will allow you to go."

"Yippee!" Ellie threw her arms around him. "I love you, Daddy." She dashed off to share her news with her cousins.

"Done some thinking, have you?" His sister grinned. "Ellie can stay the night while you *tell* that sexy lady what's on your *mind*."

"Not going there, Olivia. But thanks for watching Ellie." He slapped the hat back over her face then took off.

"And do try to be romantic," she called after him.

Olivia would think him crazy, but he knew what Cat would think romantic—him delivering her confiscated samples.

Alex jumped in his pickup, backed out of the driveway, and set out for Cowling's. He'd give her the samples then tell her what was in his heart.

Today, he'd finally gotten to kiss her, and he wanted more. He wanted to clasp her in his arms while the sun went down and make love to her until the sun came up again. He wanted to share his life with her.

She'd still have to leave. He got that. She had a job in New York City and a mother to take care of. But surely, she could promise to come back to Tide Harbor next summer. For all the moaning and bantering of his siblings, it wasn't that far from Halifax. They could meet in Tide Harbor and kiss, and . . . well, anything was possible after that.

He turned on to the road to town. But what could he do to entice her to make that promise? She'd laugh if he proposed. They'd only known each other for seven days. Too soon for forever promises.

The thought struck him. He could give her his house. She loved the design. She loved the cove. He'd sell the sloop to his brothers and use that money to settle as much of the mortgage as he could. Then he'd work hard to earn enough to pay off the rest. Maybe get a second job.

It was the ideal solution. She'd have to come back if she owned a vacation cottage here. Would she think him crazy? The rest of the town would. Who gave away a house?

He pulled to a stop at the main crossroads in town. He should bring food. Once he had the samples, he could surprise her with a frozen pizza and tell her his plan. Well, maybe he needed something better than frozen pizza— something more romantic—but what? He was not a flowers-and-candy guy. Not his *modus operandi*. Not even Helen had thought him romantic.

Alex let out a slow whistle. For the first time in a long time, he'd thought of Helen and not cringed. The memory was still there, and a trace of the emptiness, but the gut-wrenching tightness had loosened. Cat was right. He'd never forget her, but it was time to do what Helen would have wanted—move on with his life.

He slapped the steering wheel. That was what he had to tell Cat. He was ready to open himself up to have her in his life.

Now, what would be better than a frozen pizza while he regaled her with his offer? Not a restaurant—no privacy. No chance to hold her and kiss her again. The tourists who visited Rose's often built a fire on the beach, baked clams, and toasted marshmallows.

A clambake. And s'mores. He could set it up on the beach below the house. Sounded like a lot of work. But if it would let him wrap his arms around Cat and allow him to kiss her again, he'd make it happen.

He peered at the sky. A storm was coming, but the weather report assured no rain until midnight. The surf might be up, but Cat would like that. And if the wind blew cold and rain did come, they could take refuge in the house. And who knew what might happen then?

He turned toward the supermarket. He'd pick up the groceries then retrieve her samples.

Twenty minutes later, Alex drove into the Cowling lot, a grocery bag full of clams, marshmallows, and chocolate bars on the seat next to him, his head full of dreams for the evening.

He blinked, then blinked again. What was Cat's rental car doing in Cowling's parking lot?

Alex pulled up next to it, jumped out of his truck, and ran toward the building. He smashed into MacDonald coming out the door.

He pulled up, huffing. "Did you see the owner of this car? A woman with pinkish hair?"

Zack scratched his chin. "Oh, yah. She came looking for the samples I took off her this morning."

Alex scowled at him. "You shouldn't have taken them in the first place. She wasn't hurting anything. Did you give them back to her?"

"No. Already turned them over to Boss Man."

He bit the inside of his cheek. Thomas would not be happy to learn Cat had been taking water samples. Why hadn't she waited for him to pick them up?

He grabbed the door handle, and MacDonald scooted out.

Zack stopped and handed him the key ring. "Supposed to be your day off, but I'm clocked out. You get to lock up."

"Lock up?" Alex jingled the keys. "But Thomas is still here, right?"

"Oh no. Thomas and the lady went out on the pen tender near thirty minutes ago."

"Fool thing to do this late in the day." Alex scuffed his foot in the dusty gravel of the lot, a frisson of fear sparking through him. All his life, Thomas had destroyed the things he loved. Now he'd taken the woman who'd returned joy to his life and Ellie's out on a boat in a stirred-up sea.

Zack shrugged. "No worries. Said they were just going out to the pens." He gave a wave then ambled off.

Alex turned and stared out at the harbor. The sun had sunk beneath the horizon, leaving behind a sliver of golden light with a darkening, cloud-filled sky hanging ominously above it. The predicted storm was out there. He could smell the salt spray, feel the up-kick in the wind, see the chop on the water. He shivered. Cat wasn't stupid. Why would she have gone out on a boat with Thomas when a storm was swooping in?

He squinted in the direction of the pens. Surely, Thomas would have the headlamp on by now. But he saw nothing moving around the pens.

A soft chime came from Cat's car. *Her phone.*

He swallowed hard. She'd left her phone behind. If she was in trouble, she'd have no way to call for help.

Alex tried the door and found it open, her pack resting on the seat, her phone in the front pocket. He swallowed hard. She hadn't taken her phone. If she were in trouble, she'd have no way to call for help.

He glanced back at the pens. Should he call the police? Cat and Thomas were probably having a grand old time and were on their way in right now. And when they found he'd panicked, he'd look like the fool he was.

There was nothing to do but wait.

Alex breathed in the salt-tinged air that did nothing to calm him and wandered down to the wharf. It was near high tide. Waves slapped around the piers. He stayed back on dry land and fought off the memory of the pen tender bringing in that dead boy's body.

He clenched and unclenched his fingers. Thomas knew boats. Had been on the water all his life.

They'd be here in minutes.

Cat would be fine.

Alex heard the boat engine before he saw the masthead light. Thank goodness. He ignored the splash of the incoming waves and the tremor in his legs as he stepped onto the wharf.

He'd see her in moments. He'd hug her. Kiss her. Tell her how he truly felt. And he didn't care what Thomas thought or said.

The aluminum boat motored slowly toward the wharf. Thomas was yelling something at him, but the blood pounded too loudly in his ears.

Cat wasn't on the boat.

Alex ran and grabbed the bowline. "Where is she?"

Thomas waved his arms. "Bent way over the side to see something and went overboard. I tried and tried, but I couldn't find her in the dark and the surf. Call 911. We need to search the harbor."

Adrenaline zipped through him. Cat was out in the water. In the dark. In the rising tide. *Drowning.*

No. It couldn't happen again. Shaking violently, he looped the bow rope around his bent arm. "It will take too long for them to get here. We have to search now, before the storm fully hits. Where'd she go in?"

Thomas leaped over the side. "You can't. Boat's near out of gas."

All he could see was Cat sinking into the sea, just like Helen.

"Maybe I can keep her afloat till recue arrives." Alex tossed the rope in and put his hands on the gunwale.

Thomas grabbed his shoulders and pulled him back. "Don't be a fool. She doesn't need a man terrified of the water." He gave him a shake.

Alex tore free. "Call emergency rescue. Send them after me. We need lights and a boat that can work in this chop." He stepped out of reach. "Where'd you last see her?"

"Near ten cable lengths west of Whaleback. Tide this strong—she could be anywhere by now. Think it through, man. It's too late."

Alex shook his head. It couldn't be too late. Cat had to survive. He had to tell her that he loved her.

Fighting down the rising nausea, Alex leaped into the boat and started up the outboard. He scanned the gauge. Thomas was right. There was barely enough gas for a trip to the pens and back. For a moment, he hesitated. Then he threw caution into the oncoming storm winds, and sped away from the dock.

The twenty-foot open-back outboard wasn't intended for more than ferrying a few men and gear back and forth from the pens. The aluminum hull was battered, and water seeped in through corroded rivets. It didn't even have a name, only a number—478. Still, the craft fought against the tide and the swells, rocking wildly as he cut across the current and steered toward the mouth of the harbor.

He squinted against the darkening sea. Time was of the essence. Staying afloat in these seas would be a struggle.

He gripped the wheel tighter as the stomach-knotting edge of panic crept over him like the incoming tide. The splash of water coming over the sides of the boat weakened his knees. Nausea pooled in his stomach.

Thomas was right about the panic. But he couldn't let it stop him. Cat needed him, and he was the closest. He knew the waters and the islands.

He choked down the rising panic, kept his eyes on the horizon, and pushed the throttle all the way up.

Chapter 24
CAT
Sunday Night

Cat bent down for the hundredth time and snatched at the netting wrapped around her leg. There was barely any light left. Below the surface, lay nothing but blackness. If she only had her scuba knife and her headlamp, this would be so easy.

She choked on another wave. Well, not easy, but surely easier.

Cat spat out another mouthful of saltwater. Had she actually told Alex the sea was their friend? She gulped a breath of air as another wave washed over her head. It sure wasn't being friendly right now. It was cold, relentless, and nasty.

She tugged, and twisted her leg again, hoping this time it would miraculously slip loose. It didn't. Instead, the hook embedded in her calf dug in. In spite of the numbing effect of the cold water, pain shot up her leg. But it wasn't as sharp as before.

And that was worrying. Up until now, she hadn't been concerned about the temperature of the water. It was summer, and in the harbor, it hovered around sixty-five to seventy degrees. But the water washing into the harbor ahead of the storm was colder. Any drop below sixty put her at high risk of hypothermia. At fifty degrees, without a wet suit, exhaustion and unconsciousness would set in between thirty minutes to an hour. And it must be nearly thirty minutes by now.

She held her hand in front of her face and estimated the time she'd been in the water by her wrinkled fingertips. From past experience in chill saltwater, she knew it took about twenty-five minutes to go from smooth to pucker. That meant the tide would be turning soon, pulling her toward the rocks and the tangle of rope, tree limbs, and net at the same time she would lose consciousness. Once that happened, she'd be a goner.

Poor Momma. Her mother would never recover if she died out here, injured, just the way Momma always dreaded.

A hollow formed in her chest at the thought and sapped her dwindling strength. All her life, she'd been a disappointment. She'd never been the ladylike little princess her mother had desired. No ruffled dresses for her. No elaborate hairstyles. No fawning boyfriends. No invitations to dances and parties. But it was the scar and crooked mouth that had hurt her mother the most.

Momma blamed herself for that scar and all the pain and struggle that had gone into making her appearance normal on the outside.

Cat spat out another mouthful of water.

But it hadn't made her acceptable on the inside.

For a moment, she stopped fighting and let the waves crash over her. She wasn't strong. She wasn't bold. She wasn't the in-your-face, pink-haired Cat Silva at all. That was a mask.

Inside, she was the teary-eyed little girl who'd been tormented and bullied. The girl with the scarred face, who had spent her school days hiding out in bathroom stalls or reading in the darkest corner of the library.

A cross-wave caught her by surprise, and she choked. Cat coughed it out and shook the water out of her eyes. The tide was higher, the surf wilder. The hook deeply embedded. She had to be losing blood. Soon, she'd be too weak to stay afloat, and under she'd go.

Death was coming. For a moment, it sounded tempting. She'd no longer have to pretend. No longer lock her heart inside a cracked clamshell. No longer disappoint her mother. One of those ambitious men would teach her students. Another marine biologist would publish research on fish farming pollution. Some other woman would hug Ellie and kiss Alex.

She let her body rock with the current. The warmth from the memory of that kiss did little to warm her limbs, but at least she'd die with that tiny glow buried in her heart. If she'd been more like the Cat Silva she pretended to be, she'd never have stopped kissing him. She would never have run away. If she hadn't panicked, she'd never have gone to Cowling and gotten into the boat with Thomas Cowling.

Who would have thought such a self-centered, clean-cut man would risk everything in an attempt to kill her? She'd signed his paper. She was no threat whatsoever.

Except . . . she pictured the look of hatred he'd given Alex at the festival. What had Alex said? Thomas Cowling had always wanted everything he had. Maybe it had nothing to do with her research. Maybe she was here, drowning, because Alex's boss was jealous enough to murder?

If she drowned, Alex would be devastated. He'd lost his wife in the same way. Ellie would struggle to understand.

Fury filled her. She couldn't let that happen. Alex and Ellie needed her alive, not dead. They needed to know the truth. They needed to know Thomas Cowling was to blame for Helen's death.

With the last of her strength, she dived under and jerked on the lines trapping her. She twisted the hook, not caring about the pain and the damage she was doing to her leg. She'd yank her leg off if she had to. Better she never walk again than let that monster get away with murder.

The need to breathe grew painful. Cat ignored it. She bent lower, hooked a finger under the ropes cinched around her calf, and pushed down. It slipped a few inches, tearing the skin as it raked over her calf. She pushed again. It moved again, loosening at her ankle. But no matter what she did, she couldn't get it over her heel. She cursed her big feet. Good for swimming—built-in flippers, her brothers had always teased—but they might just be the death of her tonight.

Her lungs burned, but she kept at it. She might not get her fingers in next time. She strained and heaved with her remaining energy. No luck. No air. Lights flashed behind her eyes. Her lungs threatened to explode. Still, she tore at the rope in one last furious attempt, and . . .

Pop, her foot was free.

Cat let go and rose.

Chapter 25
ALEX
Sunday Night

Alex shifted his weight on the rolling boat and fought the panic whipping through him. Thomas was right. He was the wrong person to search for Cat.

Despite the chill air, cold sweat beaded his brow. His stomach pinched. His breath lay sodden in his throat. Waves slapped against the sides in time with the throbbing in his head. The fuel gauge indicated barely any gas left. Everything was telling him to turn around.

He swallowed hard. Just being on a boat was turning his knees weak and setting his heart pounding louder than the surf. Someone petrified of the water was the last person to rescue someone lost beneath the tide. But he was all she had. So somehow, he would.

He braved a glance over his shoulder. The lights of Tide Harbor lay small and faint on the opposite shore. Behind him, the pole lights on the wharf flickered. The Cowling offices and parking lot lay dark.

Alex blinked. *Dark?* The place looked deserted. That made no sense. Thomas should have all the lights in the place blazing. And why hadn't the police and EMRs arrived yet? They didn't have that far to come.

Alex glanced at the gas gauge again and remembered the expression on Thomas's face. It hadn't been anguish creasing his brow and stiffening his cheeks. It had been hatred.

His gut tightened. The gas was disappearing too fast. It wasn't just low. He should never have trusted Thomas. He might spout magnanimous words, but Thomas had never forgiven him for winning Helen. No. Stealing Cat from him was pure revenge.

He'd have to call for help.

Alex removed a hand from the wheel and searched for his cell phone. He patted his jacket pockets before he remembered he'd stuck it in his back pants pocket after his dip in the pond. He pulled it out just as the boat tipped. The phone flew out of his sweaty hand and, by some evil stroke of fate, went over the side.

His head throbbed. No one knew they were out here. No one would be coming to his or Cat's rescue. Now Thomas Cowling would get his revenge, and no one would ever know what had happened.

He slapped the bench seat. He was a fool. He'd allowed Thomas to bully him for years. Always gave him the benefit of the doubt. Never saw him for the cruel man he was. He should have stood up to Thomas years ago. He should have told the authorities about the request to move the dead body. Now it was too late.

Alex slowed the boat to the lowest speed to better maneuver through the increasing chop. There wasn't enough gas to go back. He might just reach Whaleback

Island before it gave out completely. He willed the boat forward. That was where Cat had gone in, if Thomas hadn't lied about that, too.

He refused to believe Cat was dead. She was too full of life and too comfortable in the water. She'd figure out a way to stay afloat. She could do it. It hadn't been long. Cat was out there somewhere, and he had a feeling she was the only one who could save them both.

Eyes peeled for a pink-haired woman floating on the waves, Alex held himself rigid, breath trapped in his chest, and fought the wind and waves. Up ahead lay Whaleback, a smidgeon of land, more rock than anything else. At high tide, only the top of the tallest boulder showed, rounded like the hump of a whale. Laying outside the channel, it was unmarked. But he knew that beneath the water hid more rocks and the treacherous mess of driftwood and fishing debris that could sink a boat or steal one's wife.

Helen. Long-dreaded memories of that day surged through him. The kayak tipping. Diving in and pulling his daughter free. Saving her. But when he had gone back for Helen, something had changed in him.

Diving under, the water had closed in. His head pounded like explosions going off. Every move sapped his strength. For the first time in a life spent on the water, he'd felt afraid.

He'd struggled against it. He'd worked his way through rope tangles, squeezed between rotten logs, and gotten caught again and again until his body had screamed for air. Helen needed him.

He'd dived deeper into the dark. He could only feel his way through the slimy, seaweed-draped rope and netting. His arm had caught, and the panic had hit full-on.

He didn't remember rising to the surface, but he did remember the pain cinching his chest. The utter terror. The weight of impending doom.

It had never left.

He'd probably missed finding Helen by a few feet, at most.

He wiped a hand down his face and squinted harder. He couldn't miss Cat.

Crash.

Alex gripped tight to the helm. He hadn't found Cat, but he'd run up on Whaleback, invisible in the dark. Now he was truly in trouble.

The boat spun and hit again. The engine stalled out. Without power, the boat turned sideways and smashed again and again into Whaleback's submerged rocks.

He grasped the wheel, steering into the waves as the outboard propeller scraped and bumped along the hidden underwater boulders. Seawater splashed. The bottom of the boat smacked again then leaned to the side and became lodged among the rocks. Water whooshed into the boat and crawled up his legs.

Shivers racked his body. It was only a matter of time before he would be dumped in the water and swallowed up like Helen had been. The thought turned him weak.

Oh, Ellie. He was going to die here and leave her an orphan. Olivia would take her in and love her, but it would never be the same. She'd lost her mother. He'd assured her that she wouldn't lose her father. All her life, she'd believe him a liar.

He gazed toward Fletcher's Cove. Once upon a time, he could have swum that far. Now, just imagining it turned his muscles to jelly.

He clung to the rail and stared down into the water. In seconds, the sea would claim him. He would not survive. A few minutes in the pond was one thing. This water was cold, deep, and hungry. Was this how Helen had felt when she'd gone under?

Perhaps it was fitting he drowned, too. He'd failed her. He'd failed Cat. He'd failed his daughter.

He peered into the dark. Not that he could see much. Ahead, the sky was black. The water was black. The future black.

He took a breath and yelled Cat's name over and over, but his throat was so tight that only croaks came out. His heartbeat blasted his ears like an interminable foghorn. Even if Cat answered him back, he'd never hear her.

Not that it mattered. It was too late. Water splashed into the boat and crept up his legs. Panic built. He wasn't even underwater yet. But he soon would be.

If only he could stave off the panic attack a few minutes longer. The tide was retreating. If he could cling to Whaleback's boulders, he might survive.

Alex took one measured breath after another, like the therapist had taught him, and removed his sneakers. The sinking boat shifted beneath him. The water rose higher. His chest tightened more. The side leaned farther over, water surged in, and under he went.

"Alex . . ."

A voice saying his name penetrated the fog of his mind.

"Alex?"

He heard his name again and half-opened one eye but saw only black. He shut it again. If this was death, it was colder than ocean ice in midwinter.

Water splashed over him.

"Wake up."

Something shook him.

He choked, turned his head, and vomited out the sea.

"Alex, please. Come back to me." Warm lips met his.

He gasped and opened his eyes.

A pale-faced mermaid with dripping hair hovered over him. A mermaid that looked a lot like Cat.

"Cat," he croaked out. "You're alive?"

Her face pinched. "Yeah. Alive. Sort of."

He reached toward her. Pain racked through him.

"Don't move. You nearly drowned, and I think your leg or hip is broken, and certainly a few ribs. You were being slapped against the rocks when I found you."

Alex peered into her eyes and spoke through the pain, "How bad?"

"Bad. I'm afraid I may have made the injuries worse, moving you here."

"You saved me."

"But we can't stay here. It's too exposed."

Alex raised his neck. Pain ripped through him. He let it drop. "Where are we?"

She brushed her hair out of her eyes. "I assume this is Whaleback Island. The tide has turned, and I found a sort of flat spot between two boulders." She gave herself a hard shake. "Not dry, though. With the rain and the surf pounding, it's certainly not the best place for someone with injuries. We need to get to shore, pronto."

"The boat?"

"I didn't see a boat." Her hand came to rest on his upper arm. "I'm hoping others are searching, besides you."

Alex pictured the dark warehouse. "No. That slimeball Thomas didn't call the EMR. He didn't care you'd fallen overboard."

"*Fallen?* Is that what that scoundrel said? Cowling pushed me in, Alex. The man's crazy. He's the one who created these mounds of debris in the harbor. He's placed them around his pens to prevent anyone getting close."

"What debris?"

"Cowling's planted nets and fishing gear underwater to discourage or trap unwary swimmers coming too close. Deadly things. There are a ton of sharp objects, like anchors and hooks, embedded in them."

Alex shivered. "I bet that's what killed that student."

"I was thinking the same thing."

"And it's my fault. Thomas knew I wasn't able to patrol out in the water . . ." He grimaced. "That's why he kept me on, even though my fear of the water made me unqualified for the job."

"Not your fault." She pressed against him. "I should never have gone in a boat with the man after I told him I knew about the debris traps." She let out a long sigh. "But he's not going to win."

"*Win?*"

"Get away with trying to kill me to keep me quiet." Her voice quavered. "Once I am sure you won't slip underwater, I'll head for the shore."

"No. You'll never make it."

"I'll make it." She placed her hand lightly on his chest. "It's you I'm worried about. I hate to leave you so exposed here in the rain and the wind."

She was as cold as he was, but where her hand rested, heat burned through him.

"Stay with me. Maybe Rosie will notice you're missing."

"She might. But not till morning—hours from now. You don't have hours. You need help immediately."

He half-raised his hand. "Fletcher's Cove is to the northwest. It's near a mile." Pain shot through him. He half-choked and dropped his hand. "It's too far."

"What about directly across from here? West."

"Nearer a half-mile."

Cat shifted beside him. "Fifteen minutes tops. A piece of cake."

"The . . . the thing is, past the cove . . . the cliffs come down to shore. The way up . . ." A wild gust of wind carried away his words. A shiver racked his body. Cat was right. Hypothermia was setting in.

"Tell Ellie . . ." His brain fogged, and when next he came to, Cat was gone, and he could no longer feel anything except failure.

He struggled to draw in a breath, and then another.

Cat was risking her life for him. And he'd never told her that he loved her.

Chapter 26
CAT

Sunday Night

Cat knew she wasn't going to make it. She could easily swim half a mile. She could even do a mile. But not in rough, freezing water.

Shivers ripped through her. Any body heat she'd had was fast dissipating. She'd been in the water for over an hour by now. She could barely lift her arms above the surface. Every other wave broke over her. And somehow, she'd gotten muddled. The lights of Tide Harbor that should be behind her to the east had disappeared. For all she knew, she could be swimming in circles.

She treaded water and swiped the rivulets of rain from her eyes. No matter which way she looked, no lights appeared.

Forget the lights. She didn't have time nor energy to waste. Alex was at far more risk of hypothermia than she was.

She took a breath and plunged in the direction the waves were moving. She felt the tug of the outgoing tide, fought against it, and kept going. Beneath her, the surf built, a sign she was in shallower water. For a moment, her hopes rose. Maybe she was nearer than she thought?

She'd only gone a few more strokes when a wave lifted her up and smacked her against something hard. A rock? There were plenty along the coast. The surf tossed her against it again, and the invisible object bobbled.

Not a rock. Cat ran her numb fingers along its side. It was too textured and warm to be stone. Perhaps, it was a large piece of debris or a boat gone astray. Didn't matter. It could float.

She thanked whoever the unfortunate boater was who'd lost it. That loss would save her. She could ride the surf to the shoreline.

Cat threw her arms over the top and clasped on. With her remaining strength, she wiggled atop. She recognized the feel of it instantly. It was a kayak.

For a moment, she let her weary limbs go limp with relief. She knew what to do with a kayak.

She began to rock it up and down until it popped free of the rocks and floated toward what she hoped was the shore.

Whirling and splashing, the kayak rode up and over the waves rolling in. Eyes peeled for rocks, Cat clung on like a limpet as the plastic boat caught one wave then another, hurtling toward shore.

The kayak washed up on a cobble beach with a crunch. Cat pulled herself up and gazed at dark cliffs, even blacker than the black sky above, looming over her. Then she slid off the boat and dropped onto the pebbly beach. Sucking in welcome breaths, she collapsed. She'd think about climbing in a few minutes.

The cold nose of a dog sniffing her face, stirred Cat awake. She pushed up on her elbow.

"Glad to see *you.*" She really was. If there was a dog, there'd be people.

She put out a hand and let him sniff. She felt for a collar. None. A stray, then. Her hopes of quick rescue sank.

Cat looped her tangled hair behind her ears. She had to get moving. Alex's situation was dire. She glanced back toward the white foaming rollers pounding the shore. If it wasn't too late.

Struggling to her knees, she ignored her injured leg and stood. Between the cross-current and the wind, she had no idea how long it had taken to swim from Whaleback. Her limbs wobbled like rubber, her mind remained fogged.

But Alex was out there, being lashed by the storm. She had to keep going.

Cat drew in a sluggish breath and staggered forward. The dog barked and ran ahead. Cat stumbled after. Somehow, the dog had gotten down on the beach. Hopefully, he knew how to get back to the clifftop.

But she didn't have the strength to reach the top.

Somewhere along the almost vertical trail, she flopped down. Rescue came in the form of a pair of strong arms. How she wished it were Alex's arms around her, not this rough-looking man's. Still, he'd saved her and would do his best to save Alex.

Ensconced on a cot in his tiny cabin, Cat forced herself to sit upright while her rescuer called the paramedics. Every muscle in her body wanted to run and get help for Alex, but the strength wasn't there.

Shivering, she wrapped the down sleeping bag, smelling too much like dog, more tightly around her and prayed the paramedics would reach Alex in time.

The tall, scruffy man in a red plaid flannel shirt pocketed his phone. "They'll have Alex off Whaleback in no time, and as soon as you warm up, I'll drive you to the hospital. That's a pretty bad cut on your calf. Someone should look at it."

Cat lifted the sleeping bag and peered at the gash. "Oh. I'm so cold and numb I forgot I had it."

"Lucky it wasn't worse." He handed her a mug of steaming coffee.

Cat took a sip. Coffee was her least favorite drink, but the hot liquid chased the chill from her insides.

She gave her head a shake to slosh the water from her ears. "I can't thank you enough for saving me. And you are?"

He held out a hand. "Will Young."

She grasped it. "Thank heavens you were there. I could never have made it up that cliff."

"Followed the dog barks. She yipped and yapped like crazy. Thought it might be another animal in need. People seem to like abandoning their pets in the middle of the night."

Cat looked around the cabin. Animal eyes peered from cages encircling the room. Birdcages hung from the rafters. A cat with three legs curled at the foot of the borrowed sleeping bag.

"You rescue animals?"

"Yep." Will gave her a broad grin. "And occasionally, mermaids."

Cat nodded. "This is one mermaid very happy to be on dry land."

Hand trembling, she set the empty cup on the rickety table next to the cot. She wasn't fully recovered, but nothing would feel right until she knew Alex was safe. "Can we leave now? I'm terribly worried about Alex."

"Of course. But I'd better cover that wound to keep it clean. My pickup is a mess." Will knelt down and wrapped a bandage around her injured leg. Then he put his arm under hers and helped her out into the predawn.

------------◆------------

The whole way to the regional hospital, Cat worried. She refused to wait while Will parked his pickup.

Stumbling into the lobby, she limped her way to the reception desk only to be told that Alex Harris was in emergency and his condition being assessed.

Cat drew the too-large flannel shirt Will had lent her more closely around her. *He was alive.* The worry that had consumed her lessened slightly, but it did not leave.

She twisted her hands together. She'd gotten help in time. Now she had to pray the doctors could fix his injuries. Meanwhile, she had to contact the police and report Thomas.

She stepped away from the desk and waved to Will, who was crossing the lobby. "Can I borrow your phone?" She held out her hand and was surprised to see it still shaking violently.

Will reached out to steady her. "I think you need to head to the emergency room yourself before you pass out."

A burst of familiar voices came from behind. She spun around. Olivia and Ellie rushed toward her.

Ellie lurched ahead. "Oh, Cat." She wrapped her arms about her legs.

Cat winced.

Will bent down and lifted Ellie up. "Be careful. Cat has a cut on her leg."

Olivia nodded at Will then addressed her. "What happened?"

Cat glanced at Ellie. She didn't want to upset her. She settled for the simplest explanation. "We had a boating accident."

Olivia's eyebrows flew up. "*Boat? Alex*? Is he all right?"

"I'll explain later. They just brought him into the emergency ward. He's being evaluated."

Ellie's lips trembled. "Is Daddy okay?"

"I think he might have broken his leg." Cat prayed that was all.

She pictured Alex when she'd left him. If he'd broken his back, he could end up paralyzed. Or he could have internal injuries. Ellie had already lost her mother. She couldn't lose her father, too.

"Finally found a parking spot." Matt Harris joined the group and lifted Ellie from Will's arms. "Thank you, Will. Sorry you got dragged into this."

"Glad to help." Will nodded. "See that this mermaid goes to emergency and gets her leg looked at. She swam from Whaleback to get help." Then he slipped away, silent as a ghost.

"*Whaleback*?" Matt sputtered.

Cat clasped her hands together. "That's where we washed up."

Both Harrises stared at her. Then Olivia buried her in a huge hug. "Oh, Cat."

At that moment, two RCMP officers strode across the lobby.

"Cat Silva?" the taller one asked. "We need a statement from you."

She extracted herself from the warming hug and nodded. "Of course."

"Wait." Olivia took her by the arm. "She needs to be seen by a doctor. You can interview her in the emergency ward."

She turned to Matt. "Take care of Ellie."

She patted Ellie's knee. "And don't you worry. I'm going to find your daddy and let you know right away how he is." She looped her arm around Cat's waist and guided her toward the emergency wing, the two officers on either side.

Chapter 27
ALEX

Monday Morning

Alex woke with a start. Cat was flying out today, and he was stuck here, constrained by a broken leg and a sister who refused to let him out of bed, if you could call the cot set up in Olivia's living room a bed.

He called out, "Olivia."

No answer.

Where had his overprotective sister disappeared to? With his own phone on the bottom of the ocean, he needed to borrow Olivia's and reach Cat before she was on the road and out of his life.

He pushed up, the weight of the thigh-high cast on his left leg sending a shock of pain through his bruised body and setting his head spinning.

Alex pressed a hand to his temple and shouted again, "Olivia."

Dead silence answered.

Everyone must have gone out while he'd been sleeping.

With a groan, Alex sat all the way up. Slowly he swung his legs over the side of the cot until his bare feet touched the floor. He let the pain wash over him and shook off the dizziness.

He had to get to Cat, even if it meant crawling the whole way. But how?

His crutches rested against the wall farthest from his cot. Olivia knew him well. She really didn't want him to try something foolish. But he couldn't let the woman he loved leave without talking to her and telling her how he felt.

Click.

The back screen door squeaked open.

Alex looked toward the kitchen. Thank heavens. Olivia was back. He could use her phone.

"Hey, sis."

Footsteps tapped across the kitchen tile.

Thomas loomed in the doorway. "Sorry to disappoint."

Thomas?

Alex gripped the edge of the cot. Senses on alert. "Why aren't you locked up? I thought they arrested you?"

Thomas smiled. "I have an excellent lawyer. And good old Mom paid the bail. Besides, there's no proof. Who's going to believe the owner of Cowling, the largest employer in Tide Harbor, tried to murder you and that eco-freak?" He stepped into the room. "Of course, your crazy story could still make some problems for me. He moved closer. "I'm here to make sure that never happens."

Alex's breath froze in his chest. "You plan to murder me here in my sister's living room? You'll never get away with it."

Thomas laughed. "I'm not that stupid. You're going to have a terrible accident."

"*Accident?*" Alex struggled to wrap his head around Thomas's words. "Can you hear yourself? For a man who has everything . . ."

"*Everything? Bah.* All my life, I've been compared to you by my mother, by my teachers, even by the men at the plant. 'Why can't you be more helpful, like Alex?' 'Why can't you tell the truth, like Alex?' 'Why can't you get good grades, like Alex?' 'Why can't you give us an afternoon off, like Alex?'" Thomas's face flushed beet-red. His voice became a hiss. "'Why can't you find a nice girl, like Alex did?'"

"But Helen chose me." It was the wrong thing to say.

Thomas roared, "Helen was meant for me! I saw her first. But you took her away from me."

"We loved each other."

"Fool woman. I offered her everything, and she still chose you. But I fixed it. I killed her."

Thomas's words knifed through his heart. He gripped the edge of the cot. "You murdered Helen? How? She drowned. Caught in the fishing debris."

"Remember that high school club I was the patron of. The one that cleans the beaches? One day, I was looking at the day's haul, and I had an idea. Why not use the stuff to protect the fish pens? At first, I planted the debris around the pens to keep the seals and those eco-freaks away.

"But my best idea was adding to the windfalls around your favorite picnic spot—Whaleback. You even told me when you were going out there that day. Unfortunately, Helen wasn't the intended victim—you were." He grinned. "Though I have enjoyed watching you suffer over her death these past years.

"You won't get away with killing me or with the other murders. Surely, after they find my body, one of the neighbors will remember your truck was here."

"Oh, you're not going to die here. A watery grave seems more appropriate for a man scared of the water. And once you're fish food, I'll take care of that pink-haired meddler."

"*Never.*" Alex leaped up, but Thomas was quicker. He lunged forward and knocked him back onto the cot. The lightweight-aluminum frame creaked, wobbled, and toppled to the floor.

Freeing his arms, Alex pummeled, pushed, and scratched, but Thomas's weight pressed him down into the tangled mess of blankets and bent cot frame so every punch lacked force.

In seconds, Thomas overpowered him. He caught one arm then leaned on his chest to trap the other with the same hand. "Heard you had some broken ribs." Thomas pressed harder. The pain rocketed. Alex's vision blurred.

"Gotcha." Thomas drew a large sea-rounded rock from his jacket pocket and held it over his head. "Now say goodbye."

The rock came down. The world whirled.

And Alex heard no more.

Alex came to in the cargo bed of Thomas's monster-sized truck where he'd been thrown like a piece of trash. The stink of dead fish assaulted his nose. Every bump shot a lightning bolt of pain through his head. Burlap bags and empty cartons threatened to land on top of him. He gritted his teeth and swore that Thomas would not win this time. And he would never get near Cat.

He studied the gray sky overhead trying to figure out where Thomas was taking him. But the clouds held no clue. He needed to see over the side. Using his uninjured foot for leverage, he flipped onto his stomach and seal-flopped over to the side of the bed. He put a hand on the edge. At the same moment, the truck made a hard turn to the left, throwing him back into the mess of bags and boxes.

The truck hit a pothole. Then another. There was only one road in Tide Harbor this miserable. They were heading for the old dock where he first saw Cat.

He had only minutes to be ready for Thomas. Using his head and good leg, he pushed the boxes toward the tailgate until he had a wall of cardboard. Then he slid toward the boxes.

Thomas thought him dead. The three-foot wall of boxes was flimsy but should provide some camouflage. Maybe that little bit of time would be enough to surprise Thomas with his attack.

Alex lay on his back and prepared to kick his traitorous friend in the face the moment the truck stopped and prayed he didn't miss.

But the truck didn't stop. Of course, not. Thomas, lazy as always, pulled as close to the water's edge as possible to make it easier to dump his body. The pickup rumbled over the old planks of the dock then halted. Waves lapped the concrete supports. The timbers under the tires creaked. Alex's pulse skyrocketed.

The were on the very edge, and the old dock couldn't support the weight of this truck for long.

Thomas's feet thumped on the planks. He unlatched the swing-door tailgate and shoved at the cardboard. "What the heck?"

This was it. Alex pulled back his foot and aimed for where Thomas was standing.

Smash. His foot made contact. Thomas wailed, teetered, and then fell back. There was a splash then nothing.

Alex slid down off the truck bed and peered into the water. "Thomas?" No one splashed and sputtered. No one called for help.

He squinted through the swirling silt. There. Several feet away, Thomas drifted below the surface like a rag doll. Blood curled into the water from the back of his head. He must have hit the sunken cement abutment supporting the crumbling dock.

With a gasp, Alex jerked back. He didn't need to get close to know Thomas was gone. Only bubbles remained floating on the surface.

A wave of sadness rippled through him. Thomas hadn't always been nasty. They'd had plenty of good times together until Helen came between them. His mother would be devastated.

The dock shook beneath his feet. He had to get off it pronto and call 911. If he remembered rightly, Thomas kept his phone in the holder on the dashboard.

Groaning, Alex held on to the side of the truck and slid casted leg forward inch by painful inch across the creaking dock.

His head might be pounding. His ears might be ringing. His ribs might be on fire. But nothing was going to stop him from telling Cat that he loved her.

Chapter 28
CAT
Monday Morning

Cat gazed out at the blue water of the harbor. She should have argued more with Olivia. Surely, Alex wasn't so injured that he couldn't come down to the beach with Ellie and watch her search for a shell to remind her of her mother.

Ellie walked slowly along the water's edge, peering down. It was low tide, the waves breaking far out, the sand hard-packed and strewn with easy-to-find shells. Somewhere was the one-and-only seashell. It wouldn't take long.

And it didn't. In minutes, Ellie came up to her, hands full. The wet shells glistened in the sun. "They are all so beautiful."

Cat gazed down at her collection. "Yes, they are. But only one can be special. Let's put them down and see which one is special to you."

She looked over to where Olivia was standing. Should she insist she go back to fetch Alex? He'd been asleep, she'd claimed, and didn't want to disturb him. But this was such a momentous occasion for Ellie. Her father should be here.

Cat sighed. But she was just a visitor. She had no right to make demands on this wonderful family. They knew each other best.

Ellie plopped down on the sand and dumped her shells in front of her. "Tell me their fancy names."

Cat squatted beside her, picked one up, and placed it on her hand. "I bet you know what this one is called."

Ellie nodded. "A clam."

"Its scientific name is *mercenaria*. See how nice and smooth it is?"

Ellie rolled it around on her palm then bent over to show it to Dorchester. She shook her head and put it back in the pile. "There are lots of those. To be special, it has to be the only one."

"Let's make groups and see which one doesn't fit." Cat spread the shells out on the sand. They were all common species—small, tough shells, capable of surviving the surf and being cast up on the beach without being crushed. The fancy, delicate ones that decorated the glossy covers of seashell guides never made it to shore, or if they did, were broken. The same way hearts broke when they chose wrong.

Cat sat back on her knees and squinted down the beach. If only Alex were here. He needed to see his daughter being comfortable with the water. He needed to heal and forgive himself for the loss of Helen.

But mermaid stories and special shells wouldn't work for a grown man.

She peered at Ellie. With her tongue poked between her lips and her brow furrowed, the child worked with the intensity of a graduate student identifying subspecies. Ellie had Alex's black hair and dark brown eyes, but the rounded shape of her face and the stubby nose must have been inherited from her mother.

Ellie held up a periwinkle, one of at least ten she'd gathered. "This one is different."

"Is it?"

Periwinkles were the most common shell on the Atlantic shores, carried across from England and Ireland on boats bringing settlers to the New World.

Cat bent over to look more closely at the tiny shell in the child's palm. Unlike the others, with their light and dark brown stripes, this one was smaller, paler, and had a white line extending from the tip to the mouth of the shell. Many periwinkles had markings like that, but none in Ellie's pile.

Ellie looked up at her. "I like this one." She ran her finger over the line. "It isn't perfect."

Cat sucked a breath through her teeth. If she agreed, would the child feel betrayed when she found hundreds of look-a-likes? Should she steer her to a different one? Maybe a small scallop? Those had more design variations.

No. That was what her momma had always tried to do—direct her to what she thought would be best for her. It was the child's choice that mattered.

Just like it was the heart's choice that had to be accepted.

Cat wrapped her hand over the Ellie's. "A perfect selection and just the right size for a pocket."

Ellie studied the shell in her hand then peeked up at her. "Are you sure you're not a mermaid?"

Cat folded Ellie's finger over the shell. "I'm sure. And neither is your mother."

Ellie looked out at the water. "She's not coming back from the sea, is she?"

Cat enfolded her in her arms and drew her into a hug. "No. People need air to breathe, and when your mother went under the water, she couldn't breathe anymore, and she died."

Ellie nestled against her. "But you go underwater."

"That's why I have all that equipment. I take air with me. It's in those oxygen tanks when I swim underwater. You've seen them. And I can only stay under for a short time."

"Can I go with you sometime? See the fishes?"

Cat wondered what Alex would say. This was his child. It had to be his decision.

"Someday. First, you have to learn to swim. And until you do, you obey your daddy and stay away from the water, and the mud flats, and the boats unless you have someone with you. We all want you to be safe."

"Can Dorchester learn to swim, too?"

Cat laughed. "Of course, he can." She pushed up from the sand. "Now, let's go show Olivia your special shell."

Ellie bounded up, her feet throwing sand in all directions, and ran to her aunt.

Cat followed, dragging her feet. It was good she would be on the road in the morning. Alex and his daughter had weaseled in under her defenses. She wanted to stay. She wanted to see Ellie learn to swim. She wanted to see her grow up.

Cat touched her tongue to the tiny scar on her lip. Most of all, she wanted to kiss Alex again. But would he still want to if he knew that she'd spent her childhood having one operation after another? That any child she had might be born with a cleft palate, too

A siren blasted, drowning out the lapping waves.

Cat looked up.

Alex had come.

At the top of the dune, he held on to Olivia for support and had his arm around his daughter, hugging her, laughing with her.

"Come on, Cat," he yelled. "We need to talk."

The setting sun caught the far-from-ordinary face she'd come to love. This Alex Harris was a happier man than the one she'd met just days ago. He still had the sea captain crinkles at the corner of his eyes. But even after the ordeal he had been through, the frown lines had lessened. The tightness around the mouth had lifted. Facing his fear of water and helping his daughter cope with her mother's death had lightened some of the inner pain he'd been carrying.

She'd helped make that happen. A miracle, he'd called her.

If only some miracle could wash away the pain she was feeling.

Cat climbed the side of the dune, wedging her feet into shifting sand. She'd had many successes in her life. She'd survived the teasing and bullying, and the surgeries, that made her childhood a misery. She'd faced down the deprecating men and gotten her degree. She'd made a name for herself as a brilliant researcher no matter what her sniping colleagues had said. But seeing the joy on Alex's and Ellie's faces filled her with more happiness than she'd ever had. That was something she'd take with her and keep close forever.

Maybe she'd never check off all the boxes on her Happiness List, but she could check off a new one—making Alex and his daughter happy.

As she neared the top, Cat hesitated. What did he want to talk about? With every word, her heart would plummet more. No. Spending more time with Alex and Ellie was impossible. She needed to keep things brief.

As soon as she packed her last items, she'd be in her car and driving like a crazy woman to the airport in order to make her flight. She had to go back to her old life, never to return. Better to make the break irreversible, as much as it hurt.

She gazed out at the cove. It was a beautiful spot. A beautiful sunset. An idyllic place to say goodbye to two people she'd never forget. Because, even though it had been only a week, she loved Alex. And she loved his daughter.

She reached the top of the dune.

That man, who'd once seemed unnoticeable, stuck out his hand. "Cat." There was a world of meaning in the way he said that word. He cleared his throat. "Thank you for rescuing me and for taking care of Ellie."

Cat put her hand in his. "Thank you for risking a boat ride to save me."

Where their hands touched, she could feel the heat and strength of him. She could smell his unique salty scent. She inhaled and held it in. Something else to cherish on those long, empty days ahead. She'd never find another man like him. She'd never love this way again.

He squeezed her hand. "I don't want you to leave. Please, stay a while longer. Ellie and I owe you so much."

Every fiber of her being yearned to say yes, but she couldn't. A whole other life waited for her.

She withdrew her hand and forced the words out. "I think not, Alex. I have a good job. I have a mother to care for. I have my research to redo."

She bent down and gave Ellie a hug. "Best I say goodbye now."

Ellie wrapped her arms around her legs. "Don't go. You have to stay."

She swallowed and patted the girl on the head. "I wish I could. Maybe next summer, I'll be able to come back."

Ellie's eyes filled with tears. "But we won't be here. We're moving."

Cat knelt down. "How about we write letters to each other? You can tell me all about your new home and school. I'll tell you about my ocean discoveries."

Ellie frowned. "I don't write very well yet."

Alex rested his hand on Ellie's shoulder. "I'll help you."

Letters from Alex? Did he still have hope that something could grow between them? Should she have told him the real reason she'd broken off their kiss? No. Better nothing was ever said. Let him remember her as someone who had passed through his life and left him a little happier.

Still, the idea of a lost future hurt.

A weight grew in Cat's chest. Tears edged their way to the corners of her eyes. She blinked them away, tugged her hat lower, and hoped her voice stayed steady.

"Sure. Exchanging letters would be great."

Alex stood completely still. "So, this is goodbye?"

Cat forced herself to push out a breath then take another in so she could speak normally. "Yes. It's been great getting to know you both. Alex"—she glanced at his sister—"and Olivia, please give your brothers my best and thank you for making my vacation delightful. Thank you for sharing your daughter with me, and for introducing me to Tide Harbor mosquitoes. I'll be scratching all the way home." She turned to go.

"What about your water samples?" Alex called after her. "Once I'm on my feet again, I could get them for you."

Heavens. Tied up with all this angst, she'd almost forgotten the whole reason she was here—her samples.

She hardened her voice to the one she used with obnoxious colleagues who tried to steal her data. "No. I'll start over nearer home. This really is goodbye."

Alex opened his mouth, closed it, opened it again. "Fine." He touched her wrist. "I'm going to miss you."

His touch zapped though her. Froze her in place. She peeked at him from under the brim of her hat. "I'll miss you, too. I wish you much success in your new job." She dug her toes into the sand. Now came the hard part. "Thank you for making this into a pretty exciting vacation for me."

She gave Ellie a last hug, regretting everything she had said, but knowing it was for the best. A vacation fling—that was all this could ever be.

Cat stared down at her bare toes. *Okay, feet, time to go.* Her overly pink nail polish winked up at her as if to say, *"No way. You're making a mistake. We're staying."*

She picked up one foot, took a step, then willed the other foot to move. These feet were going to carry her out of this man's life. If they happened to feel like they weighed ten tons, too bad.

Goodbyes were over.

Time to go.

Her phone vibrated in her pocket. Momma was hwaiting.

She had to get home.

Chapter 29
ALEX

Monday Morning

Cat's taillights disappeared down the road, taking his heart with them.

Olivia escorted him to the waiting police car. "You are a fool, Alex Harris. How could you let that woman leave without telling her how you feel?"

Alex shivered. Cat was gone, and so was her warmth. Ahead of him lay the sorrowful task of explaining Thomas's death.

He gave his sister a quick look. "It wouldn't have been fair. I have nothing to offer her. I don't even have a job anymore. Thomas is dead."

Olivia's hands flew up. "*Thomas? Dead?* How?"

Alex sucked in a breath and repeated the lie he had told the police and would tell his former friend's mother. Lillian Cowling didn't need to know her son was a murderer.

"Committed suicide. Jumped off the old pier and right into a mess of rocks. I tried to save him, but he'd hit his head."

Olivia's face paled. Her mouth moved, but no sound came out.

Alex took her hand. "I know you were sweet on him."

"Once. When I was young with an easily turned head, but . . . I can't believe he's gone. He was a such an important man in Tide Harbor, and your best friend." Her voice rose. "And what do you mean you *tried* to save him?"

"He came 'round your place to talk, and I asked him to bring me here to say goodbye to Cat. But he was depressed over that boy who died two weeks ago. Near the salmon pens. He was facing a major lawsuit from the parents. And there was an attempted murder charge hanging over him.""

Olivia shook her head violently. "*Depressed? Murder?* But why? He had everything. That incredible mansion. That looker, Gloria. And a wildly successful business." Olivia's forehead creased. "Have they said what will happen to Cowling?"

"I assume it will be up to his mother. But she doesn't know yet. Sergeant Murray"—he indicated the police cruiser parked across the road—"and I will be heading over there now."

"Oh, Alex. Can't you just let the police tell her?"

"Thomas was my best friend, and his mother was our lifesaver when Mom died. It is the least I can do."

Alex watched his footing as he crutched his way through the fog. Tide Harbor's cemetery sat in a stand of pines above the town, well out of sight of the sea.

Alex set a hand on the Harris tombstone, a block of granite with his parents' names and a carving of the sloop, based on one of Olivia's childhood drawings. The surface was wet from the fog swirling around him. It was always foggy when he came here.

He'd asked his mother why they'd located the cemetery here when he was a boy.

"The sea can be cruel, Alex," his mother had said. "Those who've lost loved ones to the sea don't feel too kindly about it. It's quiet here. Peaceful. With just the birds and the trees."

Alex had nodded. But he always wondered if that was the truth of it. Nowhere in Tide Harbor was far from the sea. The thump and swoosh of the surf and the horn blast of the lighthouse were always with them, even here.

He wobbled on his crutches down the gravel path to the gravesite where Thomas would be interred next to his father. The Cowling tombstone was far more elaborate than his parents', but Alex didn't begrudge him that. He much preferred his family's personalized stone.

He took his place beside his brothers and sister and listened to the minister say all the things expected. Inside, his mind whirled.

Thomas's murderous rage had been totally unexpected. Yes, his friend had been egotistical and willing to cheat. Alex regarded Thomas's mother. No question she had spoiled him, as had his father. But that didn't turn someone into a murderer.

He rubbed his hands together. For a moment, the foggy air became too thick to breathe. The cold too bitter. It had been self-defense . . . an accident. He'd tried to save him.

If only the ending had been different.

In front of him, Lillian Cowling blotted her eyes and stifled a sob. Alex moved forward and gathered the frail woman in his arms. Her whole world lay fractured in the grave before them.

He swiped his tears away.

He was leaving. The woman he loved was gone. And the future lay before him as blurry as the fog.

Chapter 30
CAT
Monday Night

All the nail polish was gone, and her nails were bitten to the quick by the time Cat's flight landed in New York. She shoved and squeezed her way through the milling crowds at LaGuardia and hustled as best she could with her still sore leg to the taxi stand.

Cat slid into the first available taxi, gave the address, then hung on as the driver swerved out into the stream of traffic, heading toward the city. She placed her briefcase on her lap. All the research inside that had seemed so important before was like a deadweight dragging her down. How could she have left her momma on her own for days? She'd been enjoying herself, acting silly over a guy, getting involved in someone else's family, so much so she'd stopped answering her phone?

She pulled out her cell and reread the text message from her brother, composed in his minimal style. *"Momma. Hospital. Asking for you."*

Hospital? Tears filled her eyes, turning the passing cars and ever taller buildings into a blur. She was a terrible daughter. She'd finish out the next semester at NYU then find a job at a community college where she wouldn't have to publish or perish, and she could spend more time with her mother. No more jaunts out to sea. No more research studies in places like Tide Harbor. No more getting dreamy-eyed over a man.

She didn't need money. She didn't need renown. She didn't need love.

By the time Cat reached the hospital, her mother was already in surgery, and her brothers were in the surgical waiting area, lined up like a row of football players waiting to be sent in the save the game, each one of them bigger and burlier than the next.

Feeling small and vulnerable, Cat settled down on the hard, plastic chair next to Rob then peered up at the patient portal board, searching for her mother's name. "How much longer will she be in surgery?"

"Doctor said the hip replacement will take four hours. It's been like two."

"I'm so sorry I wasn't here to help with all this."

"No sweat, sis." Rob patted her knee. "Momma's going to be okay. She's tough."

Cat wrung her hands together. Not that tough, or she wouldn't be here, having surgery.

She let her chin fall against her chest. "If I hadn't gone away, I might have prevented this."

"She got her sleeve caught on the doorknob as she was going outside and lost her balance. Took a tumble down the front steps. Nothing you could have prevented."

Cat jerked her head up. "She was going out? Where? She never goes out without me."

Down the row, Angelo laughed. "Ha. See what you know, Pumpkin Head. Of course, she goes out. Does her rounds."

"What rounds?"

Frank gave her a look. "You live with her, and you don't know she organized some local reading program through the library? Calls it the Reading Stars. She goes to shut-ins and reads books to them. Has a whole crew of volunteers. Been doing it for years."

Cat looked up and down the row of handsome hulks. They had to be joking. "You guys make that up?"

Frank rolled his eyes. "A reading program? Come on, sis. We're not that creative."

She glared at the three of them. "So, why was this kept a big secret from me?"

Rob pinched his lips together. "Not sure. She swore us to it. Maybe she thought if you knew she wasn't as doddering as you believed, you'd go off on your own and end up drowned on one of those expeditions of yours."

Cat jumped up and shook her fist at them. "How dare you not tell me she was tricking me? It's fine for you guys to go off and bash your heads in playing sports—probably had a million concussions—but I aced my swimming, earned a master certificate in diving, and take a few dips in the ocean each summer for my research and, oh no, can't have that. Silly Catalina might get sucked down into a whirlpool or something." Cat snapped her mouth closed. She had almost drowned—*twice*—in the last seven days. She inhaled. The key word was *almost*.

Rob reached out to take her hand. She jerked it away. He caught it and held on tight. "She loves you, Cat. She's got three of us. You're her only daughter."

"Thanks for the honor." She headed for the door. "I'm going to take a walk."

"Look, go home. Get some rest. You've got owl-eye circles under your eyes. We'll call with any news. She's going to be all drugged up when she gets out, anyway, not wanting visitors tonight. You can come back in the morning."

Cat shoved her hands in her coat pockets. She had a lot to think about. "You know, that's exactly what I'm going to do. I can be back in fifteen minutes if need be. Text me updates, okay?"

At Rob's nod, she fist-bumped her brother in the shoulder then took off through the swinging doors.

Cat rushed down the hospital corridor as fast as she could. She had to get out of here before she screamed. How could her mother have manipulated her like that? How could she be so competent in her career yet unable to see through the twisty plotting of an old woman?

Momma loved her more than her brothers? Right. Smothering her as a child. Disparaging every single thing she had accomplished. Tricking her into living with her. Calling her a failure because she couldn't land a man. That wasn't love.

That was some warped idea of motherhood.

Later, she would have trouble remembering how she had gotten on the beach and how she'd fought the surf until her muscles tired. But she would always be glad that she had ended up lying on the clean-washed sand as the tide went out and the sun came up.

It was a new day. She had things to do. A sneaky mother to go visit. A letter to write.

Chapter 31
ALEX

One Week Later . . .

Despite the closure of Cowling Fish Farm after Thomas's death, Alex would still move to Halifax. Even with his broken leg, Lillian Cowling thought him the best person to oversee the Halifax office until the business sold. If he were lucky, the new owner might keep him on.

Alex surveyed the boxes stacked in the living room. Only a few more items to pack up—Helen's things. He was dreading that task. But he'd promised Ellie they'd do it together, so he would. Only, where was his daughter?

He peeked in her bedroom. With all her toys and wall posters packed, the space looked as cold and sterile as the rooms he'd looked at when apartment hunting in Halifax.

His sister was right. Life in Halifax was going to be a lot harder than he'd thought. After being surrounded by sea, sky, and pines, living cooped up in a tiny two-bedroom with a galley kitchen and a miniscule shower would feel like living in a bait bucket with the lid on. Smell as bad, too. He still hadn't recovered from breathing in the mix of cooking smells that filtered through the apartment corridor.

But that's what he could afford if he was keeping this house. And he was going to keep it. Not that it would be easy. Even though Thomas's mother had forgiven his mortgage, he still had to pay the taxes and upkeep. But it would be worth it. He didn't intend to stay in Halifax forever.

He looked around. How could he sell it when everywhere he looked, there was a memory? Helen washing dishes at the kitchen sink. Ellie cuddling her imaginary puppy. Cat in her outrageous pink tee, throwing open the drapes and letting in the light.

Halifax would always be temporary. Fletcher's Cove was where he'd come home to. He might even find a job here. Rumor was some businessman from New Brunswick was interested in buying Cowling and converting the open pens to an on-land operation.

Now, where had Ellie disappeared to?

Alex crossed over to the window and looked out. She'd been wandering around the house minutes ago, looking for a piece of paper and a soda bottle.

He crutched his way out onto the deck. The yard was empty.

He slapped his head. Paper? Bottle? Ah. He knew exactly where she was.

Grasping his crutches, he worked his way down the steps and stumbled toward the cove, his heart thumping a thousand times faster than normal.

Ellie was sitting on the beach at the high-tide mark.

Heart-rate dropping, Alex slogged his way across the sand. He squatted down beside her. Her little body shook with sobs.

"What's wrong?"

She looked up at him, tears streaming down her face. "It's not working."

He caught sight of the clear plastic bottle lying at the water's edge. A wave broke, rushed in, picked up the bottle, carried it out, then brought it back in again. Over and over, the bottle floated in and out, as if the sea couldn't make up its mind on whether to take it or not.

He felt a lot of sympathy for that bottle. It was exactly the way he felt—should he or shouldn't he?

He drew Ellie against him. "Is there a message inside?"

She nodded. "But the ocean is supposed to take it to her like in the book Miss Paquette read to us, and it won't, and she will never know."

"*Know*?"

"That she has to come back. Cat belongs here. With us."

He ran his fingers through her curls. "I agree."

Ellie pulled her head away. "You do?"

"I miss her, too."

"Why did she leave us, Daddy?"

"Her mother fell and had to have an operation. Remember, it was in the letter she sent you."

Ellie pinched her moon shell pendant between her fingers. "The letter didn't say she'd come back."

"No, it didn't."

"She's angry about the water thing you lost."

"Who told you that?"

"I heard you talking to Aunt Olivia."

"It's rude to listen to adult conversations."

"But you were talking so loud."

He had been loud—and angry. He'd been yelling, spouting a load of nonsense. Having a whole sniffling, choking breakdown just because Olivia thought he should go to New York and apologize for whatever fool thing he'd done. Like he could just pick up and leave to chase a woman he'd known for a week.

A woman who'd made him laugh again. A woman who'd given his daughter peace. A woman who'd seen into his heart. A woman who made him a better man.

He watched the bottle float in, float out. Float in again. It was never going to reach New York that way.

Alex got up, made his way to the water's edge, picked it up, and looked at the crayoned message folded inside. He hated to say it, but his sister was right.

He came back up to Ellie, swung her up into his arms, and gave her the bottle. "I know a much better way to get this message to our Cat."

He gazed out toward the fish pens. But he had to do something first.

It had taken some time to for his leg to heal and to gather the equipment, and to ready the boat and his mind, but the day was finally here.

Wearing a life jacket, Alex gripped the side of the kayak and slipped into the cockpit. For three years, the blue and white Skipjack had sat tucked away in his father's boathouse, gathering dust. He'd never thought he'd use it again.

Matt passed him the paddle. "You sure you want to do this by yourself? We could—"

Alex held up his hand. "It's less than a thousand feet to the pen. I think I can paddle that far."

Besides, he had to do this. It was time. It would make Cat happy. And maybe—just maybe—if he was willing to take a chance on himself, she'd take a chance on him.

He looked out across the glistening aquamarine water. It wasn't the distance that would stop him or his motivation. It was the shaking in his arms. The pounding in his chest.

He flexed his biceps and checked that the sampling equipment was latched tightly to the hatch. He had all the right stuff, thank heavens. It helped to have a brother studying marine biology. Logan had been able to borrow test equipment, like Cat had been using, from his lab at Dalhousie.

"Daddy." Ellie ran down to the water's edge. "I want to go, too."

Olivia pulled up behind her, huffing. "I tried to stop her, but she heard Logan talking about the kayak."

He'd known launching from the cove was a mistake, but it somehow had seemed the perfect place to get his feet wet, so to speak.

Alex looked at his daughter. She deserved to be part of this. Cat belonged to them both. Or, at least, he hoped she would. And his brave little daughter had been acing her swimming lessons.

He waved toward the beach where he'd left his towel and the pink child-sized life jacket he'd bought after the accident, as if that made up for its lack on the day it was really needed.

He'd intended to give Ellie a ride in the kayak later, after he'd gotten the shivers out, but why wait? Any one of his siblings could swim out to the pens and back if he totally blew it.

"Put the jacket on her."

Olivia's eyebrows rose. Then she smiled. "Aye, aye, Captain."

In minutes, Matt had Ellie ensconced in the front cockpit.

She peered over her shoulder. "Let's go, Daddy."

Alex wedged his knees against the thigh braces and pressed his spine against the back band. His whole body shifted and became one with the kayak.

It was true what they said about muscle memory—the body never forgot. His challenge would be making his mind forget that the last time he'd sat in this boat, it had led to disaster. But he'd been through two weeks of swim therapy, and he had a woman to impress.

He signaled his brother. "All set. Let her go."

Matt leaned in. "You need help, just shout. We're all here for you."

Alex glanced back at the beach where Logan, Olivia, and her boys stood waving. He waved back. His parents might be gone. Helen might be gone. But the Harris siblings would never turn their backs on him.

Matt released his hold on the stern. The kayak drifted with the waves. Alex dipped a paddle in the water and felt the boat respond. Water sloshed against the hull as the boat moved sideways. He dipped the other paddle, the boat straightened. Another pull, and it was slicing through the water, wind whistling past, the prow rising and falling on the swells.

Elli held up her hands. "This is fun, Daddy."

He dug the paddle in. It *was* fun.

He and Helen had loved racing through the water without a care in the world. He'd loved sailing the sloop. He'd even loved going out on the lobster boat with his dad, despite the backbreaking work on the coldest days of winter.

Olivia was right. The sea was in his blood. Helen wouldn't have wanted him to give up his life on the water because she was gone.

A breath of wind brushed his cheek like a caress, and he knew he was right.

Within minutes, he'd reached the side of the fish pen and pulled alongside. Using the technique Logan had taught him, he released the sampling vial and lowered it to the prescribed depth.

Ellie watched the tube sink. "Cat's gonna be happy to have her fishy water, right, Daddy?"

He sure hoped so.

He gave her a smile. "Of course."

When the cord reached its limit, hand-over-hand, he drew the tube back up and out of the water. The sample inside was dark and murky. Not water he'd choose to swim in. Not water his Tide Harbor neighbors would want in their harbor.

Alex gazed across at the Cowling Fish Farm facility on the opposite shore. He sure hoped that the rumors were true and these polluting pens would soon be gone.

"You hold this, Ellie." He passed the tube over to her.

She clasped it tightly. "I won't drop it, Daddy."

He turned the kayak back toward the cove and dug in the paddles.

Ellie glanced over her shoulder. "Can we take it to Cat tomorrow?"

Alex shook his head. "No, sweetheart. We need to take samples six more times on six more days."

"Then we can go to New York?"

"Yes. Then we can go to New York."

Chapter 32
CAT

A Month Later . . .

Cat folded the letter in half and tucked it into her briefcase. There, that was settled.

The A train rattled to a stop. Clutching the leather case to her chest, she exited the station and hurried toward 65th Street and home. It was time to tell Momma the truth. No more vying for the full-time position at NYU. She'd found a better one.

In minutes, Cat was at the door of her mother's small brick house. For a moment, she slowed and peered down the street, toward the boardwalk. If you had to live in the city, this was a wonderful place to be. But it wasn't the only spot on earth within walking distance of the ocean. There were others . . .

Cat drew out her key, inserted it in the lock, and opened the door. Raised voices and laughter washed over her. It sounded like a party.

She stepped into the living room and stopped dead. Her mouth dropped open. Her briefcase tumbled to the floor. It *was* a party.

All the neighbors and a crowd of strangers, who must be members of Momma's Reading Stars, surrounded her mother as she lay on the recliner and stuffed her mouth with a mini-sized cupcake.

The crowd hushed.

An elderly woman grabbed Cat's arm and whispered in her ear, "Perfect timing. We're just about to induct a new member." She took a big bite of her own cupcake and pointed.

Sitting on a low stool at her mother's feet was Alex Harris, looking not so ordinary in a neat, navy-blue suit and a pink tie decorated with—she narrowed her eyes— mermaids. Then she noticed what he was reading from—her Coleridge.

He held the battered book from her childhood like it was a treasure and read the opening line of one of her favorite poems, "The Rime of the Ancient Mariner." If she remembered correctly, she'd crayoned pictures of sea monsters all over the page.

But forget the book. She focused on the man ensconced in the middle of her mother's living room. Alex's voice rose and fell as enticing as that of the ancient mariner. She could hear the sea. Feel the storm.

Cat gave herself a shake. She'd forgotten he was an English major. She'd forgotten how rich and strong his voice could be. But she hadn't forgotten how he made her heart toss and twist like a ship in a storm and how he had turned her traitorous body into mush with a single kiss.

It took all her willpower to take a step back, then another, and another, until she was out the door and running down the street.

Several hundred yards along the boardwalk, Cat found an empty bench. She lowered herself onto the seat and stared out at the surf breaking against the shore. But it wasn't the ocean she was seeing. It was Alex. Here. In her house. Entertaining her mother.

Saying goodbye hadn't been enough. Ignoring his phone calls hadn't been enough. He'd come, bringing cupcakes from a little café in Tide Harbor.

What would he want from her? What did she want from him? Surely, more than a thank you.

Cat sat back on the bench and took in her surroundings. The expanse of ocean. The briny scent of the sea. The people passing by.

There were the mothers pushing baby carriages, enjoying the sun. Skatcboarding teenagers, not yet back in school, wove in and out of the huffing joggers. In the ocean, a kayaker paddled his boat through the surf like she used to do with her brothers.

Far Rockaway wasn't that different from Tide Harbor. Waves lapped the shore. Seagulls swooped overhead. Sunlight glinted off the rollers. Except it was.

Between the boardwalk and the beach, there were probably as many people enjoying this sunny September day as lived in all of Tide Harbor—all of them strangers. In Tide Harbor, people weren't strangers. They knew each other.

"There you are." Alex, with Ellie hitched up on his hip and a small daypack on his shoulder, pulled up in front of her. He was no longer rule-follower neat. He'd taken off the suit jacket, loosened his tie. Sweat dripped from his brow. His hair stood up at odd angles. He looked messy, and real, and wonderful. He looked happy.

Alex set Ellie down, and the child flung her arms around Cat.

"I thought we'd never find you. It took hours, and hours, and hours to get here."

"How did you?"

"Daddy drove."

Cat looked over Ellie's head at Alex. "You didn't come in the sloop?"

Alex shook his head. "Sorry. Not all dreams are meant to come true. I gave the boat to my brothers. Though they let me keep a quarter ownership out of the kindness of their hearts. The plan is to run harbor cruises in the summer.. We're asking Nick to come back and captain."

Cat shuffled her feet. "Haven't met that brother."

"We're hoping you will." He signaled his daughter. "Ellie, you ready?"

The child nodded.

He drew a crushed plastic bottle from his knapsack and put it into her hands.

Ellie held it out to her. "For you."

Cat took the battered bottle and turned it over and over. "Looks like this bottle has traveled a long way."

"It did." Ellie frowned. "I threw it in the ocean, but the waves kept rolling it around and wouldn't take it to you like what happened in the storybook. And Dad said it's better we bring it ourselves. So, we did." She put her hands on her hips. "And we're here."

"You definitely are." Cat winked at Alex and tapped the bottle. "So, what am I supposed to do with it? There is recycling in Tide Harbor, you know."

Ellie giggled. "It's a special bottle. There's something inside."

Cat held the battered bottle up so the sunlight silhouetted the crumpled paper. "I see. Now, let me think . . . Is that a—"

Ellie jumped up and down. "It's a message, Cat. For you."

"A message in a bottle? Oh my, I've always wanted to find one of these." She unscrewed the lid, flipped the bottle upside down, and gave it a shake. "Not going to come out that way." She turned the bottle sideways and peered through the scratched plastic. "Can't quite make it out."

Ellie tugged on her hand. "It says, 'Come home.'" The little girl threw her arms around her again. "I missed you."

Cat smiled. "I miss you, too." She looked up at Alex. Did he miss her? He wasn't saying, but he sure was looking at her. "Ellie"—she pointed out toward the beach—"do you want to go down onto the sand? We're farther south here. I bet you could find new kinds of shells."

Ellie clapped her hands then ran down the ramp to the beach. Alex and she followed.

Alex stopped at the high tide mark and took off his pack. "I almost forgot." He reached inside and drew out a slightly smashed chocolate cupcake in a red-and-white striped baking wrapper. "I saved you one." He passed it to her.

Cat stared down at the lopsided chocolate confection. "You brought cupcakes all the way from Tide Harbor?"

"I did. As I remember, you were in ecstasy over that particular flavor."

"*Ecstasy*, huh?" She took a bite and chewed slowly. It tasted exactly like she remembered—rich, and sweet, and magical.

As she chewed, she waited for him to say more. He didn't, though she sure liked the way he was staring at her lips.

Cat took another bite and swallowed. "Okay. Explain. Why did you come?"

Alex grinned. "So, I could see that look on your face again."

Cat lowered the cupcake. "What look?"

"The look of pure love." He ran his finger over her lips. "Got a dab of chocolate there."

Their eyes met. Sounds faded away. The people around her became blurs. Her heart fluttered.

"Love?"

Alex gazed out at the surf. "Yeah. Love those cupcakes, don't you? I brought two dozen, but your mother thought they were for her. I didn't think it wise to disagree. By the way, she's not at all what I expected. Rather a lively gal, just like her daughter. Anyway"—he shifted closer to her—"we were just starting to get into a very interesting conversation about you when all those people showed up, and your mother made it sound like I'd come to join them or something. Somehow, I ended up reading a poem. Then you arrived. But when I disengaged myself from your mother and her crew, you'd run out the door." He stopped to take a breath. "I thought I'd scared you off. But your mom said you'd be down here at the beach, that you always come here to think."

Cat shook her head. "I wasn't scared. There were too many people there. I didn't want to share you."

"Almost ran by you. Luckily, Ellie caught sight of your hair."

He moved closer and picked up a strand. "Flamingo Pink again?"

"I like pink." Cat popped the rest of the cupcake in her mouth and let the creamy fudge do its thing.

Alex grinned. "Sorry. My plan was to woo you with cupcakes, but you've eaten the last one. I guess I'm going to have put that look of love on your face in a different way."

"You've taken up cupcake baking?"

His lips spilt into a wide grin. "No, kayaking. I've brought you your water samples."

Cat winked. "I kind of knew."

Alex's eyebrows rose.

"You're not the only Harris." She waved to Ellie, who was busy filling her hands with what were probably teeny tiny shells. The surf here was much wilder than in Fletcher's Cove.

He drew his lips together. "Olivia?"

"We've exchanged a few texts. She's let on that you've been out in the kayak, did some sampling. But that's not surprising. You're a brave man. You risked your life to save me. I knew you'd find your way back to the sea. You and Ellie being here, though . . . that is a surprise she didn't mention."

"So, we're a surprise? A good one?"

"I guess." She twisted her fingers together behind her back. Was that hope bubbling up inside her? Should she tell him what she'd done?

She glanced over at him. "I told you not to come."

He moved closer, his eyes narrowed against the sun, creating those little crinkles in the corners that she loved so much. He clasped her hand and pulled her to a halt. "No, you didn't. Not once. You didn't call. You didn't text. You sent a letter. It said give Ellie a hug. It said good luck on the new job. It said you were sorry to hear about Thomas. It said you were too busy and not to expect to hear from you again." The hurt in his voice was as sharp as a fishhook.

She bent down to pick up a tiny jingle shell—*Anomia simplex*. So delicate light could pass through the shell and yet strong enough to survive the roaring surf. Was that the kind of outer shell she wore? Could Alex see right through it?

Cat looked out at the water. A huge cargo ship was steaming up the channel. "I've been busy."

"I've been busy, too. Getting ready to move to Halifax."

Her heart rate rocketed. She whirled around. "So have I."

"Move? Out of your mother's? Olivia mentioned that."

"Out of the country."

"Where to? The South Seas?"

"No." Cat grabbed on to his tie and yanked him to her. She wrapped it around her hand. "Where in the world did you get a tie with mermaids on it?"

He lifted the brim of her hat. "Same place you get hats saying, 'I'm a Hooker.'" He put a finger under her chin and lifted it. "Your mother told me about the cleft palate. How they had to put your face back together. All the surgeries you had." He ran his thumb over her upper lip. "I don't care if your hair is pink, or you wear funny T-shirts, or have a scar. All that pain, all that fighting to make your dreams come true, has made you strong and wise. You can see inside people's hearts because you know what it is like to dream things differently. That little scar is what makes me want to kiss you. It's what makes you—you."

"You want to kiss me?"

"Always. Once was not enough. I think you have me hooked like your hat says."

His head came down, and their lips met. Everything faded away except the sound of the sea beating against the shore in rhythm with the thumping of her heart.

Cat pulled away and stared into his eyes. It was time to tell him.

"I have a surprise, too. I'm moving to Halifax. Got a visiting professorship at Dalhousie." She gave him a wink. "Could maybe turn into something more?"

Alex threw back his head and laughed. "I will definitely turn that into something more." And he kissed her again.

Epilogue
ALEX

A Year Later . . .

Matt joined Alex at the water's edge. "Fletcher's Cove is the absolute craziest place to hold a wedding ceremony. With our luck, everyone will get wet." He bent down and shook the kinks out of the microphone wires. "And definitely sand in their shoes."

Alex peered at the waves lapping at the shore. Not too long ago, he wouldn't have stood this close to the water. The fact that he could now, he owed to one incredible woman. "I think it's perfect."

Matt gave him a knowing look. "Maybe Cat did pick the right venue. Or should I say, man?"

"Of course, she did." Alex smiled. "I've checked the tide tables twice. The tide is going out. Besides, she did write 'bathing suit and shoes optional' on the invites."

He squinted out to where the fish pens used to be. A lot had happened in the last year. Cowling Fish Farm had been bought by Jason Burke, a cracker jack of a fellow. He'd shut down the open-water pens and was in the process of setting up one of the biggest enclosed, sustainable salmon tank farms in the province. Neither the fish nor their waste would ever come near the sea.

Tide Harbor would return to the pristine condition it had been when they were young. Alex was happy to see the changes the new owner was making. He was not so happy about Jason's burgeoning interest in his sister. But he'd have to trust Olivia to be sensible. He had his own life to enjoy. And enjoy it, he would.

"Hey there. Give me a hand," a voice called up.

Alex spun around. Speaking of the new man in Tide Harbor, here he was.

Jason strolled down the beach.

Alex waved. "You got everything set up for the clambake?"

"Of course. Olivia has outdone herself. There's enough food for every man, woman, and child in town. I donated some of our first sustainable salmon, too. Should be great advertising what with all the city folk coming to your shindig."

Jason looked toward the dunes. "That woman you are marrying is something else. She actually tested the fish for contamination. Fortunately, she gave my fish an A plus rating. And have you seen her dress?"

Matt put his finger to his lips. "*Shh.* He'd better not have."

Alex looked back and forth between them. "Is that just the typical the-groom-can't-see-the-bride thing or should I worry?"

Matt swung his head from side the side. "Well, let's just say all eyes will be on her."

"Of course, they will. She's the bride."

Jason laughed. "They won't just be looking because she's the bride."

Alex looked down at his navy suit and mermaid tie. She'd specially asked him to dress up.

He rubbed the back of his neck. Surely, she wouldn't totally flaunt wedding traditions. But this was Cat, and she did have an outrageous collection of clothing. Over the past year, he'd gotten to see most of it.

"She's not wearing one of her funny T-shirts, is she?"

Matt and Jason looked at each other.

"No," Matt said. "It's definitely a dress."

"So, what is it that's got you two looking like a pair of seals who've just swallowed a tuna? She hasn't changed the color of her hair again, has she?" In the last two months, she'd gone from pink to purple to blue. But at the wedding rehearsal, she'd been her natural blonde.

Matt finished laying down the wires for the mic and hooked them to the solar panel. He stood. "I guess you'll be finding out soon enough. Your guests are arriving."

Alex turned to see Olivia and Kate at the head of the first comers.

Kate held her fisted hands above her head. "The cupcake queen is here to report mission accomplished. Two hundred Death by Chocolate cupcakes, iced and delivered. Though, I still think a cake would have been way easier."

Alex gave her a hug. "Cat and I have a special fondness for those little chocolate wonders. I can't wait to feed her one later."

Olivia looped her arm into his. "I hear that the two of you have tried out for the next production of the Shakespeare Club."

"You did?" Matt punched him in the arm. "What are they putting on?"

Olivia grinned. "*The Taming of the Shrew.*"

"Hey, what part did you and Cat get, bro?"

"Don't know yet. But we're hoping for the leads."

Matt looked him up and down. "Cat will make a great female lead, but I'm not sure about you playing Petruchio."

"Don't think I can control my Cat?"

Matt shook his head. "You haven't seen her dress, little brother."

Olivia held up her phone. "Well, he's going to see it soon. The bridal party just disembarked from the limo. They'll be promenading over the dune in five minutes."

Alex moved into position under the seashell decorated trellis, set into the sand so that it framed Whaleback Island. The wedding guests settled on the blankets spread on the sand. Matt, serving as best man, came and stood beside him.

Alex gave him an elbow. "You have the rings, right?"

Matt patted his jacket pocket. "All taken care of."

Off to the side, Ellie's teacher, Mia Paquette, strummed a chord on her guitar and, in a clear, pure voice, sang the opening stanzas of "Fishing for Love." The children's lullaby, with the slightly changed lyrics he'd written, was perfect. He especially liked the line that went, "*Fishing for love in Tide Harbor.*"

Alex scanned the faces of the people who'd come to witness his marriage to Cat. On the right sat Momma Silva and two of Cat's three brothers. The hulking athletes, who overfilled their chairs, were certainly causing a stir in town. Behind them, sitting on the bride's side, seemed to be the entire unmarried female population of Tide Harbor—all of whom had come in swimsuits.

On the left sat his family. Olivia and her three boys, his brother, Logan, and an empty chair. The empty seat made his stomach twist. Nick. He'd promised to come, but no one had heard anything from him in weeks. He hoped his brother was okay.

He understood why Nick had left Tide Harbor. He'd had his personal tragedy, too. But it was time to forgive himself and come home. Alex crossed his fingers. He might still make it.

Cheers and gasps rose from the crowd. Alex looked up. The bridal party had arrived and started down the dune. Leading the procession was Ellie.

No frilly dresses for her. Not with Cat as a role model. But he didn't care. She was bright, and smart, and happy. She looked adorable in her neon pink bathing suit and bare feet. On her head, she wore the traditional flowers in her hair as she carried a basket of tiny seashells, which she was enthusiastically throwing in every direction. Behind her came Rosie, who Cat had chosen to be her maid of honor. After all, she'd said Rosie had been the one who'd given him the push to ask her out in the first place.

Rosie looked like she was in heaven. Arrayed in a dark burgundy dress and a mile-wide smile, the Ottawa import was not going to be treated like a stranger anymore, not with the way Matt was gazing at her.

For a moment, there was a gap in the procession. Then there she was. His Cat being Cat. The woman who'd saved his life. The woman who always knew how to make him smile. The woman who'd brought light back into his life.

Holding on to her brother, Rob's, arm, she put one bare foot and then another on to the red carpet, spread across the sand and leading straight to him.

Alex tried not to shout aloud his joy or rush to crush her against him. He held his arms at his sides and let her come to him, the way they had rehearsed it.

Cat came closer, her gaze wholly on him, her mouth partially open, inviting him to kiss her, and kiss her he would as soon as the minister had his say and the vows had been given.

He didn't even notice the dress at first. Then he did.

The dress, in many ways, was traditional. The silvery pink, strapless, sequined bodice was form-fitting to mid-thigh. Below, a swirl of toile flared out like a mermaid's tail. But his mermaid didn't carry the expected flowers. Instead, in her hand was Ellie's bottle, carefully preserved over the year in a place of honor on her desk at Dalhousie, a pink ribbon tied around the neck.

Across the front of her dress were silver letters. But before he could decipher them, she was standing next to him, ready to pledge her life to his.

Cat took his hand and turned to face him. Caught in the rays of the sun shining on the water, the dress sparkled and the words on her dress glittered with reflected light. His breath caught. The message shone clear. In curlicue letters, the words, *I Love You, Alex*," danced in front of his eyes. Now there was a slogan he'd be happy to see her wear every single day.

Cat stage-whispered in his ear, "Like the dress?"

Alex squeezed her hand and whispered back, "How could I not? You're wearing it, it's pink, and Cat, I love you, too."

The End

SNEAK PEEK

ADRIFT ON THE TIDE

Book 3 in the Tide Harbor Suspense Series

When a tractor trailer carrying a million dollars' worth of lobsters goes missing on his watch, Will Young, Tide Harbor's reclusive logrolling champ and wildlife enthusiast, becomes the butt of jokes on local and national news.

Angry and embarrassed, Will sets off to find the missing truck, little knowing that the more dead bodies he stumbles over, and the closer he gets to the criminal operation that stole the lobsters, the more his life—and that of the gorgeous undercover environmentalist masquerading as a birdwatcher, who's attached herself to him like a tidewater barnacle—are at risk.

ADRIFT ON THE TIDE
Prologue

Will Young's stomach clenched tighter than a seaman's knot. He checked the bill of lading again. It couldn't be wrong. It just couldn't.

His boss, Bertram Miller, strode up and down the loading dock, the sun glistening off the top of his bald head. The man stopped and glared at him. "So, where's the truck?"

Will looked out at the tractor-trailers lined up in the lot and counted again. Nine. How could there be only nine?

He shook his head. "I swear I counted ten, sir. The last one came in at 5:04 p.m., just like I marked it down. Saw the driver get out and all." He ran his fingers under his sweat-wet collar. The white semi had been there. He knew it had.

His boss's eyes narrowed.

Will tried again. "Saw it clear as a blue-sky day. It had a small dent on the door, a black scrape running along the side, and a broken chain hanging down at the back. Ontario license plate." He twisted a button on his shirt. "I guess it must have pulled back out."

"Pulled out? Through the locked gate?" Bertram Miller scowled at him. "No way, idiot. It was never there. A figment of your batty brain, that's all. Knew I should never have hired you, no matter how much your uncle begged. Felt sorry for you getting married and all with a kid on the way. Even if the babe ain't yours."

Bertram snatched the bill of lading from Will's hand and flapped it in his face. "That truck was worth a million dollars, Zoo Boy. Consider yourself fired. Now, get your junk out of your locker and scram." He turned then looked over his shoulder. "In fact, I suggest you leave town. Reporters catch wind of this, you're gonna be a laughing stock. I can see the headline now: '*World Log Rolling Champion Who Can't Count to Ten Loses Million-Dollar Truckload of Lobsters.*'"

Coming Soon!

YOUR FREE BOOK AWAITS . . .

Thanks for taking the time to read *Lost Beneath the Tide*. If you enjoyed it, please take a minute to post a review or rating on any of the online book sellers. I really appreciate your feedback, as I depend largely on word of mouth to promote my books.

To learn when more of my books are coming out and to earn a chance to win a new romance every month, sign up for my newsletter HERE. By becoming a member of my Readers Club, you will receive one of my books, *Inside the Skin*, a multi-holiday, sweet contemporary romance, and the FREE story, *The Holiday Stranger*, which tells how Nick Harris and Kate, of cupcake fame, first met.

If you would like to know more about the Nova Scotia setting and how I went about writing the *Tide Harbo Suspense* series, check out the Tide Harbor Suspense Story Bible.

ABOUT ZARA WEST

Zara West loves all things mysterious, adventurous, and heart-stopping, as long as they lead to true love. Born in Williamsburg, Brooklyn, Zara West spends winters in New York where the streets hum with life, summers in the Maritimes where the sea meets the shore, and the rest of the year anywhere inspiration for tales of adventure and love are plentiful.

In a life full of misadventures, she has had a sunstroke on the top of a Greek mountain, been partially trampled by a herd of four hundred sheep, and while she has never been kidnapped, she has been marooned on an uninhabited island in the middle of the Canadian wilderness for longer than she wants to remember.

A member of Romance Writers of America and of Women's Fiction Writers, Zara is an award-winning author of both fiction and non-fiction in the fields of ethnography, education, and the arts. Under the pen name, Zara West, she has published the award-winning romantic thriller series, *The Skin Quartet*. She is also the author of the *Write for Success* series.

Zara blogs about romance at Zara West Romance, and about writing at Zara West's Journal, and teaches numerous online writing courses. Find her current teaching schedule HERE.

OTHER BOOKS BY ZARA WEST

Tide Harbor Suspense Series
Concealed by the Tide
Lost Beneath the Tide
Adrift on the Tide (coming soon)

The Skin Quartet: A Dark, Sexy Romantic Thriller Series
Beneath the Skin
Close to the Skin
Under the Skin
Within the Skin

Historical Fiction Under the Pen Name Joan Koster
"Beneath the Mask" in *The Eve of Love Anthology*
"Solstice Promise" in *The Light of Love Anthology*
That Dickinson Girl: A Novel of the Civil War
Censored Angel: Anthony Comstock's Nemesis

Write for Success Series
Fast Draft Your Manuscript and Get It Done
Revise Your Draft and Make It Shine
Research Your Subject and Validate Your Writing
Power Up Your Language and Make It Sing

Tidal Waters Press